Love, Death, and the Ladies' Drill Team

Books by Jessamyn West

THE FRIENDLY PERSUASION

A MIRROR FOR THE SKY

THE WITCH DIGGERS

CRESS DELAHANTY

LOVE, DEATH, AND THE LADIES' DRILL TEAM

LOVE
*
DEATH
*
AND THE
*
LADIES' DRILL
*
TEAM
*

BY JESSAMYN WEST

HARCOURT, BRACE AND COMPANY

NEW YORK

The following stories appeared originally in somewhat different form in *The New Yorker:* "The Mysteries of Life in an Orderly Manner," "Love, Death, and the Ladies' Drill Team," "The Battle of the Suits," and "Learn to Say Good-by" (as "The Lesson"). The remaining stories appeared originally in the following magazines: *American Prefaces, Harper's Magazine, Ladies' Home Journal, Mademoiselle, The New Mexico Quarterly, The Saturday Evening Post,* Grinnell College (Ia.) *Tanager,* and *Woman's Home Companion.*

LIBRARY OF CONGRESS CATALOG CARD NUMBER: 55-10809

PRINTED IN THE UNITED STATES OF AMERICA

For Merle—Rusty grown up

CONTENTS

CONTENTS

Love, Death, and the Ladies' Drill Team

*

A Time of Learning

*

EMMETT MAGUIRE, hitching Old Clay to the buckboard, was suddenly convinced of folly. He became too sorrowful to slide the thin tail through
the crupper, too pensive to buckle a hame strap. He
stood in the sallow, early morning light gazing about
the farmyard. Fool, he asked himself, where'll you find
anything like this?

Just then, as he renounced it, the whole landscape so
altered that he felt that for the first time in his nineteen
years he was seeing it truly. All the familiar parapher-
nalia of the farm seemed suddenly to detach themselves
from their background, move nearer him, become lumi-
nous and significant.

Amos, the blue-nosed mule, stood out against the sul-
phur-colored sky like sculpture. Emmett could not take
his eyes from him. Now he was leaving—he had, in fact,
moved heaven and earth to get away—and what did he
really know of Amos? He had consigned himself to dab-
bling and traveling when he might have stayed home and
learned, got to the bottom of mules. Against the morning
sky, streaked now like a ripening Baldwin, Amos's head
hung more heavy and knowledgeable than the rock of

ages. Would there be any wisdom in the next county equal to what Amos had?

In the moment of leave-taking Emmett doubted it. Leaving, what could he expect? Girls and fritterings. No doubt sleep with the swine at the last, too, he supposed. But he felt as bound to move on as the prodigal himself, and for a better reason.

A sign and house painter soon paints himself out in his own neighborhood. All who incline toward paint and have money to pay for it come finally either to the end of the houses and sheds and outhouses needing a new coat or to the end of their money. All who care to have their fences decorated with signs for Hi-John Compelling Powder have them so decorated. Then the painter moves on or puts down his brush.

"Having trouble?" Emmett's father came from behind the buckboard, where with Emmett's mother he had been stowing away a round leather box of clean collars.

"No trouble," said Emmett, pulling the long switch tail on through. "I was thinking."

He was thinking, if they shed a tear, I'll have to unhitch, unpack, stay forever. But he was mistaken. Had his father laid a hand on the bridle, or his mother clung to him, he would have been off, as determined and set in his leave-taking as he had been in his preparation to go. But the leave-taking was seemly, no tears shed or protestations made. As he drove away, the known objects continued to move toward him, become big with the brightness and urgency of the willfully rejected.

His parents saw him depart, untransformed: their dear son, artist and thinker, Emmett. Though those were words they had never been permitted to say to him.

Once, in the barn, his father had come upon a picture of Emmett's painting. He had stared at it a long time. It was a big, empty picture with great reaches of unoccupied cardboard. Except for the front of a house, an expanse of white siding dazzling in sunlight, there was almost nothing in the picture at all: shallow wooden steps ascended to a partially open door; beyond the door on the dark floor boards and deep in shadow lay something crumpled, a piece of goods, a ribbon perhaps, and beyond that a naked, retreating heel.

Emmett's father would have enriched the picture with many more objects: set pots of flowers on the steps, put a window next the door and a face at the window. Still empty and unembellished as the picture was, it had a certain power. He had found himself wondering about it: about that heel, more yellow than pink, about its haste, its alarm. Then he had noticed that there was a shadow across the steps, that near the house someone, stock-still, stood and watched. Listened, too, perhaps.

But when he had said to Emmett, who came in and found him staring, "Son, you're an artist," Emmett had taken the corn knife he had in his hand, and cut the picture to shreds.

"Don't call me that," he told his father. "Never say that. I can't learn. I'm a house and sign painter."

He was a house painter, or a barn or shed painter when he could find houses and barns and sheds to paint; but in Bucklin County he was treading upon the heels of a competitor. Emmett regarded with scorn the wash of murky green that marked the man's progress. A color not fit to set to the side of a hen house, he thought, not good enough for any privy I'd paint. He thanked God for his contract and painted signs.

He had known for some time that he was being watched. That didn't trouble him. It was almost as if the eyes that followed the movements of his hand gave it added force. It was talk that troubled.

"What's 'Crossing and Un-Crossing Powder?'"

"I don't know," Emmett said, painting on.

"Would you make a sign for what you don't know?"

"Yes," said Emmett, "I would."

"I wouldn't."

Emmett said nothing.

"What's 'David the Fearless Floor Wash?'"

Emmett set his brush in the can of linseed oil, turned away from the granite rock on which he was lettering freehand.

"What's a kid who stands asking questions while you're trying to work?" he asked.

The boy was big but round, round as an apple, and his round black eyes were swallowing the lettering like quagmire.

"A nuisance," Emmett told him, shortly.

"What's the sign for?" the boy asked, as if he hadn't heard.

"Make people buy the stuff."

"How can they buy it if they don't know what it is?"

"You couldn't buy if you knew. You haven't got any money."

The boy's pants were tight, his pockets taut, his hands fat; still he managed to squeeze a quarter up to the air.

"All right," said Emmett. "Read that and be quiet."

He tossed him the Occult Supplies Catalogue, turned back to his painting.

"Bat's Blood Oil," the boy said and Emmett could hear him moistly swallowing.

"Shut up," said Emmett, "or I'll take it away from you."

The boy shut up. Except for the swallowing he didn't make another sound until the sign was finished. The minute Emmett stepped away from the boulder to judge his completed work, he began again. "Which would you buy," he asked, "Graveyard Dust or Oriental Lover's Powder?"

"Graveyard Dust," said Emmett.

"Not me," said the boy. He pushed his quarter to the surface again. "I'll take three packages Oriental Lover's Powder."

"I don't sell the stuff," Emmett told him. "I just paint the signs. You write them," he pointed to the catalogue, "to get the powders."

"Have you got a pencil so's I could write it down?" the boy asked.

Emmett tore a sheet from the little notebook he carried, handed it and a pencil to the boy.

"What do you figure to do with it?" he asked, watching the boy, who wrote with his tongue as well as his fingers.

The boy looked up, but a sudden film came over his eyes. "None of your business," he said.

"That's right," said Emmett, "It isn't."

He took back the pencil and began to collect his gear.

"That your horse and rig by the bridge?"

"Yes," said Emmett.

"I'll help you carry your paints."

Emmett handed him a bucket. "Watch your step," he advised. "That's valuable."

The boy planted his bare feet as carefully as if walking through nettles. He looked over the amount of material in the back of the buckboard. "Takes an awful lot of paint to paint signs," he said.

"I paint houses, too," Emmett told him.

"Barns?" asked the boy.

"Sure," Emmett said.

"We got a barn to be painted."

"Who's we?"

"Us. My father. He wanted the other man to do it but Ivy said his paint looked like scum on a frog pond."

"Who's Ivy?" Emmett asked, thinking she'd picked the right word for it.

"My sister. But Ma said, 'There's things worse than scum, Miss Ivy.'"

"Don't your mother want the barn painted?"

"Oh, sure."

"I'll apply for the job," Emmett said. "You want to ride on home with me?"

They went by the river road. Red dust clung to the lush green growth that arched above their heads and Old Clay methodically lifted more of it to their faces. Even in the gloom of red dust and green shadows the boy bent over the catalogue, reading or rereading, Emmett didn't know which, the wondrous items. Emmett himself was rehearsing a sales talk; reassuring himself, before he tried to convince others, that he was the man for the job.

When they turned away from the river, made for the open, rolling farm lands, Emmett asked the boy his name.

"Oral," he said, not looking up from his reading.

"Oral," Emmett repeated. "How do you spell that?"

Oral spelled it. "I'm named for a bird," he said, keeping his place in the catalogue with one finger. "A yellow, singing bird that sang where my mother used to live."

Emmett looked at the cannon-ball boy, his black eyes and white hair. "You're not very yellow, Oral," he said. "Can you sing?"

The boy didn't smile and he closed his catalogue. "No," he said, "nor lay eggs, neither."

"Excuse me, Oral," Emmett said.

There was no more talk for a time. Finally Oral said, "You're not very big for a man."

"Big enough," said Emmett.

"You ain't bad looking, though."

Emmett nodded his thanks.

"You got a girl?" Oral asked.

"No girl," Emmett said. "I'm off girls."

"Not me," said Oral. "I got two."

"You don't look very old to be having girls," Emmett told him.

"Old enough," said Oral and went back to his reading.

He roused to point out his home before they got there. It and its outbuildings were planted on a gentle rise of land, visible, as they approached, from every hill-top: a substantial brick house and a big weather-beaten, two-story barn. Three-story, it proved to be when they arrived, the hillside on the back having been scooped away to make room for stalls for the animals.

Oral's father, who was Oral expanded and coated with hoarfrost, heartily welcomed Emmett.

"I'm C. B. Lish," he said after Emmett had stated his

own name and business, "and I'm pleased to make your acquaintance. The barn needs painting the worst way."

Emmett then delivered the rehearsed speech, speaking, as he thought right, of the quality of his paints: linseed base, lead content, color, time a coat would last; of his own work, skillful, experienced, painstaking. But C. B. Lish was reading.

"Candle Powder," he said wonderingly. "Now the way I always heard that was candle *power*."

"This is something different," Emmett explained, wishing the catalogue had never fallen into Lish hands. "This is a powder."

"Now, how," said C. B. Lish, "do you recken they go about getting a Candle Powder? Grind 'em up?"

"I don't know," Emmett said. "I just paint the signs."

"Bible Bouquet Oil," he said reading on and sniffing as he read. "There's a concoction ought to be mighty sweet. You sell this, boy?"

"No, sir," Emmett said, "I don't. I'm a painter. I'd like to get the job painting your barn."

C. B. Lish was turning the pages. "Jinxers. Four inches tall."

"I don't sell that stuff," Emmett reminded him. "I paint."

C. B. Lish nodded, but didn't look up. "That's what you told me before. You walk on up to the house and talk to Emma and Ivy. They're the ones to decide."

Emmett never forgot the room he stepped into. After the summer dust and heat it was as if he had plunged into water, shadowed and cool. He closed his eyes once or twice as he would have done under water, to feel the coolness on his eyelids. The bricks, he supposed, were what made the room cool, the pulled blinds kept it dim.

The room was a kitchen because it had a stove in it: unlit, cool-looking, even, black and shiny like a stoat fresh from a shady wallow. But besides the kitchen furniture—the safe, the cabinet, the set table—there was much else in the room. There was a sofa, a small bird in a big wooden cage, a secretary whose space was about evenly divided between books and dishes, a diamond-shaped mirror with pegs for hats and coats at each corner. Beneath one of the pulled blinds, Emmett guessed, a prism was hanging, for onto the bleached floor boards fell shafts of multicolored lights.

And there was a girl in the room. Emmett saw her last of all. She stood in the darkest corner of the room, leaning against the sink, grating nutmeg on a pudding of some kind. Emmett could smell the vanilla, sweet and sharp, above the sweet muskiness of the nutmeg.

The girl looked up at Emmett, then grated away, not saying a word. Emmett prepared to speak, but could not for a minute. He knew what a beautiful girl should look like; he had often thought about it; he knew exactly what it took. So far as he could see, nothing was missing.

The girl had on a white dress. She curved in and she curved out. Her waist went in to a span as narrow and supple as a grapevine; elsewhere she had the fullness of the clusters. Her hair was like Oral's, but her eyes when she had looked up at Emmett were like the best milk-agates he had ever owned. O God, Emmett silently prayed, I thank thee for not letting me stay home and study mules.

She was a calm-looking girl, but seeing Emmett, she

dropped the nutmeg, and the sound it made rolling along the bare floor boards brought him back to speech.

"Your nutmeg, Miss," said Emmett, getting it before it stopped rolling.

"Thank you," said the girl.

"I'm Emmett Maguire, house painter," Emmet told her.

"I'm pleased to meet you," said the girl. "I'm Miss Ivy Lish."

That night in the south upstairs chamber, a hot little room where a full-leafed chinaberry tree shut all the air from the single window, Emmett lay in a kind of trance. Sometimes he slept but more often he was awake, and every time he awakened he rejoiced as though he were Lazarus newly come to life. Sleeping, he dreamed of Ivy, but awake he thought of her. And, since he reckoned thinking to be one step nearer reality than dreaming, he hated to lose time in anything as second-hand as sleep.

He would awaken, wonder for a minute where he was, hear the leaves of the chinaberry tree moving outside his window with a watery ripple, say, "Ivy, Ivy." Inside himself he would feel a happiness so great it made him a little sick: a feeling like that he had tobogganing each winter on Sugar Slide, when at the final curve he always thought, I'll die this is so wonderful—joy and pain being at that point so delicately balanced.

Once he got out of his bed and laid the palms of both hands first against the west wall of his room, then against the east, telling himself as he did so, one inch of wood may be all that separates us. But all he heard as he stood, hands pressed to either wall, was a serene snoring: too delicate for Oral, probably C. B. Lish himself.

He had been in love before but always unlucky, and never able to do much but suffer. Once with a girl who was engaged, who had bent down and kissed him twice on the eyelids, but would have no more to do with him; once with a girl whose father had promised to shoot any man or boy who came on the place, and Emmett, after hearing the first load of buckshot whistle past his legs, had never again been able to feel the same about her; the last time had been with a girl in Mercer, but before he had a horse of his own, and in the weeks when he had not been able to see her, she had met and married a coffee salesman.

But now he was lucky: in love and beneath the same roof with the girl he loved. And going to be beneath the same roof with her for two more weeks at the least. For the barn painting, if he did a good job, would take that long; and he intended doing not only a good job, but a job so wonderful people for miles around would marvel at it. He intended to paint the Lish barn as if it were a miniature, with every brush stroke being set on ivory.

The last time he awakened the summer night had ended. The air in the room had cooled and outside in the chinaberry tree the awakening birds were whetting their bills and stretching their throats.

I could paint her, Emmett thought. I see just how to do it, where she should stand, how turn her head. I would paint her in her white dress, full length, a shadow at the base of her throat. In his hand he already felt the brush and the strokes it would make so that Ivy would stand curving in, curving out, alive upon cardboard. Alive with a reality beyond life because to her store of realness he would add all of his own.

✦

There was nothing in the next week he did not do well. He was so filled with power and sureness he walked about his scaffolding as if gravity were a force from which he was exempt. He laid the brush against the barn each day in strokes so solid that the barn rose up clear and bright again, rebuilt, it almost seemed, as well as repainted.

At night, untired after the day's work, he washed first in turpentine and then in water, and talked with the family.

Privately, he said to C. B. Lish, "I'll paint the tool shed free if I can borrow your buggy, Sunday."

"What you want of the buggy?" Mr. Lish asked.

"I want to take Ivy to church."

Mr. Lish whistled. "So that's the way the wind blows."

"Yes, sir," said Emmett, "it is."

"Ivy's no churchgoer," Mr. Lish told him.

Emmett was taken aback. He had supposed all nice girls were churchgoers. He had no idea where else he could take a girl on Sunday, or what other entertainment she could want. Though he would never have denied that for himself coming and going would be the best part of it. Still this was Bucklin County, not home, and he hated a man who was set in his ways.

"Wherever she wants to go, I'll take her."

"The novelty of it," her father admitted, "might appeal to her."

Ivy said yes when he asked her, as if novelty had nothing to do with it.

Upon himself, upon Old Clay and the buggy, Emmett had done an amount of polishing just short of abrasion. A stroke or two more and varnish and hide, human and horse alike, would have given away. Tender and glittering, they drove churchward.

There was nothing Emmett could think of to say which did not seem too personal for words. His mind was filled with Ivy: her sweet, flowery smell, which it was probably wrong even to notice, let alone mention; the blue vein in her forehead; the way a fold of her full skirt lay across his shinbone, where its lightness weighed upon him like a burning glass.

They drove through heat waves rippling like lake water. Already the leaves hung downward, giving the sun only their sharp edges to taste. Old Clay was discolored by sweat and on the fence rails the birds rested with lifted wings.

"Ivy," said Emmett, "will you let me paint your picture?"

"Can you paint people, too?" Ivy asked. "Besides barns, I mean?"

"Yes," said Emmett, with sudden knowledge, "I can," and he used the word he had forbidden his father "I'm an artist."

"Perhaps you would make me look funny," said Ivy.

"Funny," repeated Emmett. "What do you mean, funny?"

"Queer," Ivy told him. "Not pretty. Maybe you don't know how to paint well enough. Maybe you would make my eyes look funny. Eyes are very hard to paint."

"I know how to paint eyes," Emmett said. "I know how to paint all of a person. I would make you look the way you are, Ivy."

"How am I, Emmett?" asked Ivy.

"Beautiful," said Emmett, trembling with frankness.

From there on, the drive to church went by in a flash, the church time, too, though Ivy was unable to attend the services with Emmett. In the churchyard Arod Johnson had awaited her. His mother was sick, pining to see Ivy, and with Emmett's permission he would drive Ivy to his place, have her back by the time church was over. He was considerably later than that, and Emmett was sorry for Ivy cooped up with a sick old woman while he sat in the shaded churchyard. Still, he had been so deep in thought about his painting of her that he had not had time for much pity.

"Let's go home the long way," Ivy said when she got back.

They went home the long way through the hot afternoon.

"Tell me about my picture," Ivy said.

"I will paint you," Emmett said, "in the parlor bay window. I will push the lace curtain back so that on each side of the picture will be just their ripple. You will stand in your white dress before the clear glass and behind you will be the mock orange."

"How will I look?" asked Ivy.

"You will look," Emmett said slowly, seeing her like a white column budding for flowers—"fine."

"We came home the long way," Ivy told Oral, who was in the barnyard when they drove in. "We came home the long way and had to go slow because of the heat." She gave Emmett both her hands when he helped her from the buggy and walked at once to the house.

Oral helped with the unhitching.

"I reckon you seen Old Arod," he said.

"Arod Johnson?" asked Emmett.

"You know any other Arods?"

"No," said Emmett, "I don't. His mother was sick."

"She seems to be a mighty weak old lady," Oral told him, he himself leading Clay to the barn.

In the second week Emmett began work on the barn each morning at sunup. In that way he made time for his painting of Ivy. He had never supposed hand and brush could work so well together. It was as if the lines of Ivy's body flowed downward of themselves, through his arm and hand, and onto the cardboard; it was as if her colors stained his fingers and he had only to touch his brush for them to be left where and as they should be.

"What do you think of while you paint?" Ivy asked.

He thought of very little. Then he was lost in the work; in the brush strokes, in the leaf-shaped shadows on the white dress, on the way Ivy's roundness and solidness were transferred by means of his skill so that in thin paint and upon a flat surface, still she was round and solid.

Afterward, when he was not painting, he thought: in later days the picture will hang in a special place in the house and I will say to visitors, that is my beautiful wife, Ivy Lish Maguire; and to the children I'll say, that is the first picture I ever painted of your mother. And I will never part with it, no matter what I should be offered for it.

"I would like my eyelashes made longer," said Ivy.

"No," said Emmett, "that would be wrong."

"Wrong?" said Ivy. "They are longer."

"But not looking at you," Emmett told her, "this way against the light."

If someone had told him, you have never said the word

love, he would have been surprised. Everything he did said the word, every look, every tone, every gesture. He himself heard no other sound.

"Is it finished?" asked Ivy.

"One more day," said Emmett. "Do you like it?"

"The eyelashes should be longer," said Ivy, but Emmett could tell by the way she stood looking at the picture, turning her head, smiling, that she liked it.

That night he worked until late on the barn and went early to bed. He lay in his upstairs bedroom listening to the chirr of summer insects, and thought, tomorrow night the picture will be finished and I will put, in one corner of the picture, my name, in the other, hers.

He was still awake when Oral came in, noisy in his unaccustomed shoes, and sat on the edge of his bed. Oral moved his feet back and forth across the floor boards, the bed squeaked as his weight shifted, a bird sang a note or two as if, awakening suddenly, it had mistaken the moonlight for dawn.

"Well, Oral?" asked Emmett.

"I got me a date with one of my girls," said Oral as if answering the question.

"Which one?" Emmett asked sleepily, not caring, thinking, he's got no one else to talk to about his girls.

"The best one," Oral said.

Emmett yawned silently, shut his eyes. The moonlight here in the corner, he thought, isn't strong enough for him to tell whether my eyes are open or shut.

"Two's too many," Oral said, "if you've got one good girl."

"One good girl's enough," Emmett agreed, smiling at

Oral's wisdom. "How's the other one taking it?" he asked.

"She's down in the mouth," Oral admitted, "but she'll get over it."

"Sure," Emmett echoed out of his drowsiness, "they all get over it."

"Emmett," Oral asked, "who's that picture belong to, you or Ivy?"

"Ivy," Emmett said, wanting to say her name, though he had thought of the picture as theirs together.

"That's all right, then," Oral said getting off the bed.

"It's Ivy's and mine together," Emmett amended.

"She's given away your half too, then," Oral told him. "Both halves together to Arod Johnson."

Emmett sat up in bed. Oral was standing where the moonlight from the window fell across his broad and sorrowful face.

"I could've told you," he said, "but there wasn't ever a time when you'd hear to it."

"It's gone," he assured him, as Emmett got out of bed. "Wrapped in butcher paper and given away."

Emmett sat down again.

"My girl's waiting for me," Oral said. At the door he turned back. "Ivy's a born two-timer. You ain't the first."

For a long time after Oral left, Emmett sat on the edge of his bed. He felt numbed, beyond feeling anything, but when he stood up his hands and face were wet, and he saw that without knowing it he had been crying.

The thing to do, he decided, is to get out, pack and leave. Get gone before I have to look on any of their faces again.

Outside, his carpetbag in his hand, he stood for a time in the barnyard. He could see that it was still early, a moonlit summer night, cooling off now so that the river mists were flowing up into the draws. He could hear the soft, slow movements of the animals in their stalls and once in awhile, as the air freshened, a slight fluttering of leaves.

Old Clay came quietly to the fence, hung his head across the top rail, and, with eyes glassy in the moonlight, looked at Emmett.

"Let's get out of here," Emmett said.

But when he saw the ladder and scaffolding still against the barn, and the unpainted section around the haymow door, he determined, stubbornly, to finish the job. "I'll not go and leave a stroke undone," he told Old Clay, as if his horse had argued with him about it.

Once he was on the scaffolding, brush in hand, another idea came to him: she took my picture and gave it away. I'll leave another here that can't be given away, and I'll paint her this time as she really is, so no eye can miss it.

He went down the ladder and brought up his other paints, and while he was doing this he was filled with hate and scorn, thinking I'll put her on the barn so that everyone can see what a slut looks like. But he could not do it.

He did not know which way it was: whether he was unable to paint and hate at the same time, or whether actually he would never be able to hate Ivy, no matter what she might do. Whichever way it was—whether the brush strokes took away his hate, or he was without real hate to begin with—he was painting a picture not much different from his first. And better, too, he knew; though whether on that surface, with the paints he had, it would show as much, he couldn't tell. There would be no rippling lace curtains in this picture because it would be Ivy herself, unobscured by any of his imaginings. He remembered what he had thought: a tower of white. And budding; and remembering, spat with disgust over the edge of the scaffolding.

From below someone whispered, "Look out for me," and there in the moonlight, gazing upward, was Oral.

"What you doing out this time of night?" Emmett asked.

"Getting home," Oral whispered, so that Emmett, answering, whispered too—though the house was far enough away to keep anyone from hearing. "You better get on to bed. You'll catch a strapping, staying out all night this way."

"Strapping," Oral scoffed. "I'm not sleeping in the house anyway," he said. "I'm sleeping in the haymow." He stood, stocky legs far apart, head thrown back so that his white hair shone in the moonlight like dandelion fuzz.

"What you painting her again for?" he whispered scornfully. "Whyn't you paint something nice for a change? Whyn't you paint something pretty up there? A big sunflower or a rooster?"

"Be quiet, can't you?" Emmett said. "This makes me feel better."

Oral went inside the barn and Emmett could hear him mounting the ladder into the haymow, then rustling about as he hollowed himself a place to sleep.

Long after Emmett had supposed him to be sleeping, he heard Oral's voice very near at hand as if he were speaking with his mouth close to a knothole or crack.

"Emmett?"

"What you want now, Oral?"

"Whyn't you get some of them powders, Emmett?"

"Powders?" asked Emmett.

"The ones from the catalogue. They work good Emmett." Oral's voice was filled with kindness.

"I didn't know they'd come."

"Oh, sure, they came. They're strong and good. I wish you'd try some, Emmett."

"No," Emmett told him, "they wouldn't work for me. No powder'll do me any good. I've just got to learn."

"Don't waste any more time on her," urged Oral. "Paint something nice. Paint a picture of a field of punkins."

"When I finish this," said Emmett, "I will."

The moon was still bright when he finished, but the stars had begun to dim and the sky's darkness was fading. He hitched and loaded his stuff into the buckboard, but before he drove away he stood looking up at his work.

"I can paint," he said looking at his picture of Ivy, forgetting Ivy herself.

He had driven down the slope from the house and up the first little rise when he heard a clear but controlled halooing behind him. Turning about, he saw that Oral had opened the door of the haymow so that his picture of Ivy was cut in two: a head, then where the upper part of her body should have been, the empty space of the open door, and below that the swelling white skirts.

"Emmett," Oral halooed quietly.

Emmett waved to show that he heard.

"You forgot your catalogue, Emmett."

"Keep it," Emmett called back. "You keep it, Oral. I can get another."

Their gentle voices carried on the quiet morning air.

The last stars had faded and the river smell was fresh and sharp.

"Good-by, Emmett," Oral called as Emmett, waving, drove on.

For as long as Emmett could be seen, Oral stood in the open doorway, not waving, himself, but following the buckboard with his eyes until finally it topped a distant rise and dropped from sight.

*

The Mysteries of Life in an Orderly Manner

*

IT WAS initiation night, a candle-lighting ceremony, a big night in the lodge, and through the spring twilight of the California hill town, past the parking meters and the street-corner loungers, the matrons carrying their candles unlit drifted like moths. Not mothlike certainly in their plumpness but varicolored, fluttering, and pleasure-bent.

Emily Cooper (Mrs. W. H. Cooper—William H. Cooper, Inc., Insurance—"See Us B 4 U Burn") sat with her husband in their car, parked at the curb. Across the street from them, and a little way down, was the Vasconi Building, where the initiation was being held. Emily was herself to be initiated that night, but she didn't know the Pocahontas women very well and she was sitting for a time with her husband, gathering up courage from his matter-of-factness and checking the suitability of her dress against what she could see of the evening dresses of the other initiates, passing in the fading light. Only the initiates wore evening dresses (formals, formals, Emily reminded herself to say). The established lodge members, the Pocahontases in good standing, went to their meetings in Indian regalia. Emily watched them

24

go by in the twilight, coats thrown back, because the evening was warm, fringes swaying, beaded headbands gleaming, moccasined feet silent on the sidewalk. Emily was proud to recognize some of them.

"There's Mrs. Asta Bell," she said to her husband. "She's Keeper of the Wampum."

"Keeper of what?" asked Mr. Cooper, himself no lodge man. Emily got into Pocahontas because of her father, Clement McCarthy, a long-time Redman, though not a resident of the state. "Join, join," her father had always urged her, but Emily would not as long as the children were little.

"Wampum," said Emily. "Indian for money. She's treasurer."

Mrs. Edna Purvis went by, black-haired and straight, most Indianlike of all, and Mrs. Wanda Turner, married to the county sheriff, and Ruby Graves, married to no one at all, the only unmarried Pocahontas in the lodge. When Emily had remarked on this to some of the other lodge members, she had been told, "Most single girls are too frivolous for lodge work. Can't concentrate on ritual and memorizing, let alone beadwork. Spend their time mooning about, thinking of . . ."

Emily, anxious to appear quick-witted before her sisters-to-be, had suggested in this pause "men," and her informer had repeated the word, but it had seemed not quite to fill the bill. "Yes and no," she had told Emily. "Yes and no." But Ruby Graves was an exception—no mooner, they said, and, though maiden, as brisk in ritual and beadwork as any married lady.

More officers, some of the most important, passed by on

the sidewalk. "Look, look," said Emily, whispering, "but not right away. Now, that's the Grand Prophetess."

Mr. Cooper looked. "Couldn't tell her from an ordinary prophetess," he said calmly.

"Oh she's full of authority," said Emily. "A power in the lodge, believe me."

It was exciting for Emily to sit in the car with her husband, pointing out to him the town's leading ladies. It was a novelty, too, for it was he who had usually known everyone and done the pointing. But they were new in Los Robles, the insurance office had been open only a couple of months, and Mr. Cooper's work in opening it had kept him too busy for getting acquainted with the Pocahontas ladies.

"That's Mrs. Pleasant Jones," said Emily. "She's First Scout, and the one with her, the tall one with the red headband, I can't remember her name but I know she's the Second Runner."

Following the Second Runner were the Guards of Tepee and Forest, and Pocahontas herself—Mrs. Virginia Smiley—with feathers in her headband. Emily knew all three of them and pointed them out as they went by carrying their candles and squares or oblongs of home-baked cake. They passed on foot, by twos and threes, or alighted, singly, from cars driven by their husbands. They were laughing and talking, but their voices were low; an initiation by candlelight was solemn and secret; it was spring, it was almost night.

"They shouldn't have candles, really," Emily explained to her husband.

"No candles?" said Mr. Cooper, who had been watching the Second Runner. "Why not?"

"It's not in the Ritual. But the Grand Prophetess says we're so far off the beaten track here in the hills that we can plead ignorance in case of criticism."

"Why, sure," said Mr. Cooper. "Sure you can. Why not?"

"We shouldn't be hit-or-miss," explained Emily. "The lodge treats of the mysteries of life in an orderly manner."

Mr. Cooper looked at his wife inquiringly.

"That's what I was told," she said. "And the candles aren't part of that order."

"Maybe they're part of the mystery," suggested Mr. Cooper.

Emily supposed that her husband was smiling, but no, he was serious, looking intently into the creamy blooms of the laurel trees that lined the sidewalk, and listening to the birds that were singing on into the night because of the springtime.

"It's the second spring," said Emily.

In California, the first spring is in November. March only echoes it. In November the first spring is brief and sharp after the early rains. Then the grass flares up like fire; dry stream beds, as dead to the eye as old snakeskins, revive, all their bends and shallows filled with the curve of bright water; quail call; mushrooms push their blunt heads through the sodden leaves under the valley oaks; and at the end of the town's short streets, early sunsets and winter barley, alike green, meet. Spring is sharp in November—a slap, a blow, a kiss, soon over, soon forgotten, colder weather to follow. In March it is easy, gentle, nothing to wonder at, it will last a long time. Summer will come, the hills be brown and faded, no one able to say just when the rains stopped or the grass withered.

"Counting November, it's the second spring," said Mr. Cooper.

"I *was* counting November," said Emily, dangling a hand out the car window to test the air. It was still warm, though the sun was down, no color left behind, the sky as drab as a cast-iron skillet. Emily pushed her feet, slim in pointed satin slippers, up the incline of the floor boards until they cleared her full, white marquisette skirt. She reset the white daphne she had pinned in her hair and redampened her handkerchief from the bottle of Hoyt's perfume she had in her purse.

"Do I look all right?" she inquired anxiously of her husband.

"Fine, fine," said he. "Couldn't look better."

"Do I smell too strong of cologne?"

"Look fine, smell fine."

With sudden energy, Emily gathered her coat about her shoulders, grasped her candle, prepared to depart. "I always look fine," she said irritably. "I always look fine and I always smell fine to you. You don't give me any confidence."

Mr. Cooper leaned over, detained her with his hand on her arm. "But you do," he said. "You always do. What do you want me to say? Want me to be a liar?"

"No," said Emily, "but if I knew you were critical, it would give me more confidence."

"Oh, critical!" said Mr. Cooper, surprised. "Why, I'm critical, critical as all getout. That Second Runner, now. She's bandy-legged. I criticized it in her first thing. They'd ought to have given her the wampum job. Something she could do sitting down, not put her to running."

Emily opened the car door, jumped out, and banged

it behind her. It was dark enough for the first stars to show, not distinctly, a little blurred in their outlines, as if the moist spring air had caused them to run a bit. The birds were still rustling and chirping in the laurel trees, unwilling for this day to end. Down the street the neon signs said "Eat," said "Drink," said "Short Orders," said "Church of the Open Door." There were no Pocahontases in sight and Emily felt a little strange, on the street after dark in her long white dress. A man paused under the "Drink" sign to look at her before pushing the swinging doors apart. She lingered at the car side.

"Don't joke about serious things," she said fiercely. "It makes me nervous. And I'm already nervous to begin with."

"Don't be nervous," said Mr. Cooper. "I'm critical and you look fine and smell fine and you are going to see the marvels of life in an orderly manner."

"Mysteries," said Emily, *"mysteries,"* and she turned away without so much as a good-by and started toward the Vasconi Building. But before she had taken two angry steps, Mr. Cooper had caught up with her.

"Mysteries was what I meant," he said contritely, and they walked on together arm in arm, past the birds and the trees and the plate-glass windows and the men going in for a drink. "The mysteries of life in an orderly manner," he said, "was what I fully intended to say."

Love, Death, and the Ladies' Drill Team

*

EMILY COOPER, the newest member of the Pocahontas Drill Team, was the first to arrive at the
Burnham Building, where the morning practice,
called by their drillmaster and team captain, Mrs. Amy
Rotunda, was to be held. She stood for a while enjoying
the wind—California's warm, dry September wind—before starting up the stairs to Burnham Hall. Burnham
Hall was less pretentious than its name, being no more
than the drab, unfurnished second floor of the building
that housed, on its first floor, Burnham's Hardware, but
the only other hall available in the small town of Los
Robles was, though its rent was lower, unfortunately
located above Sloane & Pierce's Undertaking Parlors.

Emily was halfway up the stairs when she was hailed
from the sidewalk below by Mr. Burnham himself, holding a key aloft. "You one of the Pocahontas girls?" he
called.

Emily turned about on the stairs and gazed down at the
wide-shouldered old man. The wind was lifting his coattails and tossing his white hair about in tufts, like those of
the bunch grass she had known as a girl in the Dakotas.
She hesitated for a moment before answering. She was

30

a Pocahontas, all right, but "girl" was a different story. She was thirty-six years old, had been married half her life, and had only an hour ago started her youngest off to his first day of school. Then, left without a child in the house for the first time in fifteen years, she had told her passing image in a mirror, "This is the beginning of middle age for you, Emily Cooper." Now "girl."

Mr. Burnham, as if understanding the reason for her hesitation, smiled as she came back down for the key. "My youngest is fifty," he said. Then, perhaps fearing that she might consider such confidences too personal, coming from a stranger, he spoke reassuringly of the weather. "Nice blow we're having—nice touch of wind." He faced about for a second after saying this, to get the full force of the warm, lively agitation, which had everything movable in Los Robles moving.

Actually, this talk of the wind was far more personal to Emily than Mr. Burnham's remark about his children. When he put the key in her hand, she said, "It's wonderful weather. I love the wind." Then she, too, was overtaken by a conviction that there was something unseemly in so much openness with a stranger, and she said a quick thank you and started back up the stairs. As she was unlocking the door, Mr. Burnham called, "Throw open the windows, will you? Modern Woodmen used the hall last night and they're a smoky lot."

Mr. Burnham was right about the Woodmen. Emily felt as if she were stepping into the bowl of a pipe still warm and filled with fumes. There were windows across the entire front of the hall, which faced on Los Robles' Main Street, and she opened them all. Then she pulled a chair up to the middle window and sat down to await the arrival of her teammates. There was not much to be seen on the street below her. Ten o'clock on a Monday morning is not an hour for shoppers, and the children who yesterday would have been out in the wind, shirt-tails lofted for sails, diving and swooping like birds, but much noisier, were behind closed doors, with shirt-tails tucked in, and speaking only when nodded to by Teacher. She thought of her own Johnny and hoped he was finding school the wonder he had imagined it. He had left her without a tear, without even a backward look, declaring, with the pleasure of a man who has arrived at a goal long deferred, "Now I am a scholar."

Emily leaned out the window to watch a tumbleweed, blown into town from one of the surrounding barley fields, cross Main at Brown, traveling west swiftly and silently. In the vacant lot across the street, the tall, switch-stemmed dust flowers were bent down almost as low as grass. Beneath the window, the Burnham Hardware sign was swinging, and the awning was bellying and snapping with the sound, she supposed, of a ship under full sail. A few merchants were beginning to go up the street to the Gem for their midmorning cups of coffee. Merchants, the wind revealed, had bodies. Inside their usually unyielding tubes of serge and herringbone, their legs were astonishingly thin. As if in restitution for this exposure, the wind parted their coattails to display their firm and stately bottoms. A black cat passed below, its black-ness not even skin-deep, for its hair, wind-blown, exposed a skin as white as that of any butcher-shop rabbit. Emily thrust her hands out across the window sill, feeling through her outspread fingers the full force and warmth of the blowing—as if I were the one true gauge, she thought, the one responsive and harmonious harp.

She was leaning thus, and by now almost half out of the room, when Mrs. Rotunda, the drill captain and coach, and Miss Ruby Graves, the team's star performer, arrived. Emily was new not only to the drill team but to the town of Los Robles, and was still able, she thought, to see people as they really were, unlabeled by a knowledge of their professions or reputations. But "Miss" and Mrs." are in themselves labels, and Mrs. Rotunda's gray hair, elaborately waved and curled, with a fancy off-center part at the back and sculptured bangs arranged with all the finality of marble, said widow, said woman without a husband, filling in an empty and lonesome life with what, in the old, rich days, she would never have wasted time on. While, somewhat contradictorily, Miss Graves's black hair, long and innocent of the slightest ripple, said spinster, said woman without a husband and reconciled to the idea that her hair, curled or uncurled, was never going to be a matter of moment to any man. But without that "Miss" and "Mrs.," without her knowledge that Amy Rotunda was Fred Rotunda's widow, and Ruby Graves was Milton Graves's unmarried daughter and housekeeper, would she have had all this insight about hair? Emily couldn't say.

It was the same with Opal Tetford and Lacey Philips, who arrived next. Mrs. Tetford's husband was an official in the local Bank of America, while Mrs. Philip's husband owned and operated a big grain ranch out on the edge of town. Knowing this, Emily thought Mrs. Tetford's soft opulence was suited to the protection of vaults and burglar alarms, while Mrs. Philips's rawboned frame was right in its austerity for a background of endless barley fields and rolling, cactus-covered hills.

Mrs. Rotunda said, "I am going to demand that the Woodmen do something about this tobacco smoke. Do they think they're the only ones who use this hall?"

Miss Graves, who prided herself on being unprejudiced about men, though with every reason to justify prejudice, said, "I expect they are chain smokers, Amy. One cigarette after another all evening long."

Mrs. Rotunda, who had no need to conjecture, said, "Well, they could at least use a little Air-Wick afterward." She went to a window and leaned out for a breath of uncontaminated air. The other ladies drew up chairs at the windows. Beneath them, Mr. Sloane, of Sloane & Pierce, passed by on his way to the Gem for his midmorning cup of coffee. Mr. Sloane, like many undertakers, was the picture of rosy durability, an evidence to mourners that though one life had ended, life itself endured.

Mrs. Rotunda withdrew her head from the window and began to pace up and down behind her seated teammates. "No," she declared. "I could never bring myself to do it. Not for a mere two-fifty, anyway."

Emily looked inquiringly at Lacey Philips, who was seated next to her. "The Sloane & Pierce hall rents for two-fifty less than this one," Mrs. Philips explained.

"Save two-fifty at the price of drilling back and forth, quite possibly, over the body of your own dead mother? Not I," said Mrs. Rotunda firmly. "It would take a lot more than two-fifty to reconcile me to that."

Ruby Graves, who, in the manner of maiden ladies,

combined extreme idealism on some subjects with extreme matter-of-factness on others, said, "If your mother passed away, Amy, wouldn't they hold the services for her down in Anaheim?"

Mrs. Rotunda replied with patience. "Ruby, I was speaking hypothetically. Mother has owned a plot at Rosemead for I don't know how long, and will, of course, be laid to rest there—not be brought up here to the Sloane & Pierce funeral home to be marched across by Odd Fellows and Knights of Pythias and others for whom such things don't matter. But I only mentioned her as an example. I would have exactly the same scruples about marching over *your* mother."

Ruby turned away from the window. "Mother passed away a year ago Labor Day, Amy," she said in a voice that forgave the forgetfulness.

Mrs. Rotunda put her hands to her head. "Ruby, I could bite my tongue out!" she cried. "My point was—anyone. I'd have too much fellow feeling to be willing to meet above the remains."

Emily said, "I think Sloane & Pierce is a good place for Jehovah's Witnesses to meet, though."

"Do they meet there?" Mrs. Tetford asked. Mrs. Tetford had a reputation for asking questions—trained, they said, by Mr. Tetford, who was a man who liked to supply answers.

Emily nodded.

"Why?" Mrs. Tetford asked.

"I don't know," Emily said.

"I mean why do you think it's a good place for them to meet?"

"Oh. Well, that's one of the things a church is for,

isn't it?" Emily asked, and, thinking of her children, seeing them already grown and scattered, and herself and John left alone with their memories, she added, "To remind us that all earthly things pass away?"

Mrs. Rotunda, at the words "pass away," stopped her pacing, and the hall had the silence of a room in which a clock suddenly ceases ticking. The women turned toward her and she extended her arms as if about to ask some extraordinary favor. "Oh, girls!" she cried. "My dear girls! Let's not be morbid. Let's not dwell on the inevitable or we'll have no heart for our practice."

Her life is drilling, Emily thought, smiling. The lodge is her husband and we are her children. She admired Mrs. Rotunda and hoped that, should she ever be left alone, she could be as sensible. Mrs. Rotunda came to the window before which Emily and Lacey sat, and perched between them on the window sill. Gazing down into the street, she shook her head. "Poor girl. Poor, poor girl," she said.

"Imola Ramos?" Emily asked, though there was not, at the moment, anyone else in sight who could possibly be called a girl. Imola was a black-haired, brown-skinned woman of about her own age. Her red-flowered dress, which looked as if it might have started life as a window curtain or a tablecloth, was cut like a Mother Hubbard and belted in closely with what appeared, from the second story of the Burnham Building, to be a piece of gray, frayed clothesline. It was plain to be seen that she wore no brassière—and not much else, for the wind plastered the big red flowers as close to her thighs as if they were tattooed there.

"Ramos!" Mrs. Rotunda said. "Why, Emily, Imola's name's no more Ramos than yours is. Her name's what it's always been—since she was married, anyway. Fetters. She married LeRoy Fetters so young it's hard to remember that she was born a Butterfield. But it's Fetters now. That Mexican never married her. Couldn't, to do him justice, since LeRoy would never divorce her. And anyway why should he have married her? She was willing to live with him."

"Live with him as man and wife," Ruby explained.

"I never knew they weren't married," Emily said. "I've always heard her called Mrs. Ramos."

Mrs. Rotunda excused this. "You haven't been in Los Robles very long. It takes a little time to catch on to these things."

Imola, who was carrying two shopping bags heavy enough to curve her square shoulders, stepped off the sidewalk and into the vacant lot opposite the Burnham Building. There she set the bags down amidst the blue dust flowers, and while the disturbed cicadas one by one ceased shrilling, she hunted in her purse for her cigarettes. By the time she had her cigarette lighted, the cicadas were once again filling Main Street with their country cries, and Imola, her head on one side, appeared to be listening with pleasure to the sound.

"Why did she leave her husband?" Emily asked.

"That is the mystery," Mrs. Rotunda admitted. "There never was a better man on earth, to my mind, than LeRoy Fetters."

"LeRoy used to wash Imola's hair for her, regular as clockwork, every ten days," Mrs. Philips said.

"Why? I always wondered," Mrs. Tetford asked.

"Pride," Ruby said. "Pure pride in that great mane of black hair."

They were all watching Imola, standing at her ease in the vacant lot, the wind outlining her sturdy body—a woman obviously well and happy.

Disagreeing with Ruby, Mrs. Tetford answered her own question. "In my opinion, LeRoy did it to save the price of a beauty parlor."

Contradicted about motives, Ruby took a new tack. "They say, Mrs. Cooper, that this Mexican manhandles her."

Mrs. Rotunda sniffed. "They say," she said. "I *saw.* Just a week ago today, I saw them having breakfast at the Gem, and Imola had black-and-blue spots the size of quarters on her arms."

Ruby said, "Poor Imola."

"What were *you* doing down at the Gem at breakfast time, Amy?" Mrs. Tetford asked.

"Who said anything about its being breakfast time? As a matter of fact, it was three in the afternoon, and I was having a root-beer float. But those two were having fried eggs and hot cakes, bold as brass, not making the least effort to deceive anyone."

"Why?" Ruby asked. "Why were they having breakfast at that hour?"

"You may well ask, Ruby," said Mrs. Rotunda shortly.

"I feel so sorry for Imola," Mrs. Tetford said.

"They live out near our ranch, you know," Mrs. Philips told them. "They're on the edge of the irrigation ditch, in one of those three-room shacks that the water company furnishes its Mexican workers. Two rooms and a lean-to, really, is what they are. Mattress on the floor, in place of a bed. Old, broken-down, rusty oil stove. Chesterfield with its springs half through the upholstery."

"I wonder how Imola's mother *bears* it," Mrs. Rotunda said.

"Do you ever see them?" Mrs. Tetford asked Mrs. Philips.

"Many's the time. Manuel doesn't seem to have any regular working hours, and in the summertime they do a lot of sporting around together, in and out of the water. And the shoe's on the other foot this time so far's washing is concerned. Imola's the one who does the washing now."

"His hair?" asked Ruby.

"Well, just generally," Mrs. Philips answered.

"A Butterfield washing a Mexican! Sunk that low! It doesn't bear thinking about," Mrs. Tetford said.

"I expect he's pretty dark-skinned?" asked Ruby, who evidently could bear thinking about it.

"They both are," Mrs. Philips explained. "After they finish swimming or washing, whichever it is, they lie around in the sun, sun-tanning. And, like as not, Manuel will play some music for Imola on that instrument of his. That banjo or guitar—I never can tell the two of them apart."

"Fred used to play the clarinet," Mrs. Rotunda said. "He had a natural ear for music and could play anything he'd heard once."

"Is it flat-backed or curved, Lacey?" Mrs. Tetford asked. "This musical instrument?"

"I never did notice."

"Big or little, comparatively speaking?"

"Big," Lacey Philips said.

"It's a guitar, then. I thought it would be. That's the Spanish national instrument."

"He is dressed, I suppose, by the time this music-making starts?" Ruby Graves said.

"Dressed!" Mrs. Philips exclaimed. "Why, Ruby, he sits there strumming out melodies and flinching off flies as innocent of clothes as a newborn babe!"

"And Imola?"

"Naked as a jay bird. Lying in the grass kicking up her heels. Sometimes silent, sometimes singing."

Mrs. Tetford shook her head. "The poor girl."

"Play to her, hit her. I guess Imola runs the full gamut with that man," Ruby speculated.

"Speak of the devil," said Mrs. Philips, motioning with her chin up the street.

Emily, who had been watching Imola as she listened to the talk about her, saw her throw away the stub of her cigarette and wave at the man coming up the street toward her. Ramos was a short, stocky man with a strong, toed-in walk and, when he reached Imola, a quick, white smile. Imola stooped down when he turned in at the vacant lot and brought up out of one of her shopping bags an enormous bunch of purple grapes.

"Isabellas," said Mrs. Philips. "First it's a feast, then it's a fast with them, I guess."

"He's a big, burly fellow," Mrs. Rotunda admitted.

"Naked and singing by the irrigation ditch," Ruby marveled as Imola popped grapes alternately into her own own mouth and into that of the Mexican.

"LeRoy Fetters was a registered pharmacist," Mrs. Rotunda told Emily. "A very responsible man. He always took a real interest in whether his prescriptions helped."

"Breakfast at three o'clock," Ruby murmured as the feeding below continued, interspersed with considerable affectionate horseplay. "I wonder what it tastes like at that hour."

"Not a thing in the world to keep you from finding out, is there, Ruby?" Mrs. Rotunda asked.

"I doubt it would be the same alone," Ruby said.

Across the street, the grapes finished, Imola, there in the broad daylight of midmorning and in the middle of Los Robles, first kissed the Mexican full on the mouth, then put a cigarette between his lips and, while he shielded it with his hands, lighted it for him.

The ladies were silent for quite a while after this. Finally, Mrs. Tetford said, "Poor Imola! Where is her pride?"

Imola now lighted a cigarette for herself. Emily, watching the two of them at their ease amid the weeds and dust flowers, the wind carrying their cigarette smoke streaming away from them in transparent plumes, said, to her own surprise, "Pride? Why, Mrs. Tetford, pride doesn't enter in. She loves him."

There was another long silence in the hall. A number of additional members of the drill team had arrived, and Emily felt that her unconsidered word was settling among them like a stone in a pond of still water. But just at the moment when she supposed the last ripple had disappeared, Mrs. Rotunda repeated the word, in a voice that lingered and explored. "Love?" she asked. "Love?"

Is she asking me, Emily thought. But evidently she was not, for before Emily could answer, Mrs. Rotunda had turned her back on the window and was calling the team together. "Girls, girls!" she cried. "Let's not moon! We won't wait for the others. Now, hands on shoulders, and remember, an arm's length apart."

Mrs. Rotunda turned them away from the windows and got them linked together. They reversed by eights, went forward by twos, and formed hollow squares. Emily, still thoughtful, still lingering by the window, saw Imola and the Mexican pick up the shopping bags and proceed, together and equally burdened, down the street. She saw Mr. Sloane return, refreshed, from the Gem to his work. She saw Mr. Burnham out on the edge of the sidewalk, face uplifted as if searching the wind for scents of some lost place or time. She saw how the wind, swooping down off the dry, brown hills, wrapped the soft prints of her drill mates' dresses about their vari-shaped bodies, so that they moved through the elaborate figures of Mrs. Rotunda's planning like women in some picture of past days. And Mrs. Rotunda's brisk commands—"To the rear by twos!" or "The diamond formation!"—were like a little, inconsequential piping, the way the wind, veering, shrills for a second or two through a crack before resuming its own voice, deep and solemn and prophetic.

*

Home-Coming

*

HENDRICKS lifted himself on his elbow. He thought he knew all the sounds that were to be heard at that time of night: the soft relaxed coughs of those who coughed without awakening: the hard bitter coughs of those who had no hope of sleeping longer, and who sat up in bed and held their sputum cups in straining fingers; the distant muffled clink and thud of the night nurse as she started her final rounds in Culbertson; the heavy sighing groans of Kurtz as his two o'clock codeine began to wear off; and far above in the hills the crying of the last coyotes before dawn.

Hendricks was accustomed to listening to these sounds each morning, as his own procaine lost its effectiveness. Only a few moments before, the hearse had crept down the hill with that silence which the management hoped minimized for those who remained the import of its journey. The velvety throb of its engine still pulsed in his ears, and he had to wait until that echo had faded before he could be sure that he had heard anything else.

As he strained forward in his bed, supporting himself on arms that quivered a little from the unusual effort, he heard, not a continuation of the light gritty sound to

43

which he had been listening, but the first cocks crowing below on the valley ranches.

He slumped back on his pillows. Sometimes he forgot that other world where men left their beds in the morning and went to work, and he was happier when this was so. He could manage to live in the abnormal and isolated world in which he found himself only by dint of forcing himself to forget that another existed. When he thought of the men on the ranches below plunging out of their beds into the gray morning coolness with responsive bodies, he hated them, as though their health was the result of some thievery from him.

He grinned to himself at this warped fancy and wondered which young rancher pulled on his pants with extra force that morning, because to his energy had been added all that he, Hendricks, had lost. Pull 'em on with a will Buddy, he thought, for God knows how soon you may have to shed them permanently. He felt his own limp pajamas, still damp from his heavy night sweat, with bitter distaste. Better rivet them on Buddy, then they'll never get you in a joint like this.

He turned his face unconsciously toward McRae's bed. This was only the second morning McRae had been gone, and after seven months of hearing him say at this hour, "Well, Hendricks, another day, another bug," he missed him. It was a ritual with them, a T. B.-er's salute to the dawn: "Another day, another bug," McRae would say.

Hendricks would answer, "What do you mean, kid? Another bug manufactured?"

And McRae would answer with scornful conviction, "Hell no, Rick, another bug *dead!*"

Somehow Hendricks was always comforted by the assurance of McRae's voice. He liked to think that his early morning depletion was the result of a nightlong struggle with a bug, who at morning light was in worse case than he.

McRae's conviction seemed to have some basis in fact, for two days ago the doc had said he could go home. Not that his fibrosis really warranted it—he should have had another six months in the san—but McRae was a level-headed guy and he had a wife whom he missed and who clamored for his return. Hendricks had seen her a couple of times, and listened through many a twilight to McRae talk of her.

No T. B.-er had a higher color or more transparent skin than McRae's wife. She was always late when she came to see McRae, and bubbling over with a pretty breathless penitence, which tried to say, Hendricks thought, "Darling, I've come to you in spite of really ghastly difficulties." McRae ate it up and didn't even notice that her act was as much for Hendricks's benefit as his own.

After her first conversational bubble had burst she hadn't much to say. She sat there and let McRae entertain her. Hendricks could feel the poor kid go taut with the effort to convert the dreary tragic routine of their days into something sprightly and amusing for her. That cockroach on his tray, which had really ruined a meal for him when meals were important, became simply a funny story for Nella, and his eyes were anxious and bright until she smiled.

And he gave her that horrible story of Kurtz's signing his name in his hemorrhage blood mockingly and lightly as if he had not been aware that many of them in just such blood would sign their final signatures.

McRae gave her everything he had; all the energy he had conserved through weeks of discipline and denial he drained off now recklessly for Nella. Hendricks supposed he wanted her to feel that he was no invalid, not really sick, washed up, but just a guy taking a little time out and amused and a little touched at what was going on around him.

He'll have to have a triple dose of Amytal tonight, Hendricks would think. Why in God's name doesn't she tell the kid something? Tell him how a streetcar looks, or what the fellow in the drugstore said when he mixed her frosted chocolate, or whether the peach trees are in bloom yet. All the sights her eyes see and all the sounds her ears hear that are denied McRae. Why doesn't she bring them to him? Why doesn't she tell him that the guys at the plant miss him? Why doesn't she tell him what Martin said to Lewis in the show last week, or how the air smells outside these antiseptic halls?

Then he'd think, Oh hell! This isn't the way McRae looks at her. And he'd try to see her through McRae's eyes. She wasn't hard to look at through his own eyes. Pink and clean, and plump in all the right places, and wearing her clothes so that all of the right places showed. And smelling sweet and fresh, too. If he could remember sleeping with her, as McRae could, he'd probably be sending his own temp up in an effort to keep her interested.

Hendricks looked out at the morning, gray now like a mouse, or a skillet, night's blackness completely gone. He reluctantly put his hand out for his temp stick, shook the bichloride solution from it, and slid it under his tongue. He was unconcerned over this ritual. The morning subnormality didn't faze him; it was the afternoon's horrible upper oscillation that made his chest heavy and tight as he waited to see how high the mercury had risen, to gauge again the heat of that fire which consumed him.

So, with his temp stick in his mouth, he lay over on his side, happy to have the dark uncharted night behind him, to be caught up, once more, into that ordered and methodical routine which made his days tolerable; a routine in which he lost his identity and became simply a cell in the great sanatorium organism.

He looked down the slope of the hill toward the administration building where a clump of eucalyptus was just moving, gray-green, in the gray air. The thud of a closing door made him drop his eyes, and he saw a man emerge from the administration building. Someone on the way out, he thought, if they're getting relatives here at this time of the morning. Some poor kid up to see his wife off. Agony and relief all in one. He's thought of her as dead for so long that it will rest his mind not to have the contradiction of her live eyes looking at him from the pillow. He raised himself to have a better look at the young husband.

"McRae," he called, half swallowing his temp stick.

McRae heard him, gave a little gesture, half of recognition, half of warning to be quiet, and came on, slowly, up the path.

Hendricks looked at his temp stick, saw the usual 97.4, and put it back in the glass, irked that not even McRae's appearance had jarred his egocentric interest in his body's heat.

McRae was at the door. "I hope I didn't send it up a couple of degrees."

"Kid, what are you doing here?"

McRae eased himself onto his old bed, and lay face up as if dead beat. He shut his eyes, and pulled his coat around his throat.

"Come on, McRae, get out of your clothes," Hendricks urged. "You'll freeze there. Get on a pair of my pajamas. Take it easy, but get into them, and get in bed. I thought I heard something a half-hour or so back. Was that you? I'll ring for Samuels to help you; you're all in."

"Samuels is busy. It was me you heard, all right. I was going to come up and just slide in, but Samuels saw me, made me wait while she phoned the doc if it was O.K."

"Why didn't she come up and help you?"

"A girl's hemorrhaging down in Ballard."

"Samuels can smell arterial blood a mile off. She's like a fire horse smelling smoke. I've seen her flanks heave when a hemorrhage call went through. She lives on blood like a vampire."

"Cut it, Hendricks."

"Did you spit some rubies while you were gone, kid?"

"Nothing like that."

"Come on, McRae, get out of your clothes. I'll get my pajamas for you myself."

McRae sat up, his eyes still closed, as if the effort to open them was beyond what he could endure. He pulled off his tie, got out of his coat, stumbled over to the chest of drawers where Hendricks's clothes were kept.

"The middle drawer, Mac. The flannel ones are there on top."

Hendricks watched McRae get out of his clothes with

pitying and speculative eyes. He's lost weight, he thought, in the last forty-eight hours. Lord, how his phrenic scar shows up when he's cold. Looks like something tattooed on him.

"Don't be a fool, Mac. Let 'em lay. Samuels can put them away. What's she paid for?"

McRae got into bed with the jerkiness of fatigue and cold. Hendricks tossed him his warm pad. "Put this on your belly. It'll warm you up quicker than putting it on your feet. Now shake down, kid, and take it easy. Breakfast will be here in an hour or so, and some hot coffee will put you right."

McRae said, "Rick, it's swell to be back. I didn't know."

"Sure you didn't, kid, but you'd better catch some rest before breakfast."

"You going to sleep?"

"Hell no. I finished two hours ago. Go ahead and talk if you want to. How'd you come back?"

"Bus."

"You weren't fool enough to sit up all night on a bus? What for, Mac?"

"I wanted to get back. And I was afraid to wait."

"What do you mean, afraid? Afraid of what?"

"Afraid of myself, afraid I'd never do it if I waited."

Hendricks looked over at McRae, who was getting warmed up, losing his bluish pallor. He supposed he might as well let him talk—better perhaps. God knows what had happened to him, but it had something to do with that pink and white Nella.

"You know, Rick, I'd been counting the days until I could leave here. Had 'em marked off on my calendar like a schoolgirl. There are a lot of things here I thought I'd like to get away from."

Hendricks knew: the deaths, the smells, the sounds; the speculation about your own durability; the mechanical care; the pork and ice cream every Sunday; the feverishness of weighing day; the sound of bedpans being emptied—and filled; and above all the sense of being shut off from the world, confined, like one from whom all humanity has fled. Sure, Hendricks knew.

"Well, kid, you got away, didn't you? When did you get into Fresno?"

"Tuesday morning at eight. I felt like a convict on the train, Rick. Thought everyone could tell I'd just got out of a san."

Hendricks knew about that, too.

"Did you have breakfast with Nella in Fresno?"

"I ate there, but she had eaten already. It's hot down in the valley. She had on a white suit. You know she's been selling real estate since I've been here, with her brother. She had a big deal on. She told me about it while I ate."

"So you listened to the 'big deal' on your first morning out, kid? You hadn't planned on that, had you? Thought you'd as well be back, with Samuels giving you theosophy with your breakfast tray?"

"We went out to go to the car. It was burning hot already. Have you forgotten how the people walk along on hot summer mornings before they're tired, Rick? Stepping along on the balls of their feet, and their eyes proud because they feel so strong and fresh? Nella was like that. She pulsed and glowed when she walked. I tried to match her but I couldn't do it. How could I? I haven't walked for a year. The heat and walking along so fast made me feel damned queasy. I thought I'd lose my breakfast.

"Then Nella met a man who was in on this real-estate deal and they stopped to talk. They talked for a long time —maybe a half-hour. At first I tried to be knowing about real estate—be the little woman's husband come home to help. But I was too sick standing in that sun. I didn't know where the car was and Nella was too busy to tell me. All I could do was lean against a building and hope I wouldn't slide down.

"After a while Nella finished. She was good, all right. Plenty good. But she wasn't proud of me, gray-green and hanging on to a wall.

"Well, we started home, and I thought everything would be all right. We had fifty miles to go, and I thought we'd get to talk at last. That things would be like I used to imagine them—here. But Nella had to stop at Ralston to see the banker, and she had to think how she'd put her case to him. We left Ralston about one o'clock."

"Nothing to eat since breakfast, Mac?"

"No, but it was the heat that made me sick. Well, we got home. Lord, how I've longed to see it. I planted a lot of things there, you know. And my dog was still there. But all I could see was a string of cars in front of the house. I began to think the heat was making me see things. I'd always thought of me coming home to just Nella, and a quiet house.

"When we got out of the car a lot of people came out on the porch: mostly people from the real-estate office. They yelled all together, 'Welcome home to the invalid,' and Nella took my arm and said, 'See, I've planned a party for you.' "

"My God, kid," Hendricks murmured, "that Nella of yours is some planner. And then you had to shake hands, and say you felt swell, and how good it was to be home. And you had to stand up some more, or thought you did."

"There was a cake, Rick. It had printed on it in red icing, 'East, West, Home's Best.' I had to cut it like a bride at a wedding. I sliced that home in two with the first cut. They all looked at me."

"Yeah, I know kid." They all looked at you, Hendricks thought. They got in corners and whispered that you looked a little feverish. They wondered if you'd ever had a hemorrhage, and some said you wouldn't be much good for Nella. And you felt it all. What they had to say closed in tight about you so there was no place to turn. And you had to play up to Nella. Be gay. Celebrate. Drink some wine you didn't want. Hell, kid, don't tell me.

"They left after a while. Said they knew Nella and I would want to be alone."

"Well, that was what you wanted, wasn't it? You used to spoil your days here thinking of Nella. Now you had her, you didn't want her, eh? You thought of rest period before supper, and Blaise plumping up the pillows for you, and the towhees chirping a little, but no other sound; and you wished you were back."

"No, I didn't want to be back. Not then. This was the first moment I'd had with Nella. Sure, I was dead beat, but have you forgotten how beautiful Nella is? She put on a kimono—long and soft, and pink. Not like these damned stiff white uniforms. Thin, you know. It was still blazing hot.

"Mac, I'm not sure I like reunion scenes. Husband and wife together at last. So you took her in your arms. You're done in, Mac. Why not cut it? Breakfast's about due. What you need's food, not confession."

"I need to explain myself to myself. Why I'm back here. You don't need to listen. No use telling you t.b. doesn't make a female any less desirable."

Hendricks watched Mac put his arm over his eyes. No use telling me, he thought. Makes you concupiscent as hell. Funny thing, for a disease to make you want what will kill you quickest. Nature double-crosses you every chance it gets. He regarded the boy with the pity of remembrance.

"Well, Mac, looks to me like the perfect setup. Boy meets girl. All legal and everything. Where's the hitch? What're you doing back here?"

"I came back because I wasn't ready to die yet. I could die for some things—but not that. Nella—I didn't mean a thing to Nella, Rick. Not a thing—or only one thing. I thought she'd been counting the days and hours, as I'd been. I thought she'd be proud of what I'd done. Pulled out of this business when no one thought I could."

I'd ought to told you kid. They don't wait for you like that. They've never had the measure of their life taken on a temp stick. They've got, without turning over a finger, what we've had to work for like hell. It's like asking a millionaire to understand how a kid feels about a penny.

Hendricks saw, for a minute, both sides. Oh God, the sick and well were never meant to be together. They only hurt each other. The well could take it; but the sick died two deaths. First, the soul's death at being misunderstood; then, until its release, the sick body must go burdened with a dead soul. He watched Mac trace with his forefinger, by the feel of the ridges alone, the pattern in the bedspread. His Nella had more than health's indifference; she had health's cruelty and arrogance.

"There's no use kidding myself, Hendricks. Trying to believe now that what I felt then was the result of being upset and overwrought. God knows that's what I want to do. But it's no use. Nella has found she's as good a man as I was when it comes to making money. She's no more need for me—that way. Oh, she still had a use for me, but I didn't figure in it. She didn't love me." McRae sat up in bed. He turned to Hendricks in bitterness. "She used me, Hendricks, she used me. There was no love nor pity in her. She didn't give a damn if I died when she finished with me. When I coughed, she laughed and said, 'Cough some more, it feels good.'"

He caught his breath in an angry sob and pressed his cheek against the iron headboard of his bed.

Hendricks eased himself out of bed and into the chair by McRae's side. It was full day now. He looked with pity on McRae's drawn face and taut body.

"Lay down kid," he said. "Lay back and rest."

McRae sank back into the pillows. "I had to leave, Rick."

Hendricks knew how it was. You had to leave, all right —and you'd seen it otherwise up here: a world of good will, full of tenderness, and everybody hoping you'd have a negative test this time. "Sure, kid, you had to leave. Forget that gal. You're back home."

There were footsteps on the graveled walk. Hendricks

got back into bed, fast. "Lord," he said, breathing hard with the effort, "here's Samuels with our hot water. It's seven already. Well, kid, another day, another bug."

McRae looked out toward the valley. "Seven o'clock," he murmured. "She's just getting into her shower now."

The Battle of the Suits

JOE ORTIZ, the janitor at the Temple Home for Boys, in Reno, thought the Christmas decorations, even though it was three weeks past Christmas, made the tunnel-like main hall more cheerful. But Mr. Buchanan, the superintendent, said, "Take them down, Joe. They're unseasonable." Prettiness is always seasonable, isn't it, Joe thought, but he said nothing, naturally, to the boss. He got out the stepladder and went up it like a sailor or a monkey and began to unfasten the crepe-paper swags. It was a job his heart wasn't in, so he got what pleasure he could out of the climb itself, thinking that for fifty-six he wasn't such a bad specimen. He had a mouth full of thumbtacks and a dangle of crepe paper about his neck when he saw the boy they called the Senator come out of Buchanan's office at the end of the hall. Joe took the thumbtacks out of his mouth, the crepe paper off his neck, and climbed down the ladder. Then he stood, back to the wall, hands free, awaiting him.

The Senator was a fine figure of a man, from a distance—tall, raven-haired, and commanding. He was a little portly, but his round paunch was balanced by his equally round buttocks, so the effect was symmetrical.

56

The Senator had a loud, sweet voice or a loud, scornful voice, as the occasion required. Now it was loud and sweet. Lifting a plump arm in greeting, he called, *"Salud, Papacito Ortiz!"*

The Senator always addressed Joe in this second-year Spanish, kindly overlooking the fact that the janitor was born in San Diego and spoke English, and that what Spanish he had was pure border Mexican.

"You want to see me, Harold?" Joe asked when the Senator, a slow and stately walker, finally reached him.

"Por favor, Señor José," Harold said, as if they were two Castilians far from home and happily met amidst strangers.

Close up, the Senator's fifteen years showed on him. He had a big, round face, raw now with acne, a full, un-formed mouth, and heavy black brows. He had a good forehead and nose, and later would be handsome. Joe knew this, and the fact was not comforting. He had enough to do handling the unsightly Senator. Let the Sen-ator grow into good looks (and the Senator would be the first to know when this happened), and Joe prob-ably *couldn't* handle him. As it was, Joe was the only one in the Home who called the Senator by his proper name, Harold Whitehall.

The Senator didn't like to be called Harold. Hal he tolerated. But his proper title was the Senator. The name had been given him by the kids in the purest derision, as Joe well knew, and Harold had wrapped it around him-self with such ostentatious pride that the Home was now impressed by what it had itself created. But not me, Joe thought. I'm not impressed.

The Senator's *"Señor José,"* his big-hearted determination to make an equal of Joe, somehow managed to push Joe into a barefoot Pancho pose, as if he were a peon who had never tasted white bread or owned a pair of shoes. Joe hated himself as well as the Senator when he was overtaken by this play-acting. He, a man with three years in San Miguel High School, was, at the moment, better-educated than the Senator himself, who was now a second-year student in the Reno High School. Joe was old enough—matters accelerated a little, as is possible with Mexicans—to be the Senator's grandfather. (Though, God be praised, things had not so fallen out.) He had five grown sons, a sweet wife dead, and a sweetheart as alive as could be, and willing, any time he gave the word, to be a wife, too. He had a 1950 Chevvy, two guitars (one of them electric), and a fine library of paperbacks, and he knew probably five hundred songs. So why let a kid like the Senator get under his skin?

Besides, the boy had good traits. Beautiful traits compared to some of the young criminals at Temple. What was wrong with speaking second-year Spanish, bowing from the waist, and hating dirty stories? And sing! The Senator sang like a bird. Church, bonfire programs, funerals—wherever singing was either needed or permitted—there was the Senator lifting what in an older man would have been called his whisky tenor in song. Sometimes the Senator would go to an out-of-the-way spot and sing to himself, and even when he was pointed out, singing there, he didn't stop or become self-conscious. By God, Joe thought, I hate myself for not loving that boy. He's a good kid, though unpleasant. And he resolved never again to call him Harold.

"Kid," he said, managing to keep it from becoming "keed," "what's your problem?"

"*Señor*, it is the *patrón*. He desires word with you."

"You mean Mr. Buchanan, Harold?"

"*El patrón, Señor Ortiz*. He desires word with you about the suits."

"O.K. I been expecting it. I want to wash up first. You go tell him I'll be there as soon as I've finished."

"He told me to bring you."

"O.K., bring me. But first I'm going to wash up."

Joe's room was in the basement, down a steep flight of narrow, unrailed cement stairs. With the Senator on his tail, he took it running—showing off, risking his neck to impress another show-off.

The room was a space fifteen by fifteen, walled off from the furnace, hot-water heaters, janitor's supplies, and the like by partitions of beaverboard. From the outside, no one could guess what a pretty place Joe had made of it. Sometimes he'd leave work for five minutes and come down to take a peek at it. Just open the door and, without going in, have a quick look, the way a man will pull the picture of his baby or sweetheart from his pocket to make sure they really exist. He did not care to have the Senator in his room, but now that the Senator was there, he'd let him see how good it was, how warm, orderly, and *bright*. The two guitars were hung up on the wall by red ribbons Joe had braided himself. They were as pretty in their way as any of his pictures—the Virgin excepted, of course. His paperbacks were arranged in alphabetical order, and not one stood a fraction of an inch farther out on the shelf than another. And the shelf, like the ribbons, was red. The window, being in the basement, looked out into the bottom of the shrubbery that grew around the foundation of the building. Joe had his table against this window, and he could sit there, as if in a game blind, observing intimately the habits of cats, sparrows, and lizards. He turned to ask the Senator to enter, but it was too late for such courtesies; the Senator had walked in and was busy looking around.

He continued to look around as Joe washed. In the mirror over the washbasin Joe could see him examining his books and pictures. The Senator gave the pictures a glance that was scornful or pained or embarrassed—Joe couldn't tell which—and went on to the books. Joe hoped the Senator would not take this occasion, while he waited, to tell him sad stories of his childhood. He had heard one or two. If you were to believe them—and Joe always did —you had to hand it to the Senator for just surviving.

"What's this?" the Senator asked.

Joe shook the water out of his eyes and looked into the mirror. "Tequila," he said.

"Alcohol, *Señor?*"

"*Sí,*" Joe said, falling into the Senator's pattern in spite of himself.

"Abraham Lincoln said, 'There are many defenders of alcohol but no defense.'"

"Good man, Lincoln," Joe said. "He saved the Union."

The Senator would not be put off by such pleasantries. "You defend alcohol, *Señor?*"

Joe, in his own room, felt easily the Senator's equal. "No, I just drink it."

"It is the same thing, *Señor.*"

"No, sir. I do many things I wouldn't waste a minute defending."

"Well," said the Senator, flabbergasted, "I never heard anybody say that before."

Joe felt proud. I have the Senator on the run, he thought. "The best things I have done in my life I wouldn't defend."

A shocked darkness, like a polliwog surfacing, floated up into the Senator's bright-blue eyes. "I have never done anything in my life I wouldn't defend," he said.

"I believe you, completely," Joe said.

This lack of argument discouraged the Senator. He sat down in the chair by the window and gazed out into the shrubbery. "There is a bee out there," he said aggressively.

Joe wouldn't argue about that, either. "Must've spent the winter in the basement and just got out."

"I owe my life to bees, and in spite of the fact, I hate them."

Joe resisted saying "How's that?" and said, instead, "Let's get going." He did not want to hear how a bee had saved the Senator's life. But the Senator did not budge. He still sat gazing with melancholy into the shrubbery. Joe could not see the bee, and though he warned himself not to get mixed up with the Senator's past life, the old, natural habit of courtesy, acquired long before he had entered Temple, asserted itself, and he said, "How's that, Harold?"

"When I was a baby, still drinking milk, my folks ran out of money. To save my life, my father robbed beehives of honey. My mother diluted it with warm water, and I lived on it. It saved my life. That was a fine, unsel-

fish thing for my father to do, wasn't it? Be willing to rob
to save his child's life?"

"Yeah," Joe said. "It was."

"I don't like him, though. I have a strong antipathy to
him. You understand antipathy, *Señor?*"

"I understand what you mean, Harold."

"I got a strong antipathy to bees, too. Once, I told my
mother about this, and she said, 'Baby, bees saved your
life. You should love bees.' But I said, 'Mother, what I
feel is antipathy.'"

"How old was you when you said this, Harold?"

"Ten, maybe."

What Joe felt was strong sympathy for the Senator's
mother, but all he said was "Mr. Buchanan's waiting for
us, Harold."

The bee at that moment made a short flight, and Joe
saw it. It was a battered, ragged bee and didn't look
as if it had ever seen a flower or had anything to do with
honey.

"The bee stands in the same relationship to me as the
wolf did to Romulus and Remus. Romulus and Remus
were—"

"I know about those two kids," Joe said. "A wolf
nursed them."

He had studied classic myths at San Miguel High
School, and he had an unpleasant picture now of the Senator, a big, fat, black-haired baby, being suckled by an
oversize, hairy-legged bee. Maybe there would be a statue
of it on the courthouse lawn someday. He emptied his
Thermos bottle, in which he carried hot coffee when he
was working out on the grounds and couldn't be bothered
coming in for lunch, and began to rinse it.

"My mother really loved me, didn't she, keeping me alive on honey and water that way?"

"No doubt about it," Joe said. "She dead now?"

"No, she's alive. She's shacking up with some guy in Tucson, charming fellow. He's crazy to marry her, but she don't know if it would work out. I'd be with them now, except he's insanely jealous of me."

Startled, Joe turned, Thermos bottle in hand.

The Senator reassured him. "It's a Freudian thing," he said. Then he got up quickly. "That's a disgusting thing to do."

"What's disgusting?"

"Cleaning a Thermos that way. No scalding, no soap. That's unsanitary. All kinds of bacteria breed in warm, dark places like that. The least we can do is to be sanitary, isn't it?"

For a second, Joe was apologetic. The last thing he wanted to do was to offend anybody by being unsanitary. Then he was mad.

"Whose bottle is this, anyway?" he asked. "For thirty years I've been rinsing Thermos bottles this way. If it's so God-damned unsanitary, why haven't I been sick?"

"It makes me sick to watch you."

"Who asked you to watch me?" He grabbed the Senator's arm. "You get out and stay out. It's none of your business if I park cockroaches in my Thermos bottle."

The Senator's head dropped, but not before Joe saw the tears in his eyes.

"I'm sorry, *Señor*," he said. "Something must've happened to me when I was young. Dirt just makes me sick."

Joe let go his arm. The kid looked sick. His face between the raw spots was gray, and the tears rolled down his cheeks without losing their shape. No satisfaction, Joe thought, kicking the Senator. Kick the Senator, who needs it, and who you hurt's a kid.

"You got no right talking that way, Harold."

"I know it. But you made me feel so at home down here, *Señor*. You certainly know how to put people at their ease."

Joe, who knew a buttering-up when he got it, nevertheless responded, "I try to."

"You succeeded. You made me think we could just work our problems out together."

Joe got mad all over again. "I got my Thermos problems all worked out, kid. You just don't worry about it. You just keep your nose out of it. Now let's get going."

The Senator was once more meek. "Could I see your suit before I go?"

"You've seen it."

"Not off you."

"O.K. Look. It's there in the closet. I'm going."

He waited a minute or two at the top of the stairs.

The Senator, when he came, said in a condoling voice, "It's rather an upsetting coincidence, isn't it?"

"It don't upset me none, Harold."

Outside Buchanan's office, the Senator said, "Charming fellow, Buchanan. Regular he-man."

Joe had never thought of Buchanan that way. The Superintendent's face was veal-colored and heart-shaped; that is, if you turned the heart upside down, so that the pointed end disappeared amidst thin strands of dun-colored hair and the double curves of the top of the heart coincided with Buchanan's fat jowls.

The Senator ushered Joe into the office as if he were a stranger.

"Sir," he said, "*Señor Ortiz*, our neighbor from down under."

The Superintendent, to Joe's surprise, found this funny. He was seated behind his desk in a dark-blue double-breasted suit. "Welcome, *Señor*," he said.

Joe nodded. "You want to see me?"

"Sir," said the Senator, "before I leave, may I just say how much we all appreciate your gesture in creating the noon music hour?"

"Thank you, Senator," Mr. Buchanan said. "Will you wait outside, please? I may want to speak to you later."

The Senator left the room, and Mr. Buchanan gazed after him. "Remarkable youngster," he told Joe. Joe agreed. "Sit down, Joe, won't you?" Mr. Buchanan pointed to a chair at one corner of his desk. "How's the world treating you, Joe?"

"I got no complaints," Joe said.

"I expect you know why I asked you in for this little chat?"

"I have an idea."

"The Senator tell you?"

"There are quite a few things I know without any help from the Senator."

"Sure, Joe. There sure are. Well, first of all, let's get this straight. I don't intend to push you around any. You've been in this institution longer than I have. In fact, you're an institution yourself around here. The kids say 'Joe the Janitor' and I truly believe, Joe, it means a lot more to them than 'Buchanan the Superintendent.' I may be the titular head, but you're the heart and guts of the place. O.K., Joe?"

"O.K.," Joe said.

"So what I wanted was for us two heads of Temple to get together and talk over a little problem that faces us."

"O.K.," Joe said again. "Here we are."

"This involves you and the Senator, Joe. One of you has to give ground."

"I don't see why."

Mr. Buchanan ignored this. "Now, you know, Joe—or maybe you don't—the Senator's had a rough life. He's been very underprivileged up to now."

"I know," Joe said. " He was brought up by the bees."

"Oh. The Senator tell you?"

"Nobody could guess a thing like that."

"No. I guess not. Now, Joe, what I'd like first of all is your version of the suits. I've never heard your version, you know."

"Version? There's what happened. How do you get versions out of that?"

"O.K., Joe. What did happen?"

"Check down at the store if you want to, about what happened. They ran this ad about their after-Christmas sale of suits, and I needed a new suit. So Tuesday noon I went down, picked one out, and bought it. They had to turn up the cuffs, like they always do, and I was to get it Wednesday. Wednesday after work, when I stopped in for it, they said, 'Which one is yours?' I said, 'What do you mean which one is mine?' And they said, 'Look. Two suits just alike and both going to Temple.' They were just kidding—they knew which one was mine, all right. The other one was the Senator's. That's the only version there is of the suits, Mr. Buchanan. The Senator and I bought identical suits. Only," he added, "we don't wear them the same."

"No, you don't," Mr. Buchanan said. "That's a fact."

"Well, that's my version. Is that all you wanted?"

Mr. Buchanan rubbed his hands together. "No, Joe, not to beat around the bush, it isn't. You're a man, Joe. The Senator's a kid. I want you to make a little sacrifice for the boy."

"What?" asked Joe.

Mr. Buchanan filled his snorkel pen, seemed dissatisfied with the job, and did it again; then, having discharged all the ink, he got up, went to the window, and there alternately exposed and retracted the mechanism. Finally, he turned around and faced Joe. "It's not easy to say this, Joe."

"Go ahead. You don't have to go easy on my account."

"You know how kids are."

"Yes, sir, I do."

"Well, they're riding the Senator about his suit."

"It don't look good on him, that's a fact. He ought never to have bought it. Big pin stripe, double-breasted. It's a man's suit."

"You're right, Joe. But that's not why the kids are riding him. You know how the Senator is."

Mr. Buchanan hesitated, but Joe didn't like to say, either.

"Kids have no understanding of the dignity of labor, Joe. You know that. So they're saying the Senator's wearing a janitor's suit."

"What can I do about it?"

"If the Senator so much as puts his head around the corner, they start telling him the furnace needs attention or a john's out of order. This humiliates the boy."

"What can I do?" Joe asked again.

"I'll tell you what, Joe. You could take your suit back and get another. I've called the store. Under the circumstances, and since you've only worn it once, they'll take it back at full price."

"If the Senator don't like to wear a suit like mine, why don't he take his back?"

"Trouble is, Joe, the Senator had to have his suit altered considerably. It won't fit anyone else."

"For a kid," Joe admitted, "the Senator's got an unusually fat tail."

"Yeah. Well, there it is, Joe. You've got a chance to make a fine gesture. Do something for an underprivileged boy."

"No, sir," Joe said. "I'm not going to do it. I bought mine first, it looks good on me, and I'm going to keep it. Couple of weeks, the Senator and me wear our suits so different, they won't look alike anyway. The kids will forget they ever started out the same."

"Meanwhile, the boy has to suffer."

"That's up to him. It don't give me any pleasure having him wear my suit, either." Joe wondered how to explain to Mr. Buchanan what he felt about the Senator in *his* suit. That suit which was made to take chances, to go a few unexpected places. The Senator made it look like a uniform of some sort. "The Senator contradicts that suit."

"I don't get it," Mr. Buchanan said.

Joe shrugged. "I'm keeping my suit. If you think the Senator's suffering too much, you buy him another."

He had perhaps gone too far. Mr. Buchanan retracted his snorkel, capped it, put it in the desk drawer, and sat down.

"Joe, take the afternoon off. Go downtown. Ride out toward the mountains. Get some perspective on this. As I see it, this is an opportunity for you to make a magnificent gesture to a young person. Give yourself a little time, and I'm sure you'll come up with the right decision."

As far as Joe was concerned, he had already come up with the right decision; but he didn't have anything against an afternoon off.

"O.K., Mr. Buchanan," he said, and left the office.

He met the Senator halfway down the hall. The Senator lifted his arm in his usual salute. "*Vaya con Dios, Señor*," he said.

Go with God! Joe's skin prickled. As if God himself were a gift the Senator could hand out or withhold as the fancy struck him!

He didn't say a word, but he went down the stairs to his room, immediately undressed, and put on his new suit. Then he stood before the mirror looking at himself.

By God, he thought, the Senator's wrong. It don't look like a janitor's suit. What it looks like is a gambler's suit. It looks like the suit of somebody who don't know all the answers but is willing to take a chance. "Yes, sir," he told his suit. "You stand up for me, and I'll stand up for you. The way I've been doing."

Since his mind was all made up about the suit, there wasn't any point in going out and looking at the mountains. There wasn't any point in going out into the raw January afternoon at all. He and his suit would just stay

in here and celebrate a little. The Janitor's suit wanted to
defy the Senator's suit. He saw the Thermos bottle, and
though he'd never had anything in it but coffee before,
and though it was a little unhandy to drink from, he felt
he'd enjoy having his drink from it now. That way, he
could defy the Senator twice, be unsanitary and alcoholic
at the same time. He poured some tequila into the Thermos bottle, and when a few drops fell onto his suit, he
didn't try to wipe them off. "Share and share alike," he
said.

His first sip quieted his anger, and as his anger left him,
he felt apologetic toward his room. He hadn't really
looked at it since he came in. It could've been a jail cell
or a comfort station, for all the attention he had paid it.
He went over and stretched out on his bed. By God, he
thought, I have made myself a pretty room—warm, lively,
and bright-colored as a woman. Not that a room could
take a woman's place. A man who thought that would
never have bothered to put up the pictures he had: tele-
phone girl, girl wearing chaps, girl blowing soap bubbles.
Though the girl pictures weren't all; besides his holy pictures, he had pictures of his five sons, his dead wife, his
live sweetheart, a lonesome coyote, Segovia, and the 1955
Chevrolet. He had an eye for anything that was beautiful, he told himself—human or animal, vegetable or min-
eral. He sloshed the tequila around in his Thermos and
drank a toast to the beauties in his room, and to beauty
generally, and to the poor Senator, who had no eye
for beauty and who, though he loved himself, must be
repelled when he looked in the mirror to see the face of
the one he loved best so disfigured. The only thing about
the Senator that's really a thing he can take any pride in

is his suit, Joe thought. And me laying here on my bed of riches depriving the poor kid of his one pride.

He took another sip and thought about it some more. I'm not going to take my suit back, he decided, but what I will do is tell Buchanan I'll never wear it here at the Home. Here in my room if I want to, Reno if I want to, but noplace where any of the kids can see me. The Senator's got his world and I've got mine, and there's no use trying to mix the two.

Having made his decision, he wanted to tell Buchanan at once, so he finished his drink in a hurry and started up the stairs in a hurry.

It was the Senator, of course, lurking in that neighborhood to be the first to hear his decision, who found him. Before Joe could tell him his decision, his eyes closed and he lost for a while not only the problem of the suits but the whole world.

When he opened his eyes, the school doctor, the Senator, Mr. Buchanan, and Father Jimenez were standing by his bed. He was evidently in a bad way. Their faces were very serious.

Father Jimenez said, "Are you feeling better, Joe?"

"Am I going to die, Father?" he asked.

The doctor didn't give Father Jimenez a chance to answer. "Die?" he said, and chuckled. "Don't be silly, Joe." Then, to Buchanan, "I told you there was going to be an accident on those stairs if you didn't put up a handrail."

The Senator poked the Thermos bottle under the nose of the doctor, who was bending over Joe. "Sir," he said, "it wasn't the stairs. It was the liquor."

"Poor kid, raised by the bees!" Joe cried. "What can you expect? Father, if I die, bury me in my suit." He pulled the coat up under his chin. "It's my last request." Then, pressing his hands to his bandaged head to hold it together while he spoke, he said, "What'll you do then, Harold? You'll be wearing a dead man's suit, not a janitor's suit. How are you going to like that?"

The Senator drew himself up proudly. "*Señor*," he said, "in that case, I have no choice. I'll walk the earth in a dead man's suit."

Joe could see him doing it, could see his chance-taking gambler's suit walking the world and beginning each day to look more like the Senator. He gave a groan and fell back across the pillows, one arm across his eyes. In that case, *he* had no choice at all but to get well. He shut his eyes and prepared to continue the struggle.

Tom Wolfe's My Name

THE FIRST TIME I ever saw Sterling was four years ago in April at a place called Babe's. Babe's is a nice little tavern just outside of Burley. I'd gone up to Burley to sell an order of books to Tidy Smith, the principal of the high school there. Burley isn't very big, couple of thousand people maybe, but they've got a good-sized union high school and Tidy's been sold on Bonn and Company texts for a long time.

There wasn't anything to it—no salesmanship, no high pressure—nothing. Tidy just checked what he needed against the Bonn and Company list and that was that.

"I like the Bonn and Company line," Tidy said, "but the names you're giving schoolbooks nowadays set my teeth on edge." He flicked through one of our catalogues. "All the arithmetics are *Adventures with Numbers*. Here's a biology called *The Mystery of Life*, a history, *The Romance of Civilization*. Adventure, mystery, romance." He spat out the words as if he'd got something nasty in his mouth by mistake.

I picked up a sky-blue book spangled with stars. "What difference does the name make, Smith?" I asked. "They've got good stuff inside—the kids like 'em, and they sell."

"Don't fool yourself, boy," Tidy said. "Names are damned important. You're so glad to have a job, you'd sell books that taught kids that two and two made five if they paid you for it."

"Don't be so conservative, Mr. Smith," I said. "I'd sell books teaching kids that two and two made seven—if they paid me for it."

"Nice to meet an honest salesman," Tidy said, "but the world wouldn't be in such a hell of a shape today if people gave things their right names."

I tried to defend the titles on our list, but I guess I was pretty weak. Tidy cut me short. "O.K., Madden," he said, "I see you've got just the romantic touch they're looking for in schoolbooks today. You ought to try your hand at a geometry. Call it 'Adventures with Angles.'"

"I don't have adventures with angles, Smith," I said.

By the time Tidy'd talked himself out the school was empty except for a couple of janitors whose brooms you could hear thumping against the walls—and a bunch of kids waiting in the hall for their folks to pick them up. There was a lot of rain coming down and the wind that blows up the Burley Valley off the bay was smacking it against the windows. If there's anything drearier than an empty school building I don't know what it is. And that goes double when it's raining. I was watching the runoff wash out their new track when Tidy said to me, "Let's go out and have a drink."

I didn't know Tidy then the way I do now. I don't suppose there's another high-school principal like him in California—probably not in the United States. He's a little fellow with a pointed bald head that looks like some kind of a mushroom or tulip pushing up through the grassy fringe round his ears. He's a south of Market Street Mick—same as me—and he's come up the hard way. Now that he's cashing in on the years he spent getting an education, he likes it plenty. Snappiest dresser not in vaudeville—and if there's anything in Burley he doesn't do I don't know it. Sings at the funerals, talks to the garden clubs, plays Joseph in their Christmas plays. But I didn't know all that then, and being asked to take a drink by a high-school principal gave me a turn. I decided he must mean a cup of coffee.

I guess I must of showed my surprise. "What's the matter, Madden?" Tidy asked. "You on the wagon? If this isn't the weather for a Tom and Jerry I never saw the weather for a T and J."

"It's sure the weather for it," I said, "and I'm not on the wagon." I hated to ask him what the town was going to think of its high-school principal tossing down a quick one. The fellow was a stranger to me then—wasn't my place to be looking after his job—but Judas, any other town in California and he wouldn't have had a job next morning. Besides, teachers, the male ones anyway, give me the jumps. I'd rather go out and have a drink with a nun. You can understand what a sister's doing with her life—got her eye on God and the life everlasting. But a guy choosing of his own free will to sit down opposite a bunch of empty-faced kids every day for the rest of his life—nope, that's got me licked. So I figured it would be better for me to have my drink alone. I'd be more comfortable and Tidy'd have his job next morning and the *dinero* to buy more of those fancy clothes of his.

I guess Tidy read my mind. "Come on, Madden," he said, "they let teachers be human beings in Burley."

So we drove down to this place called Babe's, he in his car and I in mine. It was a darned nice-looking spot, even in all that rain. An old whitewashed brick building set under some peppers out on the edge of town. And it was just as nice inside. Big wood fire, stone floor, old-fashioned heavy round tables. There were seven or eight men in the place—mostly looked like ranchers killing time until the rain was over. A couple of fellows at a table by the stove were playing cribbage and their counting, fifteen-two, fifteen-four, and so on, was about all the talk you could hear above the rain.

Tidy spoke to some of the men, who called him professor. We ordered our drinks, and sat down and stretched our legs out under a table. Jeez, that's a good minute—when you've sold a big order, the day's over, and you've got a drink coming up. And it was a good drink, too.

I was just ready for my second one when another guy came in and Tidy Smith got a kind of pleased look in his eye. The look a guy gets when he thinks he's going to let you in on something special. Of course I'm writing with hindsight now, but I think I noticed it—even then. Anyway Tidy called out, "Hi, Sterling, come over and join us."

The fellow he called Sterling got out of a big yellow raincoat, banged his hat against the door a few times to get the water out of the crown, and came over to our table.

Tidy said, "Sterling, I want you to meet a book drummer, name of Madden." We said the usual howdys, and this Sterling ordered his drink, a glass of dry sherry.

To be saying something, I told Sterling wine drinking, when you could get anything else, had me beat.

"Well, Mr. Madden," he said, "I own a vineyard. The very grapes that went into this glass," and he held the leather-colored stuff up so's the light went through it, "may have been grown on my land. Beneath my soil, their million-footed roots, into my sunshine their million-fingered tendrils." He took a drink and set his glass down.

That kind of talk before a guy's got his drink down him—after, even—well, it makes you sit up and shake your ears. And this Sterling was enough to make you sit up, even without any of this "million-footed, million-fingered" stuff. He wasn't any fullback—short and slight, though he was plenty wiry-looking. What made you notice him first was his hair. I guess it was lemon-colored hair—kind of a mixture of yellow and silver and green. And instead of looking fine and kind of brittle the way most blond hair does, it looked soft like fur. It was smoothed down on top, not a ripple, but around his neck, where it was too long, either because he liked it that way, or hadn't bothered to have it cut, it went into curls.

But what really got you were his eyes. If they were any color they were air-colored—or maybe water-colored or ice-colored. Anyway they were transparent and they were bottomless. You got the same feeling looking in them you get looking down an empty elevator shaft. It's only your eyes that travel the length of that shaft, when you lean over, but your body follows somehow and you have the sensation of falling. It was the same way looking into that fellow Sterling's eyes. They gave me a sensation of falling, so I decided to concentrate on my drink.

Just then the phone rang somewhere in the back of the

room, and the fellow who ran the place called, "Professor, somebody wants to speak to you." Sterling and I drank and watched the rain while Tidy was gone.

When he came back he said, "Couple of my kids are mired down out by Lodi Lane. Guess I'll have to pull them out."

Sterling said, "Why don't their folks do it?"

"That's just the trouble. They don't want their folks to know it happened. Nope, I'll have to go. You two entertain each other. Remember Madden's a book salesman, Sterling," Tidy said, and I kind of got the feeling that that meant more to Sterling than it did to me. "You two ought to have a lot in common."

I didn't know what I could have in common with that platinum-haired grape grower, but it was still pouring and Babe's place was a damned sight more pleasant than a hotel bedroom. So I was willing to stay and find out.

When Tidy finally took off, this Sterling said to me, "What kind of books do you sell?"

"Schoolbooks," I told him.

"So," he said, "books for children."

"That's right. Kid stuff. Algebras, histories, and so forth."

"Do you ever see any authors?" he asked.

"Sure," I told him. "I've seen the author of *Our Eskimo Cousins* and *Our Mexican Cousins,* and the author of *The World We Live In,* and the—"

Sterling cut in. "You've never met any of the big authors, then?"

"You mean the best sellers?" I asked.

"No, no," he said, "the authors of the best books— regardless of how they sell. The books the critics praise."

"Nope," I said. "That lets me out. I've never even seen Kathleen Norris, and they say she's in and out of San Francisco all the time."

This all sounded right sane to me—the usual questions I get from people who hear I sell books—and don't know authors are the same tissue of artificial dentures, over-drafts, and unrequited love as the rest of us. Well, as I said, this talk about authors sounded sane to me—and I decided that "root and tendril" stuff had been just a pass-ing flight. So I chanced another look at the fellow—but jeez, his eyes were still empty and you still fell.

Anyway I decided it was time for a little reciprocity. He'd asked me about my bookselling. Time for me to ask him about his grape growing. "This late rain doing your grapes any harm?" I asked.

"No, no," he said. "It feeds them. At night I hear not only the rain falling, with a sound of bells in the darkness, but I hear the thirsty vine roots drinking. I lie awake these spring nights and hear the sounds their throats make swal-lowing—and no other sound, unless perhaps far off in the Napa Valley the clank of great wheels pounding on a rail, and a long whistle like a cry of sorrow across the hills, cutting the night air."

I sure wished I'd let reciprocity alone. But there wasn't much I could do—except to order another drink. I figured that to be an earpiece for this guy you needed to be a little tight.

Sterling emptied his third glass of sherry. "No, there's more to be heard than that. If you listen long enough on a wet night you can hear the feet of the rain on the sur-face of the little creeks: the Napa, the Feather, the Yolo, the Rio Hondo. And you can hear the voices of the little creeks deepen as they lose themselves in the mighty plunge and welter of the Sacramento, the San Joaquin. In the nighttime, while we sleep, immortal rivers flow by us to the sea."

He stopped speaking, looked out into the rain, kind of self-consciously. "Forgive me," he said. "It's very easy for a writer to start quoting himself."

"You write?" I asked. That relieved me some. The guy was just a writer then—not screwy the way he sounded.

"Yes," he said. Then he swung around from looking out into the rain. "My name's Thomas Wolfe."

I tell you that stopped me—stopped me cold. I couldn't think of a thing to say. I just sunk my face in my Tom and Jerry and gave that guy's hair and build another look over the top of my mug. Well, you can only spend so long drinking a Tom and Jerry.

So I put my cup down and said, "The author of *Look Homeward, Angel?*"

"That's right," he said.

"Thomas Wolfe," I said.

"Yes, that's right."

I didn't see any use in our going through that again.

"I understood Tidy to say your name was Sterling."

"You did—you did." The fellow was smooth as soap. "It's the name I use here in Burley. Intelligent men, men like you and Tidy can accept a writer—his differences and limitations. But if it were generally known here in Burley who I am, it would set me apart—keeping me from being one of the people—as I wish to be. No, Tidy was right. Here in Burley I'm known as Tom Sterling, but Tom Wolfe's my name."

When a fellow tells you a thing like that, blank out,

it gives you a damned funny feeling. You know that little blond cornstalk can't be Thomas Wolfe, but jeez, when that guy said, "Tom Wolfe's my name," his eyes changed. They filled in—focused. Something moved in behind the cellophane. You didn't fall any more.

But I decided to put it to him straight. "Your talk sounds like Wolfe," I said, "but you sure don't look like him. Look the opposite I should say. He's a big, dark fellow."

"You've seen pictures of him?" he asked me.

"Sure," I told him. "Who hasn't? He's a big black fellow, looks like a wrestler or a truck driver."

"That's just the reason I chose those pictures for my publicity releases," Sterling said. "I don't think my appearance suggests or is in harmony with my writing. And I feel it is important for the reader's singleness of mind that the author's face suggest his writing. You do agree, don't you?"

I told him I supposed it helped.

"Of course it helps. You were shocked just now to think that a man of my appearance should write as Thomas Wolfe writes, weren't you?"

"Yes," I said. I'd been shocked all right.

"And you do feel, don't you," he urged, "that the face I chose does represent my writing? That it has a dark October quality?"

"Yes," I said, "particularly around the mouth." And then, right away, I was damned sorry for that. I was a little tight by then, but that's no excuse for hitting a guy where he lives, and Sterling was sure living in that Thomas Wolfe fantasy. When I made that crack his eyes got empty again.

To make up for it I said, "Who is this fellow whose picture you use, Mr. Wolfe?"

My calling him Wolfe integrated him—gave him back his core curriculum so to speak.

"I don't know," he said. "I've never wanted to know. The publicity department simply furnishes the pictures for me—produces a new pose when I need one for a new book."

By that time this Sterling-Wolfe had me going. I wanted to ask him a hundred questions—just to see how he managed the practical side of impersonating a famous author. Because I was damn sure it was an impersonation. But jeez, there's so many screwy things going on in the world it could be the way he said. It would be an outside chance, but it could be. I wanted to ask him some questions but I didn't want to hurt him—so I asked the questions straight—I didn't farce them.

"Mr. Wolfe," I said, "your publicity material says you live in the South—and in New York—and your novels are about the South."

"That's right, Mr. Madden," he said. "This is more or less my hideaway. But I intend to be more than a sectional writer. I hope to speak for all of America. To do that I must know all of America. So for a part of each year I grow grapes in Napa County. But I'm not here as often as it seems to the people in Burley. Genius has a protean quality that makes it seem more omnipresent than it is."

I never expected to meet a guy who looked less like Proteus—but no use mentioning that, I figured. Besides I had a lot more questions to ask him. I wanted to see if I couldn't trip him up. No—that wasn't it exactly. I didn't think I really could—he made you feel he had the answers to all the questions. But anyway I wanted to hear a few more answers. When he finished his fourth or fifth glass of sherry, though, he said he had to leave—had a dinner date.

"I've enjoyed talking with you, Madden," he said. "Look me up next time you're in Burley. Tidy'll tell you how to get out to my place. I might be away, but I've a feeling I won't be. I've a feeling you and I will meet again."

As soon as he'd left I tried to get Tidy on the phone. I wanted to find out what he knew about this Sterling-Wolfe. But I couldn't raise Tidy. So, when I paid for my drink I asked the wop who ran the place, an old fellow with a pair of sad mustaches, about him.

"Who's the guy who was tucking away the sherry?" I asked.

"That's Mr. Sterling," he said.

"What's he do?"

"Grows grapes, like everybody else here."

"He a newcomer?"

"Nope," the wop said. "He been here before me."

"How long you been here?"

"Eleven years."

Tidy was out all evening, and I had a date with a principal in Petaluma next morning at eight. So I didn't get to talk to him about Sterling until the next April. I didn't make my usual September trip to Burley that year. I was out in the Islands then on that promotion junket.

But the first thing I did when I saw Tidy this April was to ask him about that guy. "Say," I said, "who's this fellow Sterling you introduced me to last year? Corn-silk fellow who says he's Thomas Wolfe?"

Tidy kind of laughed. "So you remember him?"

"Hell, yes. Who is he?"

"His name's Thomas Sterling. The Sterling family's lived over by Santa Rosa for the past sixty, seventy-five years."

"How long's he been saying he wrote Thomas Wolfe's novels?"

"Ever since the first Wolfe novel was published."

"You don't think he writes 'em?"

"How could he? He spends all his time growing grapes. He's got forty acres of grapes up there on the mountain, and he does most of the work himself. Besides, we never heard any of this Tom Wolfe talk until about six months after Wolfe's first novel was published. And when the newspapers were carrying accounts of Wolfe's being in Europe Tom was right up there tractoring his vines."

"How'd he explain that?" I asked.

"Promotion stunt by the publicity department. 'People like to think authors get around,' he said. 'I write the books. My publishers can do anything they like in the way of promotion.'"

I asked Tidy if he figured the fellow was crazy.

"I figure," Tidy said, "that on the subject of Wolfe he's touched. Pretty definitely touched. But he's smart as they make 'em when it comes to growing grapes."

"I'm going up to see him," I said. "He asked me to."

"O.K.," Tidy said. "You do that. It's a beautiful drive and you can't miss his place. It's the last vineyard on the mountain. But seeing his place, Madden, isn't going to settle your mind any."

Tidy was 100 per cent right—about the drive—and about my mind. The drive was beautiful—lupine and poppies in bloom and the vineyards just uncurling. I didn't have any trouble locating the Sterling place. A house painted white up there among the trees couldn't be missed. It was the neatest, prettiest little place you ever saw. Green shutters on the house, flowers in beds, bricked paths. Outside it looked like a retired lighthouse keeper's heaven.

There was a fellow down the slope a ways doing some pruning, and I knew it was Sterling from the way his hair shone in the sun—like a mirror. I gave a whoop and the fellow—it was Sterling—came up to the house.

I told him I didn't suppose he remembered me. That my name was Madden and that I'd had a drink with him a year ago down at Babe's. I called him Mr. Wolfe, too.

He was as pleasant as possible. "Of course I remember you. I don't forget people who like my books. Come in and have a drink and a chat."

"Sure I won't be interrupting your work?" I asked.

"No, no," he said. "When an idea doesn't take shape I go out and prune for a while, and there thinking only of the vines and their needs, the solution of my problem comes to me."

He took off his gloves and opened the door for me. The room we stepped into gave me quite a shock, it was so different from the yard. But in a second I realized it was just what I should have expected. I remembered the Tom Wolfe legend—shirts and socks thrown into a corner until they were all dirty. Writing done by the pound instead of the page in big ledgers. Place a jumble of frying pans and papers.

. That's the room I stepped into. That's the legend Sterling was living. The dirty shirts were right there in the corner where they should have been. I don't know which there was most of on his table—books or milk bottles. And the ledgers you read about were right there in an open packing case. I walked over and put my hand on them.

"These will all be in the Library of Congress someday," I said. I didn't suppose there was a word written in a one of them. I thought they were stage properties—duds. Sterling smiled modestly.

"*Look Homeward, Angel, Of Time and the River,* all those famous and eloquent words," I said, "here in longhand."

I let my fingers open a book, flick a few pages, but I kept my eyes on Sterling. I expected to see him wince, show some strain, suggest I look at something else. But he stood there easy and smiling.

"Every word in longhand," he said. "Terribly silly, but I can't seem to write any other way."

O.K., fellow, I thought, you asked for it. So I lifted out three of the ledgers, took up the fourth one and opened it—the pages were filled. A heavy angular hand, the hand of a guy who writes fast with his mind on what he's saying. I looked at half a dozen books. I saw the familiar words. Believe me, I felt plenty funny. This guy was a phony. He had to be. But he had sure gone to a lot of trouble to be a phony. It's bad enough when you look at something that's not what it seems—but it's a hundred times worse when you get a load of something that seems to be what it's not. I guess that's just the same thing put backward. Anyway, here was this guy who talked Wolfe, lived Wolfe, who even wrote Wolfe—but he wasn't Wolfe.

I gave up trying to get him on anything. There he stood, his face shining like a kid's at my speaking of his "famous words." O.K., fellow, I decided, you can put on your act for me. You sure spent plenty of time working it up. I've got an hour to play audience for you.

In lots of ways it wasn't a bad hour. It was a good hour, lot of ways, except for the times I got a kind of sick feeling as if I was living in a dream and might fall through any minute and hit myself hard on a hunk of reality somewheres.

He fixed me a lunch, slices of ham, steak-thick, stewed tomatoes, black coffee, a bakery cake. He stowed it away like a teamster and talked about the good food he'd eaten —and where. And he talked about his books. What he'd written and was going to write.

"I'm just a funnel through which America can pour," he said. "It has to come out the way I saw it and the way I felt it, but it will come out America, not me."

I think he smoked a pack of cigarettes while he was talking.

"When I finish writing," he said, "when I'm all through, the last book filled, the last word written, all of America will be down in print, there for anyone to sample: the smell of America—her million smells: the sweat of the Negroes, the dry smell of leaves, the autumn smell of chrysanthemums, the fish frying on a summer evening, the wind off our thousand miles of ocean, the smell of new rubber on the roads, and of asphalt, and of printer's ink wet on the evening papers, and the petunias freshly watered, and the damson plums boiling up in the little lean-to kitchens, and the girls sprinkling Hoyt's cologne on their hair."

Oh, he sure ticked them off. I didn't know America had so many smells and sights and sounds. He had them all on his tongue—in his heart, too, I guess. Before I left I went out to the car and got a copy of *Look Homeward, Angel* I'd brought with me, and asked him to autograph it. It was half a trick to catch him out, and half wanting to please him.

"I don't autograph my books," he said. "It gives books a false value too often. I want mine liked for what they say. But I'd be glad to write your name in it." He stood staring out the window for a minute, then he gave me a kind of amused look and wrote, "For Mike Madden who values good writing." But he didn't sign his name.

That was in April—and I thought about that guy off and on all summer. When I'd be talking textbooks to some principal I'd be thinking about that Sterling—what'd he get out of a racket like that—what was there in it for him? I still figured he was a phony and I still wanted to catch him out—but somehow I'd got to respecting the guy. He was sure going to a lot of trouble to be what he'd dreamed about. He must have spent half his nights after he was through working on his grapes copying Tom Wolfe in those big ledgers. He was kind of like a religious I figured. A real religious. Not one of these dames who go to prayer meeting and sing, "I Want to Be like Jesus," and let the matter drop there—this Sterling set right out to be the guy he wanted to be like. I was ready to hand it to him for doing what he was and handling it the way he was—never letting himself be cornered.

In September, just after the schools had reopened, I

was back up north, checking over the spring orders with the principals, seeing if enrollments had picked up, new classes been added and so forth. On the sixteenth I was in Ukiah. It was a hot dry morning and I was having breakfast in the William Tell Hotel where I always stay, and hating to go out of the air-conditioned grill into the heat, so I was reading the *Chronicle* through pretty thoroughly, postponing the minute. Otherwise I probably would have missed it—a little article saying Thomas Wolfe had died the day before, in Baltimore I think it was. Dead. It didn't seem possible. That big, black fellow, so in love with all that had to do with living—food, women, the sound of trains in the night, the oceans washing against the shores of America, the names of our rivers. Dead and gone to dust—no more words to write. I looked out into the sunlit street with a sad, empty feeling in the pit of my stomach.

Then I remembered Sterling, the phony Wolfe. Say, I thought, how's he going to explain this? Ukiah's only about twenty miles from Burley—so I got right in my car and drove over to find out. On my way over there I had it doped out what Sterling was going to say—that he had decided he'd written himself out in the vein of Thomas Wolfe—that he wanted to begin again—not to be saddled with Wolfe's fame or manner. That he'd told his publishers to announce that he was dead so he could start over—be a new and different funnel through which America could pour. Then, I thought, after a while he'd identify himself with the first guy who published a promising novel. I didn't think he'd say this last —but that's the way I thought he'd have it planned.

I kept an eye on the vineyard as I drove up to Sterling's place. It was picking season and I thought he might be at work. But there wasn't any work going on at his place, so I drove straight to the house. Nobody answered my knock and I figured he'd probably taken a load of grapes down to the winery. I tried the door anyway. I wanted another peek at that Tom Wolfe stage set.

I got it—and I got more than I'd figured on. There was Sterling himself stretched out on the studio couch. Opening the door turned a whole shaft of light on him. I thought he was asleep, until I walked over to him, laid a hand on him. He was dead—stone dead, and cold as a stone, too.

Believe me, I didn't lose any time putting in a call for the coroner and the county sheriff. While I was waiting for them I had a good look around. Looked to see if there wasn't a morning paper there with a notice of Wolfe's death—but I couldn't find a thing.

On the floor by the couch Sterling was on was one of the big ledgers—face down, and on top of it Wolfe's *The Story of a Novel*, and a fountain pen. It looked like the fellow had been copying the stuff when he died.

I stayed in Burley until the autopsy was over. I had to —since I'd found the body, but I wanted to anyway. I supposed the guy had killed himself—couldn't stand the letdown of not being Wolfe. But the coroner said "no" —"death by natural causes."

Tidy and I talked it over afterward in Babe's. Tidy said, "You hear the coroner says he'd been dead approximately twenty-four hours when you found him?"

"Judas Priest," I said, "you mean he died about the time Wolfe did?"

"I figure it was about the exact time," Tidy said.

"What do you make of it, Tidy?" I asked. I expected him to ring in his old line about the importance of words and so forth. But Tidy just shook his head. He just wrinkled up his long Irish lip and looked far away. "I dunno," he said. "I wouldn't know. How about having a glass of dry sherry?"

What I wanted in that heat, was a beer, but I said, "O.K., dry sherry for me." Maybe this was just a case to remember, not explain.

Tidy lifted his glass and said, "Their million-footed roots, their million-fingered tendrils."

Learn to Say Good-by

*

JOHN THOMAS had awakened thinking of Curly—
or, rather, when he woke up, he did not stop
thinking of Curly, for all night he had been with
the young steer, encouraging him, patting him on his
curling forelock, leading him before the admiring judges.
The boy was wide awake now, yet Curly's image was
still as strongly with him as in the dream—the heavy
shoulders, the great barrel, the short legs, the red coat
shining with health and with the many brushings John
Thomas had given it. And Curly's face! The boy's own
face crinkled happily as he thought of it, and then
turned scornful as he thought of the people who said
one baby beef was just like another. Curly looked at
you with intelligence. His eyes weren't just hairless spots
on his head, like the eyes of most baby beeves. They
showed that Curly knew when eating time had come
and that he understood the difference between being told
he was a lazy old cuss and a prize-winning baby beef.
You had only to say to him, "You poor old steer," and
he put his head down and looked at you as much as to
say he knew it was true and not to kid him about
it. John Thomas remembered a hundred humors and

shrewdnesses of Curly's, and lay in bed smiling about them—the way he had of getting the last bite of mash out of his feed pail, and his cleverness in evading the vet, and how he would lunge at Wolf when the collie barked at him.

"This is the day!" John Thomas said aloud. "This is the day!"

Across the hall came a girl's sleepy voice. "Johnny, you promised to be quiet."

John Thomas didn't answer. No use arguing with Jo when she was sleepy. He sat up and slipped his arms into the sleeves of his bathrobe, and then stepped onto the floor boards, which were so much cooler than the air, and walked slowly, because he wanted so much to walk fast, to the window.

There Curly was, standing with his nose over the corral fence looking up toward John Thomas's window. Curly acts as if he knows, the boy thought. I bet he does know.

"Hey, Curly!" he called softly. "How you feel this morning? Feel like a prize baby beef? Feel like the best steer in California? First prize for Curly?" Curly swished his tail. "Don't you worry, Curly. You *are* the best."

John Thomas knew he was going to have to go in and talk to Jo, even though she'd be mad at being waked so early. If he stood another minute looking at Curly—so beautiful in his clean corral, with the long blue early-morning shadows of the eucalyptus falling across it—and listening to the meadow larks off in the alfalfa and remembering that this was the day, he'd give a whoop, and that would make both Jo and Pop mad. He tiptoed across the hall, opened his sister's door, and looked at her room with distaste. Grown-up girls like Jo, almost twenty, ought to be neater. All girls ought to be neater. The clothes Jo had taken off before she went to sleep made a path from her door to her bed, starting with her shoes and hat and ending with her underwear. Curly's corral's neater, he thought, and said, "It's time to get up, Jo!"

Jo rolled over on her face and groaned. John Thomas stepped over Jo's clothes and sat down on the edge of the bed.

Jo groaned again. "*Please* don't wake me up yet, Johnny," she said.

"You're already awake. You're talking."

"I'm talking in my sleep."

"I don't care if you don't wake up, if you'll talk. I've seen Curly already. He looks pretty good. He looks like he know's it's the day."

"He's dead wrong, then. It's still the night."

John Thomas laughed. If he got Jo to arguing, she'd wake up. "It's six o'clock," he said.

Jo, still face down, raised herself on one elbow and looked at her wrist watch. Then she whirled onto her back, stuck one leg out from under the sheet, and gave her brother a kick that set him down on the floor with a thud. "Why, John Thomas Hobhouse!" she said indignantly. "It's only five-fifteen and Nicky didn't get me home until two. You're so kind to that damned old steer of yours, but you don't care whether your own sister gets any sleep or not."

John Thomas bounced back onto the bed. Jo looked at him sharply and he knew what was to come.

"What have you got on under that bathrobe, John

Thomas Hobhouse?" she demanded. "Did you sleep in your underwear last night?"

"I slept in my shorts."

"That's a filthy thing to do."

"You say it's filthy if I don't wear them in the daytime and filthy if I do wear them at night. What's daylight or dark got to do with it? Now, if I—

"Look, Johnny, let's not get started on that. There are some things you're going to have to do that aren't reasonable. Once school starts, you'll be spending some nights with the other boys, and their mothers will be saying I don't look after you, and let you sleep in your underwear."

"I don't do it away from home, Jo, but it was so hot last night. You tell Mrs. Henny to do my ducks up special for today? Boy, wait till you see me and Curly go by the grandstand! Wait till you see us in the ring when Curly wins!"

"When Curly wins! Maybe he won't win, Johnny."

"Maybe the judges *won't* see he's best—but they will if they're any good."

John Thomas lay on his stomach, hanging his head over the edge of the bed until his long pompadour spread out on the floor like a dust mop and his face was out of Jo's sight. "I prayed about today," he said.

"Did you, Johnny?"

"Yep, but I didn't think it was fair to pray for Curly to win." He heaved himself up and down, so that his hair flicked back and forth across the floor. "A lot of kids probably did pray they'd win, though."

Jo regarded him with tenderness and amazement. "I

never would have thought most of the kids who go to
the fair had ever heard of praying," she said.

"Oh, sure, they all heard of it," Johnny said. "And
when it comes to something important like this, they all
think you ought to try everything. But I didn't ask for
Curly to win. I just prayed the judges would be good
and know their stuff. If they do, Curly will get the blue
ribbon, all right. With everyone else asking to win, I
thought maybe that would kind of make an impression
on God."

It made an impression on Jo. Lord, she thought, I'm a
heathen. "What do you care whether or not Curly wins,
if you know he's best?" she asked.

John Thomas heaved his head and shoulders up onto
the bed and lay on his stomach with his face near Jo's.
"How can you wear those tin things in your hair?" he
asked. Then he answered her question. "I know for sure
Curly's best, but *he* don't. He knows he's good, but he
don't know he's that good. I want him to win so he
can have the blue ribbon on his halter and walk up in
front of the people while all the other baby beeves watch
him."

"You going to walk with him, kid?" Jo asked.

"Yep, I got to."

"Kinda nice to have the other kids watch, too."

This slyness tickled John Thomas and he laughed. No
use trying to fool Jo about anything. "Anyway, it's
mostly Curly," he said.

Jo started taking the curlers out of her hair. She tucked
them, one by one, into Johnny's bush of hair as she took
them out. "Remember when Curly got bloated?" she

asked. "You weren't much help then. You cried and didn't want the vet to stick him."

"Yeah, but, Jo, it looked so awful. To take a knife and stick it inside him. And Curly was so darned scared." He spoke dreamily, with the satisfaction and relief of dangers past. "He looked like he was going to have a calf, didn't he? And I guess it hurt more."

"Yep, Johnny. A cow's made to have a calf, but a steer isn't made to have gas. Hand me my comb. Top left-hand drawer."

John Thomas got up and stood looking at himself in the mirror. His hair was thick enough to keep the curlers from dropping out.

"You look like an African Bushman," Jo said. "Come on, get that comb."

When John Thomas handed it to her, she began loosening her sausagelike curls. He watched her turn the fat little sausages into big frankfurters.

"Time to get dressed, kid," she said. "Jump into your ducks. They're all done up fresh and hanging in your closet."

"Do you think I've been giving him too much mash, Jo?" Johnny asked. "Does he look kind of soft to you? Too fat?"

"He looks just right to me. But it's all over now. No use worrying any more. This time tomorrow, he'll be someone else's problem."

John Thomas sat down on the window sill and looked out at the tank house. The sunlight lay on it in a slab as heavy and yellow as a bar of naphtha soap. There was already a dance of heat out across the alfalfa fields. White

clouds were boiling up from behind purple Tahquitz.
The morning-glories were beginning to shut themselves
against the sun. This was the day all right, but he could
not think ahead until tomorrow, when Curly would
have been sold.

The boy made the width of the room in three jack-
rabbit hops, and banged the door behind him.

Jo swung herself out of her bed and her nightgown in
a single looping movement and stood before her mirror.
I guess it's hell to be thirteen and not have a mother,
and to love a steer that's going to be beefsteak in forty-
eight hours, she thought somberly. I ought to take better
care of Johnny, and Dad ought to wake up from remembering Mother. He's been that way ever since she died.

But the air flowed like liquid silk about her naked body,
and she lifted her arms and tautened her body, thinking
no longer of John Thomas but of Nicky. She regarded
her image with affection and pride. I don't know where
I would change it, she thought. The sound of Johnny's
leaps down the stairs—four house-shuddering thuds—and
his cracked voice calling out to Mrs. Henny made her
look at her watch. Almost six. Jo grabbed fresh underwear from the drawer and ran for the bathroom.

When Jo came downstairs, ten minutes later, all dressed
except for putting on the scarf and belt that were hanging over her shoulders, she saw her father seated at the
table on the screened porch where they ate breakfast in
summer and reading the morning paper. She was fond
of her father, but in one respect he was unsatisfactory:
She didn't like his appearance. He didn't look fatherly
to her. There wasn't any gray in his black hair or any

stoop to his shoulders, and her girl friends exasperated her by saying, "I could go for your old man."

He called to her now, "Tell Mrs. Henny we're ready to eat."

Jo went through the porch door into the sunny kitchen, where Mrs. Henny was slicing peaches for breakfast. She was already dressed for the fair, in a lavender dotted swiss with a lavender ribbon through her bobbed gray hair. "Hello, Mrs. Henny," Jo said. "Dad says let's eat. Gee, you look swell!"

"I thought I'd better wear something light," Mrs. Henny said. "It's going to be hot as a little red wagon today. Take these peaches out with you. Time you've finished them, everything else will be ready."

Jo stopped to buckle on her belt and tie her scarf. Then she took the peaches out to the porch. Her father put the Los Angeles *Times* under his chair and took his dish of peaches out of her hand. "Well, Josephine," he said, "considering you only had three hours' sleep last night, you don't look so bad."

"You hear me come in?"

"Nope, but I heard that fellow drive away. He ran into everything loose and bangable on the place. What's wrong with him?"

"Blind with love, I guess," Jo said lightly.

Her father held his third spoonful of sugar poised over his peaches. "I take it that you have no impairment in your eyesight," he said.

"Things look a little rosy, but the outline's still plain, I think."

Mrs. Henny came in with the eggs and bacon and muffins. "I don't want to hurry you," she said, pausing, on her way out, at the kitchen door, "but it's not getting any earlier."

"Where did Johnny go?" Jo asked. "He ought to be eating. He'll be sick this afternoon if he doesn't eat." She took two muffins, buttered them, and put them on Johnny's plate.

"He's out talking to Curly. You'd better call him."

"Dad, what's Johnny going to do about not having Curly any more after today?" Jo asked. "You know he acts as if Curly were a dog—or a brother."

"Oh, Johnny's all right. He knows what the score is," her father said, with his mouth full of muffin and scrambled eggs. "But call him, call him. We've less than an hour to eat and load the steer. I ought to have taken him down last night, but John Thomas was afraid Curly would look peaked today if he spent a night away from home."

"Remember John Thomas's kitten?"

"Kitten?" said her father grumpily. "He's had a dozen."

"This was the one he had when he broke his leg. Don't you remember? He said, 'Let's never let her see herself in a mirror, and then she'll think she's just like us, only smaller.' He's that way about Curly now, you know. He never lets Curly know there's any other difference than size between them."

"Doesn't he know where Curly'll be tomorrow?"

"He *must* know it, but he hasn't felt it yet."

"Well, call him, call him," her father said. He got up from the table and stood with his back to her. "He can't learn to say good-by any earlier."

He's thinking of Mama, Jo thought, and walked

slowly out through the screen door and down the steps into the sunshine, eating a muffin-and-bacon sandwich as she went. She stopped at the foot of the steps to pick up the cat, and balanced him, heavy and purring, on her shoulder, and let him lick the last of the muffin crumbs from her fingers. "Oh, Nicky, Nicky," she murmured, pressing her face close against the cat's soft, furry side. Then she saw Johnny, sitting hunched up on the top rail of the corral, looking at Curly. "Well, Bud," she called out, "he looks like silk!"

"He's kind of rough on the left flank," Johnny said as she came and stood beside him. "Been rubbing against something. Can you notice it? I been working on it."

"Can't see a thing," Jo said. "Now, look here, John Thomas, you're going to make him nervous, sitting there staring at him—give him the jitters before he ever gets to the fair. You'll spoil his morale. Dad let you keep him here till this morning when he didn't want to, so don't you gum things up now."

John Thomas slid to the ground. "So long, Curly," he said. "I got to eat now." And he ran for the house.

A little before eight, they all drove into Verdant, the county seat—Mr. Hobhouse and Mrs. Henny and Jo and Johnny in the car, and Curly in the trailer behind them. "Awnings up early this morning," said Mr. Hobhouse as they moved slowly forward in the already long line of cars. "Going to be a scorcher, I guess. Flags look dead when there isn't any wind, don't they?"

Jo, who was riding beside her father in the front seat, nodded, but nothing looked dead to her. She loved the beginning-again look of a town in the morning—the sidewalks sluiced down, the vegetables fresh and shining, the storekeepers in clean shirts, the feeling that nothing that had been spilled or broken or hurt or wronged the day before need be carried over into the new day. The heat made her sleepy, and because she wouldn't be seeing Nicky until evening, the day seemed dreamlike, unimportant. She would move through it, be kind to Johnny, and wait for evening and Nicky again. Her father swerved sharply to avoid hitting a car that had swung, without signaling, out of the line of cars heading for the fair.

"Hey, Pop, take it easy!" John Thomas yelled anxiously from the back seat, where he sat with Mrs. Henny. "You almost busted Curly's ribs then."

"John Thomas ought to be riding back there with that steer," declared Mrs. Henny. "Or else I wish I could have rid in the trailer and the steer could have set here with John Thomas. The boy hasn't done a thing since we started but put his feet in my lunch basket and squirm, till I've got a rash watching him."

"Hold out five minutes longer, both of you, and we'll be there," Mr. Hobhouse said.

Jo roused herself, lifted her eyelids, which seemed weighed down with the heat, and turned around. "Hi ya, Johnny," she murmured.

As soon as they were well inside the fairgrounds, her father maneuvered out of the line of cars and stopped. "Jo, you and Mrs. Henny had better get out here," he said. "It'll take me and Johnny some time to get Curly unloaded."

As Jo climbed out, John Thomas touched her arm. "You'll sure be there, won't you, Sis?" he asked.

"Where?"

"In the grandstand for the parade at ten-thirty. All the baby beeves."

"Johnny, where'd you think I'd be then? Looking at the pickle exhibit, maybe? Of course I'll be there. Just you and Curly listen when you go by the stand. You'll hear me roar."

"Hurry up, you two," said her father. "It's getting late."

"When's the judging, Johnny?" Jo asked.

"Two-thirty. Front of the Agriculture Pavilion," he replied.

"I'll see you then. Don't worry. I think the judges are going to know their business." She poked a finger through the trailer's bars and touched Curly. "So long, Curly. You do your stuff!"

Her father edged the car and trailer back into the line of traffic. Mrs. Henny lumbered off, with a campstool on one arm and the lunch basket on the other, and Jo was left alone. The day was already blistering and she was glad. She took no pleasure in a moderately warm day, but a record breaker, one that challenged her ability to survive, elated her. She went into one of the exhibition buildings and walked through acres of handiwork, wondering if she would ever find life so empty that she would need to fill it with the making of such ugly and useless articles. Children whimpered as mothers jerked them doggedly through the heat. Oh, Nicky, I promise you never to be like them, Jo thought.

She was in the grandstand at ten-thirty when a voice from the loudspeaker announced, "Ladies and gentlemen! The Future Farmers of Riverbank County and their baby beeves will now pass in front of the grandstand for your inspection. At two-thirty, the final judging will take place in front of the Agriculture Pavilion, and after that the steers will be auctioned to the highest bidders. I'm proud to announce that there isn't a first-rate hotel in Los Angeles that hasn't a representative here to bid in one or more of these famous Riverbank beeves. There they come now, ladies and gentlemen, through the west gate. Let's give them a big hand—the Future Farmers of Riverbank County!"

Jo craned forward to watch the long line of steers and boys move proudly in review before the grandstand. The steers were mostly Herefords, shining like bright-russet leather in the blazing sun. Jo had not realized how thoroughly John Thomas had convinced her of Curly's superiority. She looked down the long line, expecting Curly, by some virtue of size or spirit, to be distinct from all the others.

A woman leaned heavily against her to nudge a friend in the row below them. "There they are!" she said excitedly.

Jo followed their glances before it occurred to her that they were not talking about John Thomas and Curly. Finally, she saw them, well along toward the end of the line, the steer like the other red steers, the boy like the other white-clothed boys. But unlike, too, for surely no other boy walked with the sensitive, loving pride of her brother. Then she saw that Johnny was the only boy who did not lead his animal by a halter or rope. He walked beside Curly, with only a hand on his neck. Idiot, thought Jo, he's put something over on somebody; he ought not to be doing that.

She stood up and, to fulfill her promise, shouted, over and over, "Hi, Johnny! Hi, Curly!," until a man behind her jerked her skirt and said, "Sit down, Sis, you're not made of cellophane."

After the boys and the steers had circled the grandstand and passed through the west gate again and out of sight, Jo closed her eyes and half slept, hearing as in a dream the announcement of the next event. She fully awakened, though, when someone wedged himself into the narrow space that separated her from the stair railing on her right.

"Dad! Where did you come from?" she exclaimed.

"I was up above you," her father said. "Well, the boy's having his day. You're half asleep, Jo."

"More than half. Where's the car? I think I'll go and sleep in it until the judging. I've seen all the Yo-yo pillows and canned apricots I can take in one day."

"I don't know whether you can find the car or not," her father said. "It's over in the first nine or ten rows of cars back of the dining tents. Here's the key, and don't forget to lock it when you leave."

Jo slept for a long time, doubled up on the back seat of the car, and then awakened with a sudden sick start. She seemed to be drowning in heat, and the velours of the seat she was sleeping on was a quicksand that held her down. She looked at her watch and saw with consternation that it was after four o'clock.

She had a long way to go to reach the Agriculture Pavilion, and because she was so angry with herself and still so sleepy, she ran clumsily, bumping into people. I'm so full of fair promises, she accused herself bitterly, and now I've let poor Johnny down. She wanted to hurt herself running—punish herself—and she finally reached the Pavilion with a sick, cutting pain in her side and a taste of sulphur in her throat. A deep circle of onlookers stood around the judging ring, laughing and talking quietly. At last, she saw Johnny and her father in the front line of the circle, a little to her left. Paying no heed to the sour looks she got, she pushed her way to them. John Thomas saw what she had done and frowned. "You oughtn't to do that, Jo," he said. "People'll think we can get away with anything just because we own the winner."

"Has Curly won already?" Jo asked.

"No, not yet," Johnny said. "Couldn't you see the judging where you were?"

"Not very well," Jo said. "No, I couldn't see a thing."

She looked now at the animals that were still in the ring, and saw that Curly was there with three other Herefords and an enormous black Angus. He was wearing a halter now, and one of the judge's assistants was leading him. Unless one of the five steers had a cast in his eye or a tick in his ear, Jo did not see how any man living could say that one was an iota better than another. She knew the points in judging as well as Johnny himself; she had stood by the corral many half-hours after breakfast while Johnny recounted them for her, but while she knew them well, her eye could not limn them out in the living beasts.

"Why're you so sure Curly will win?" she asked Johnny.

"Higgins said he would."

"Who's Higgins?"

Johnny shook his head, too absorbed to answer her question. The judge, an old, bowlegged fellow in a pale-blue sweater, had stopped examining the animals and was reading over some notes he had taken on the back of a dirty envelope. He walked over for another look at the Ayrshire. Seemingly satisfied by what he saw, he took off his gray felt hat and with the back of his hand, wiped away the sweat that had accumulated under the sweatband. He set his hat on the back of his head, stuffed his envelope in a hip pocket, stepped to the edge of the ring, and began to speak.

"Ladies and gentlemen, it gives me great pleasure to be able to announce to you the winner of the Eighteenth Annual Riverbank Baby Beef Contest."

There was a hush as the spectators stopped talking, and Jo tried to find in her father's face some hint of what he thought the decision would be. She saw nothing there but concern. Johnny, though, had a broad and assured smile. His eyes were sparkling; the hour of Curly's recognition had come.

"And I may say," continued the judge, enjoying the suspense he was creating, "that in a lifetime of cattle judging I have never seen an animal that compares with today's winner."

The fool, thought Jo, the damn fool orator! What's got into him? They never do this. Why can't he speak out?

But Johnny looked as if he enjoyed it, as if he knew whose name would be announced when people's ears had become so strained to hear it that it would seem to be articulated not by another's lips but by their own heartbeats.

"The winner, ladies and gentlemen, is that very fine animal, John Thomas Hobhouse's Hereford, Curly!" said the judge.

There was a lot of good-natured hand clapping. A few boys yelled "Nerts!," but the choice was popular with the crowd, most of whom knew and liked the Hobhouses. The judge went on to name the second- and third-prize winners and the honorable mentions. Then he called out, "I would like to present to you Curly's owner, John Thomas Hobhouse himself. Come take a bow, Johnny!"

Jo was proud of the easy, happy way Johnny ran over to his side. The judge put out a hand intended for the boy's shoulder, but before it could settle there, Johnny was pressing his cheek against Curly's big, flat jowl. The steer seemed actually to lower his head for the caress and to move his cheek against Johnny's in loving recognition. This delighted the spectators, who laughed and cheered again.

"Now, ladies and gentlemen, the show's almost over," said the judge. "Only one thing left—the auctioning of these animals—and, believe you me, the enjoyment you've had here is nothing to the enjoyment you're going to have when you bite into one of these big, juicy baby beefsteaks. Now if you'll all just clear the ring. Ladies and gentlemen, may I present that silver-tongued Irish auctioneer, Terence O'Flynn. Terence, the show is all yours."

The non-prize winners were disposed of first and in short order. They fetched fancy prices, but nothing like what would be paid for the prize winners. The big Los Angeles hotels and the Riverbank Inn liked to be able to advertise "Steaks from Riverbank's Prize Baby Beeves." Jo felt sick at her stomach during the auction. This talk of club steaks and top sirloins seemed indecent to her, in front of animals of whom these cuts were still integral parts. But Johnny seemed unaffected by the auction. "Bet you Curly will get more than that," he said whenever a high price was bid.

"He'll fetch top price," his father answered him shortly. "You'll have a big check tonight, besides your blue ribbon, Johnny." The prize winners were auctioned last. All of them except Curly went to Los Angeles hotels, but the Riverbank Inn, determined not to let outside counties get all the prize winners, bid Curly in for itself.

"I'm not a Riverbank citizen," boomed O'Flynn, "but I don't mind admitting, folks, that I'm going to come back the day my good friend Chef Rossi of the Riverbank Inn serves steak from Curly. I know that baby beef is going to yield juices that haven't been equaled since Abel broiled the first steak. If *I* was young Hobhouse, I'd never sell that animal. I'd barbecue it and pick its bones myself."

Most of the animals had already been led into slaughterhouse vans and trucks, and the rest were being quickly loaded. A van belonging to Mack's Market, the Riverbank Inn's butchers, backed up to the ring, which now held only Curly and the Ayrshire. As O'Flynn finished speaking, two young fellows in jumpers marked "Mack's" leaped out and came over to give Curly a congratulatory pat before sending him up the runway.

"Well, kid," one said pleasantly to John Thomas, "you got a fine animal here."

Johnny didn't hear him. He was looking at O'Flynn, hearing those last words of his.

Now it's come, thought Jo. Now he's really taken in what he's been preparing Curly for. Now he knows for the first time. Don't look that way, Johnny, she pleaded silently. Oh Johnny, you *must* know you can't keep Curly—you can't keep a fat pet steer.

But Johnny didn't smile. He walked over and stood with one arm about Curly's neck, staring incredulously at O'Flynn. "Nobody's going to pick Curly's bones," he said to the auctioneer. Then he turned to the steer. "Don't you worry, Curly. That guy hasn't got anything to do with you."

There was a sympathetic murmur among the bystanders. "The poor kid's made a pet of him," one man said. "Too bad. Well, he can't learn any earlier."

The men from Mack's Market tried to take the matter rightly. "Look here, Bud," said one of them. "Get yourself a canary. This steer don't want to be nobody's pet. He wants to be beefsteaks." And he put a hand on Curly's halter.

Johnny struck it down. "Don't touch Curly!" he shouted. "He's going home, where he belongs! He's won the prize! That's all he came here to do!"

The circle of onlookers came closer, augmented by passers-by whose ears had caught in Johnny's voice the sound of passion and hurt. The buzzards, Jo thought. She saw Johnny press himself still more closely against Curly, keeping his eyes all the time on O'Flynn. She gripped her father's arm. "Dad, do something!" she cried. "Let Johnny take Curly home. There's plenty of food and room. Johnny wouldn't feel this way about him except for you and me. It's our fault!" She was half crying.

"Yes, this nonsense can't go on," her father agreed, and went quickly over to Johnny.

Jo couldn't hear what he said or see his face, for he stood with his back to her, but she could see Johnny's face, and its anguish and disbelief. At last, the boy turned and threw both arms around Curly's neck and buried his face against the steer's heavy muscles. Jo saw his thin shoulder blades shaking.

When her father turned and came toward her, eyes to the ground, she found she could not say to him any of the bitter things that had been on her tongue's tip.

"Dad," she said, and put her hand out to him.

"There's no use, Jo."

"But he loves Curly so."

"Oh, love!" her father said, and then added more quietly, "It's better to learn to say good-by early than late, Jo."

"I'm going to the car," Jo said, and she turned and ran blindly through the crowd. Because Dad's had to learn, why must Johnny, she thought bitterly.

She got into the front seat and leaned across the wheel, without any attempt to stop crying. Then, as the sobs let up, she pounded the wheel. "No, sir!" she said aloud. "I *won't* learn! I refuse to learn! I'll be an exception."

*

A Little Collar for the Monkey

*

I**T WAS** Thursday, the day the fish wagon came by, so old Mrs. Prosper shouted from her bed to her daughter in the room next to hers, "Thursday, Lily, fish day!"

The strength of her shouting lifted her momentarily above her pillows, and she sank back pleasurably, awaiting a reply. The sun was just up but it was not rising on a world in any way strange to it. It was rolling back into its own heat, heat left over from the day before. It was moving across the sky in a blaze of its own redness, mounting a streak of crimson spread out above it like a length of welcoming carpet. Outside in the growing light the birds, who for two hours had been whetting and sharpening their already thin, sharp little voices, now cut the air with razor strokes of sound.

"Poor fools," wise old Mrs. Prosper addressed them, "poor fools."

Two more hours and sparrow and linnet, towhee and mockingbird would be sitting in the umbrella tree's deepest shadow, wings extended, mouths gaping, and tongues—dry from singing and heat—shrunk to the size of little black basting threads. They would then drop down to the hydrant, dripping inside the circle of ferns, to lick up a warm drop or two.

"Poor fools," said Mrs. Prosper. "Not the least idea in the world what's good for you. Screeching now because the sun's up—and in two hours it will have you parched to the bone. Poached like eggs, and willing to pay money to be rid of your feathers."

Mrs. Prosper, herself old, thin, and unfeathered, enjoyed the heat. She let one foot dangle out from under the single sheet which covered her until it touched the uncarpeted floor boards. The floor boards were still warm from yesterday's heat, and the feel of that lingering warmth excited Mrs. Prosper. A small ripple shook her, as if she had been some variety of electrical mechanism suddenly enjoying the shock of a propulsive voltage. Be a scorcher today, she thought, be a record breaker —but probably not, she concluded. Nature continually disappointed Mrs. Prosper. It seemed capable of so much variety and actually was so repetitious. Mrs. Prosper was always searching for a wildness, a violence, nature never provided. A strangeness which any day might by very simple means provide: let only the sun reverse itself, or flowers fly; let fish sing or rain fall upward. That would do it. The possibilities were endless. Life might easily be exciting, strange, and awesome; as it was, everything was in a rut. Spring, summer, winter, fall. First the bud and then the blossom. First the egg and then the bird. And then the song at sunup. "Poor fools," said Mrs. Prosper, listening.

Mrs. Prosper wasted very little time wondering about who was at the helm of the world, who ordered matters thus tamely. That someone was there she took for granted; she wasn't a fool, only imaginative. But she had long ago concluded that it was someone either dozing or unaware of the possibilities; someone, at least, totally unlike herself.

She herself, limited as she was, had gone out one spring, when the apricot trees were smaller, and had broken from one of the sturdiest trees every single bud and blossom. Painstakingly, every one. Then, when the trees all about it had been heavy with fruit, she had been pleased to stand beside it noting its peculiarity and bareness: full of heart-shaped, shining leaves, a perfect bower of greenness, but no fruit. Looking at it, she had felt full of power and accomplishment.

"What do *you* make of it?" she would inquire, addressing it, her tree, her handiwork, turned in a direction quite opposite from what nature had intended.

Her husband, then alive, had also looked at her tree, though with no notion it was hers. "An odd business," he had said. "Gopher at the roots, maybe. Possibly gum disease."

"Possibly," Mrs. Prosper, not then old, had replied. "But it looks healthy, doesn't it? Green and flourishing."

Mr. Prosper had laid a hand on the puce-colored bark, like a father testing his child's temperature. "It does," he agreed. "It does for a fact. I can't figure it out."

"Can't you, Enos?" asked Mrs. Prosper.

"It's a mystery to me," he said, feeling and touching.

"A mystery," said Mrs. Prosper.

She liked her husband well enough, considering she despised him. But then, whom did she not despise? She could have respected only a man capable of looking at her and saying, "You don't for a minute fool me." And there had never been anyone to say that. And for her, a woman alive in a world in a rut and among men without insight, Enos Prosper was as good a man as any other and better than many.

They had walked back to the house together. "Next year I'll make it bloom and bear," she had said.

Her husband took her hand. He kissed the fingers that had broken off the buds. "I believe you could," he said. For Mrs. Prosper, who lived on irony, that was a dainty mouthful.

"Fool, fool," she said now, coming near enough the edge of her bed to rest the whole of her foot upon the floor boards, whose warmth, retained from yesterday, promised still greater heat for the coming day. The words she spoke recalled her to the present, and she listened for a sound from her daughter's room. There was none.

"Thursday, Lily," she shouted again. "Fish day. Time to curl and primp." Again there was no answer, but there were now other sounds. A car down the road. A cock crowing. A faraway tractor. Bees in the Gold of Ophir rose which had laced itself among the limbs of the umbrella tree at the corner of the house.

"Get up," shouted Mrs. Prosper. "Rouse yourself, Lily, and make yourself pretty for the fishmonger."

Mrs. Prosper got out of her own bed and walked to the front window. She unlatched the hinged screen, swung it open, and leaned out into the morning air. "Be a furnace by noon," she speculated; but the rest of the world was disappointing. With the help of a half dollar and a matchbox a child could draw it: rounds, squares, and rectangles, that was the whole of it. Round sun, round sky, and apricots and their leaves nearly round. The road itself, in front of the house, a half circle, a tunnel of green under the wholly round umbrella trees: trees round as upturned green basins and chinked only enough to let sufficient light to travel through. The ranches she looked out on were squares or rectangles, separated by a road or a row of standpipes. A world for a child to draw. But she herself, she thought, too complex for any such picturing.

She spread her unbleached muslin gown across the foot of the bed to air, walked to the old bureau, and saw herself in the mirror which was blurred with constellations and sunspots, pocked with moonlike craters. Gone sallow, gone stringy, but not flabby; tight in buttock and neat in breast; no one with a matchbox and a half dollar could draw her. She gave herself a smart slap and put on her wrapper. She lived inside herself as precisely as a walnut in its shell, nothing rattling, nothing wasting, rich and orderly, too tough a nut for time to crack.

"Get up, Lily," she called again in the hall, on her way to the bathroom. "Get up and slick yourself up for your fish peddler." But as she waited for a reply she heard Lily, already downstairs, bustling about in the kitchen.

Mrs. Prosper went down to breakfast, smooth and shiny as a beetle in her coal black; her gold brooch and earrings as many-faceted as a beetle's eye in the morning light. She found the table already set in the breakfast room, and curtains already partly drawn against the heat. From beneath the curtains, bars of yellow light slanted down onto the rag rugs; but this light was only ankle deep: above the ankles the room was dusky. Hodge, the cat, lay on a window sill, one ear cocked to follow the buzzings of a fly, self-conscious with being watched. Hodge was a fly trap more certain than Tanglefoot, more deadly than a Daisy Fly-Killer; and this lone survivor, having witnessed since sunup the engulfment of all his kind in the breakfast room, buzzed now a nervous swan song.

"Good morning, Hodge," said Mrs. Prosper. The marmalade-colored tom closed his yellow eyes.

In the dusk of the upper room Mrs. Prosper saw white sweet peas in a glass bowl on the center of the table, coffee already poured, dishes of strawberries, and a fringed napkin, covering, she knew, a plate of Lily's fine-grained scones.

Mrs. Prosper appreciated the scene, all of it, even the buzzing fly. It looks like a home, she thought. She imagined herself a stranger standing outside the windows and peering through the glass with a stranger's eyes. She saw how pleasant the surface was. It does look like a home, she thought, it looks like a nice breakfast, I look like a nice old lady come down to eat my breakfast; and Lily, there, pulling out my chair, looks like a daughter.

Only Mrs. Prosper had never been able to think of Lily as a daughter at all. She thought of her as a female relation, connected, but distantly, through Mrs. Prosper's mother's people. A niece or possibly a cousin of her mother's. Indeed, Lily looked so like Mrs. Prosper's mother that Mrs. Prosper sometimes had the feeling that she had spent her entire life with her mother, knowing her first as a mature woman and then, in Lily, as a child and girl. Now, at forty, Lily was her mother as Mrs. Prosper best remembered her: the same soft, dun-colored hair looped back in the same aimless way; the same light brown eyes, faintly pink lips, and teeth that, curving inward, gave the mouth its peculiarly childlike look. Well-fleshed, as her mother had been, but no muscles beneath the flesh, so that she was as soft to the touch as a handful of yarn. Always neat, always the same flowered dresses, white aprons, and black oxfords; shoes sensible of heel but so fancifully cut about the vamp that they contradicted everything else Lily wore.

"Good morning, Lily," said Mrs. Prosper seating herself in the chair that Lily pushed carefully in for her.

"Good morning, Mother," said Lily.

"I called you early this morning, Lily," said Mrs. Prosper. "Several times. At the top of my voice. No answer."

"I didn't hear you, Mother," said Lily. "I came downstairs early this morning."

"Then you did remember," said Mrs. Prosper. "Good. I didn't want you to oversleep."

Lily said nothing, but took the napkin from the scones and held the plate for her mother.

"Courted by a fish peddler," said Mrs. Prosper helping herself. "How does that seem?"

Lily put the napkin back over the scones and said nothing.

"Ah, well," said Mrs. Prosper, "it's an intimate subject. I don't blame you for not wanting to talk of it. What's his name again, by the way? I know, but I keep forgetting it."

"Olav," said Lily. "Olav Duun."

"Sounds like an owl hooting," observed Mrs. Prosper. "An old owl in the dead of night. He a foreigner?"

"He's Swedish," said Lily.

"He don't look it. Black. Black as soot and long mustaches like a catfish. I've heard that people who live a long time in China begin finally to look like Chinamen and that people in charge of the crazy begin after a while to look crazy themselves. Do you reckon if you sell fish long enough, you begin to look like a fish?" asked Mrs. Prosper.

"Olav hasn't sold fish for so very long," said Lily.

"He's made progress, then," declared Mrs. Prosper. "Whiskered like an old catfish already."

Lily, undisturbed, insofar as Mrs. Prosper could see, buttered a scone. "Courted by a Swedish fish peddler, name like an owl in the night! Has Hodge been fed this morning?" she asked, suddenly tiring of Lily's unresponsiveness.

"No," said Lily.

Mrs. Prosper took the saucer from under her coffee cup and half filled it with yellow cream. She handed the saucer to her daughter and Lily placed it on the sill beside the cat.

"Kit, kit, kit," said Mrs. Prosper. "Cream for breakfast."

Hodge turned his eyes for a moment away from the bemused fly, buzzing just now against the hot windowpane above his head.

"Cream," said Mrs. Prosper. "Thick cream!"

Hodge turned back to the window, with a sudden soft slap killed the sun-struck fly, and, negligently chewing it down, settled himself for sleep beside the untasted cream.

Mrs. Prosper laughed and struck her hands together. "Wonderful animals," she said, "wonderful Hodge." She glanced up at Lily and it was her mother who regarded her.

"The sugar, please, Lily," she said. She sprinkled sugar thickly over the big, deep-red berries. "I remember picking strawberries once, when a girl. A day about like this."

"Yes, mother," said Lily.

"I and a friend, a hulk of a girl, twice my size and a year or two older. Her name was Rose. Rose Vawters. Our mothers sent us over to a Jap's who had berries for sale. The berries were cheaper if you picked them yourself. It was a hot muggy day with gnats and the ground had been newly irrigated and wasn't nice to kneel on. 'You'll pick mine, too,' I told Rose. 'Why?' she asked. 'My mother only wants . . .' 'Don't talk,' I said. 'Pick.' She began to pick. 'Faster,' I said, and she picked faster. I only nudged her with my toe now and then, never kicked her or really hurt her. She was twice my size and considerably older, but she picked all my berries. A bucket for each of us. And she carried them home. 'Walk in a ditch,' I would say, and she walked there. 'Hide,' I would say, 'you've stolen the berries,' and she would hide. 'Lie flat on your stomach, they'll see you,' and she would flatten herself in the slime of an empty irrigation ditch. 'Run,' I would tell her, 'run, you're being chased,' and she would run. Pretty fast too, though the berries were heavy and she wasn't slim herself. I can still see her pounding down the road ahead of me, a berry jolting now and then out of the two full buckets she carried."

Mrs. Prosper finished her berries. "I never eat berries but I remember that morning. I've forgotten a lot of things that happened when I was a girl . . . not that morning and how I felt. But I've told you before, haven't I, Lily?"

"Yes, mother," said Lily.

Mrs. Prosper noticed that her daughter had pushed her own berries aside and was looking at nothing, or possibly a crack in the floor boards or a spot on the wallpaper. "But you don't listen, do you, Lily?" she asked.

After the breakfast work was finished Lily and her mother sat in the shadowy, still-cool living room. Tightly closed as it was against the heat, it smelled of furniture polish, of the acacia branches which Lily put in the fireplace in summer to hide its reminder of heat and burning, and of Hodge, the cat. The smell of Hodge was remarkably like that of the Shasta daisies which, like spokes from a wheel, rayed out from a bowl on the center table: a smell Mrs. Prosper had been sampling since her youth, unable to decide whether it was good or bad. On each side of the daisies were candles, which were not reminders of heat or burning since they had never been intended for lighting. They were candles by reason of their being placed in candlesticks. Actually, encrusted as they were with deep swirls of blue and green paint, they more nearly resembled stalagmites rising upward from the gloom of the center table.

In this pleasant darkness Lily sat tatting, Mrs. Prosper buffing her nails, Hodge watching the pendulum of the clock on the mantelpiece, with its movement so like that of something which might be crushed and eaten. Lily's bobbin, as the thread left it, made a very light tick, the clock echoed it on deeper note, Mrs. Prosper's buffer went over the ridges of her old nails with a dry swish. Only Hodge was silent, his eyes following the pendulum, which he believed would sooner or later forget he was there, fly out from behind the glass that housed it, and finally slide, a round juicy mouthful, down his throat.

As the clock struck ten, Mrs. Prosper put down her buffer and listened. Within a few minutes, so faint that any other sound would have drowned it, came the tootle of a horn blown three times.

"There he is," said Mrs. Prosper. "The fishman. Right on time."

Lily paused for a minute in her tatting. Then her bobbin flew again.

"Ladies a quarter-mile in each direction freshening themselves up," said Mrs. Prosper, "in order to be ready to buy a half-pound of halibut."

"He blows it so they can have their money ready," Lily said, "and a pan to put the fish in."

"He tell you?" asked Mrs. Prosper.

"Yes," said Lily.

"Money and pan ready don't seem to speed him any here."

"He's polite," said Lily. "He thinks of more than selling. He likes to pass the time of day. He don't rush."

"No, he don't," said Mrs. Prosper. "Why don't you walk down a ways to meet him, Lily? He goes clear round the section before he gets here. You could ask him which fish were most tasty this week. Inquire if the sand dabs are up to par."

Lily's shuttle went perhaps a little faster but she said nothing.

"I will, then," said Mrs. Prosper. "I'd like a little ride.

I'll catch him at the corner, ride round the section with him, ask him about his wares."

Mrs. Prosper put her buffer on the center table. "How is it exactly you say his name, Lily?"

"Duun," said Lily, "Olav Duun."

"Mr. Duun, I'll say, I've come to ride a ways with you."

That was what she did. She walked down the tunnel of green under the umbrella trees and caught Mr. Duun at the Burneys'. Mrs. Burney had just departed with her change and fish for the house. Mr. Duun stood at the back of his wagon, wiping out his scales.

"Mr. Duun," said Mrs. Prosper, "I've come to ride a ways with you."

"Duun's the name," said Mr. Duun without turning about.

"Duun," repeated Mrs. Prosper.

Mr. Duun gave his cleaver a final swipe, placed it in its rack, and closed the heavy doors of the truck upon his stock of fish.

"Hop in," he said.

Mrs. Prosper walked around to the right side of Mr. Duun's fish truck, climbed up and in, and closed the door behind her.

Mr. Duun, for whom the height of the running board had been less of an impediment than for Mrs. Prosper, was already in the cab, writing down his sales, when she got there. Without looking up he said, "Slam your door, otherwise it rattles."

"Slam it yourself," said Mrs. Prosper, settling comfortably back.

Mr. Duun did so. He reached across Mrs. Prosper, pencil still in hand, and banged the door. Then he went back to his totting up.

Mrs. Prosper watched him as he worked. In age, he was a man halfway between Lily and herself. It was untrue, what she had said about his mustache. The hairs about the mouth of a catfish are sparse, gray, and stiff. The hairs about Mr. Duun's mouth were thick, soft, and black. There was only something in the angle of their growth, their curve being long and downward, which had put her in mind of a catfish. There was no gray in either his mustache or his hair, which he wore roached back in an unstylish pompadour. From its bridge his nose ran along straight enough for two-thirds of its length, then splayed out, became thumb shaped. His eyes, Mrs. Prosper knew, were black; now, because he was looking downward and because they scarcely bulged his eyelids, they seemed very flat. He was olive skinned and smooth contoured, the smoothness being broken only by his high cheekbones and full Adam's apple. He looked a good, craggy man to Mrs. Prosper, wearing a white apron and woven straw gauntlets on his wrists, as a fish peddler ought. His hands, busy with his writing, were perfectly clean except for a splash or two of fish blood.

"You wouldn't think fish peddling would take so much book work," said Mrs. Prosper.

"You know much about fish peddling, Mrs. Prosper?" asked Mr. Duun closing his book and placing it in a little rack above his left shoulder.

"I know what I think," said Mrs. Prosper.

"Ah," stepping on the starter.

"Do you write down, five cents for a quarter of a

pound of smelts sold to Mrs. Butts's cat on Thursday?"
asked Mrs. Prosper.

"Sometimes less, sometimes more," said Mr. Duun
swinging out onto the road.

"More?"

"A word about Mrs. Butts herself, and now and again
a word about the cat."

"Have you ever put down a word about—us?"

"About your daughter."

"What did you say?"

Mr. Duun looked full at Mrs. Prosper, and she saw that
his eyes were less flat than she had thought. "It slips my
mind," he said.

Mr. Duun then picked up his horn, an ordinary cow
horn it looked to Mrs. Prosper, silver tipped at the blowing end. Neatly parting his mustache with the tip, he
blew three blasts, two short and one long.

"That like to burst my drums," said Mrs. Prosper.

"They tell me it'll carry a mile if the wind's right,"
Mr. Duun agreed.

While Mr. Duun sold fish at his next stop to the
O'Toole sisters—two plump maiden ladies who brought
him iced lemonade and warm spongecake to stay his midmorning hunger—Mrs. Prosper took a look at the cab of
Mr. Duun's truck. It was thoroughly decorated. There
were flowers painted on the glass of the dome light and
a little vase in a bracket, the vase now filled with some
wilting lop-headed fuchsias. There were tacked-up picture post cards, mostly of boats and harbors, and some
oddments, unfamiliar to Mrs. Prosper but connected, she
supposed, either with fishing or fish selling. There was

even a motto of some kind, in a language Mrs. Prosper could not read, above the rear-view mirror.

When Mr. Duun and the O'Toole sisters had concluded their considerable visit, and after Mr. Duun had written down whatever it was he did write down after such sales, Mrs. Prosper asked him about the motto.

"What language is that?" she asked.

"Swedish," replied Mr. Duun, putting his account book in its rack and his pencil behind his ear.

"It's a peculiar-looking language," said Mrs. Prosper.

"Not to Swedes," said Mr. Duun.

"So you're Swedish," said Mrs. Prosper.

Mr. Duun, busy backing his truck out of the O'Toole driveway, nodded.

"You don't look it."

Mr. Duun, now in the clear, replied, "The Lord must've thought so, otherwise he wouldnt've set me down among Swedes."

"The Lord makes mistakes."

Mr. Duun did not contradict this.

"How did you happen to come to America?"

"My ship put in here at a time when I'd decided I'd had enough of the sea. Time to learn something about the land."

"You a sailor?"

"I was."

"How'd you come to take to fish peddling?"

"Nearest there is to sailing. You move about and you move with fish. Nothing lacking but water and that was what I wanted to get away from."

Mr. Duun turned into the Smedleys' palm-lined driveway.

Mrs. Prosper, looking at the drawn blinds, the closed garage door, said, "No one home here."

"Home or not," said Mr. Duun, "every Thursday I put a lobster in the Smedley icebox."

When Mr. Duun returned from delivering this lobster, Mrs. Prosper handed him a silver-inlaid leather circlet, which she had lifted from a hook that also held a calendar, a good luck medal on a chain, and two brown shoelaces braided together.

"A nice piece of work," she said, "a pretty bracelet for a plump arm."

Mr. Duun turned the leather circlet about in his hands a time or two; then, lifting up his apron, he vigorously polished the silver work on his pants leg.

"It's a collar," said he.

"It'd take a skinny neck to fit that little circle."

"I made it for a skinny neck," said Mr. Duun, "and it fit to a T."

"You a silversmith, too?" Mrs. Prosper asked. While Mr. Duun's hands looked skillful enough to handle a fish knife, the silver work on the collar was fine and intricate —something beyond a mere fish carver.

"My father did the silver work. He was a farmer, and in the winters, when work was slack, he made collars— first for his own dogs and then for the dogs of all his neighbors, until finally he was as much a maker of dog collars as a farmer."

Mrs. Prosper took the collar from Mr. Duun and ran her fingers around its circumference. "Tiny little dogs you have in Sweden," she said.

"That was never made for a dog—it was made for a monkey."

"Where's the monkey?" asked Mrs. Prosper.

"You're ahead of the story," said Mr. Duun. "When I was twelve I got a piece of leather—that piece of leather," he said touching the collar Mrs. Prosper now held. "And I cut it just that size. When my father saw it he was just like you. 'Well boy,' he said, 'what toy neck you planning to span with this collar, what lady's lap dog?' 'It's not for a dog,' I told him, 'it's for a monkey, a little collar for a monkey.' 'A monkey!' said my father. 'So you're going to sea,' for every sailor who came home to Göteborg, which was a port town, had his monkey with him."

"You were forehanded," said Mrs. Prosper. "A monkey collar at twelve."

"So my father said. But he helped me with the collar, set in all the silver work himself, though he was against my going and needed another hand on the farm. And when the day came for leaving—I was seventeen then—I was so excited I forgot all about my little collar. My father went up to my room, and fetched it down. He opened my bag, already strapped shut for my journey, and laid the collar inside. 'There's your little collar, son,' he said, 'and I hope you find a good little monkey to wear it.'"

"Did you?" asked Mrs. Prosper.

"No," said Mr. Duun. "I found a bitch of a monkey, a regular she-devil, the devil in monkey form maybe."

Mr. Duun reached over, took the collar out of Mrs. Prosper's hands, and hung it once again on its peg. Then he started his motor and backed out of the Smedleys' palm- lined driveway.

The fish truck, because of the amount of ice Mr. Duun

carried, was cooler than the air outside, but even so it was hot. Mrs. Prosper could no more sweat than a stone, but she saw that Mr. Duun's olive skin had become ruddy and that among the black hairs of his mustache fine beads of sweat glistened like little brilliants.

He turned left and right, and then into the green tunnel under the umbrella trees. The little monkey collar swung back and forth with the momentum of his turning.

"It doesn't appear to have been much used," observed Mrs. Prosper, watching it swing.

"Two weeks," said Mr. Duun. "We were two weeks out of Montevideo when I took the collar off her neck and tossed her into the sea."

"Drowned?" said Mrs. Prosper.

"She asked for it," said Mr. Duun. "She was vicious. She had bad habits."

"So you drowned her," said Mrs. Prosper. A monkey's dying by drowning seemed somehow stranger than if it had come to its death from a blow on the head or a knife thrust.

"She drowned herself, I reckon," said Mr. Duun. "I only tossed her over the rail. She clung to the rail, she clung to me. She knew what was coming and she was suddenly loving. I threw her over and she looked like a big black spider there on top of the water. She cried out, too. Pitiful to hear, I suppose, if you hadn't known how she had asked for it."

Mr. Duun's recital was calm enough, like that of a law-respecting judge summing up a case, but Mrs. Prosper's heart was beating faster. She could see it all, very clearly. Mr. Duun, large, young then, handsome; though he was handsome now, for that matter. She could see him take the collar from the monkey's neck and hand it to a fellow sailor. And she could see the look in the monkey's eyes as he did that, the foreknowledge, and the thin black hands on the rail, and the little hands torn off, and the unbelief in the eyes as it fell, and the desperate flailing as it tried for a time to regain the ship.

"Did you ever get another?" asked Mrs. Prosper.

"One was enough," said Mr. Duun.

Mrs. Prosper reached out and touched the collar. "But you kept the collar."

"So far I have," said Mr. Duun. "To remind me."

"Did you think as you watched it drowning," asked Mrs. Prosper, "your monkey—did you think—monkey, you were born to live in a tree, but I've changed all that for you?"

"I did not," said Mr. Duun, who was now turning into the Prosper driveway.

"It would have been an interesting thing to see," Mrs. Prosper said as Mr. Duun brought his truck to a stop at the back steps of the Prosper house, "a monkey drowning in mid-ocean. I wish I had been there."

Mr. Duun took his hands from the wheel and turned sideways so that he squarely confronted Mrs. Prosper. Sitting thus, he gave Mrs. Prosper the glance she had never before encountered, but which, now that she had received it, she felt she had spent a lifetime looking for. It was a glance of recognition. It took her all in. It missed nothing. Mr. Duun sat for quite some time in this way, gazing at Mrs. Prosper; then, slowly, he turned away, and after a few seconds or a few minutes—Mrs. Prosper was too shaken by the complete reflection and recognition she had seen in Mr. Duun's eyes to keep track of time—he spoke.

"What will you have today?" he asked in the same matter-of-fact tone he had used to describe the drowning of the monkey.

"Have?" repeated Mrs. Prosper, somewhat bewildered.

"What fish?" asked Mr. Duun. "I've got some nice halibut. Sea bass. Salmon. Barracuda."

Mrs. Prosper recalled herself. "No fish today, Mr. Duun," she said.

"No fish! Don't tell me, Mrs. Prosper, you ladies have lost your taste for fish!"

"Not I," declared Mrs. Prosper. "Not I. But Lily's never cared for them and she's finicky. She says that in this hot weather the smell of so much as a fish frying would turn her stomach."

Mrs. Prosper unlatched the door on her side of the cab.

"You might ask your daughter, when you go in," said Mr. Duun, "if she'd like a little ride with me out San Jacinto way. She'd find it cooling, I think."

Mrs. Prosper let the door—which she had been holding open—come to, but not latch. "It would be better not," she said. "Lily's my daughter, Mr. Duun, but it's my duty to tell you she's at the age an old maid's likely to reach. The age when it's her pleasure to think every man has his eye on her. For harm, you understand. The milkman, a Mexican come to clean out the hen house, an agent with magazines, it's all one to Lily, so he wears pants. She's going to make trouble for some man someday. And I wouldn't want it to be you."

Mrs. Prosper looked upward, once again searching Mr.

Duun's glance for that shock of recognition—for that reflection of her whole self.

It was there. It was fully there. While Mrs. Prosper was using it, making up for what she felt to be a lifetime's lack, Mr. Duun suddenly opened his own door and stepped out.

"It would be better, I see, for me to ask her myself," he said, and went into the house without a knock at the door or even a pause. Mrs. Prosper climbed slowly down out of the fish truck—and stood for a minute in the driveway, enjoying the sun, now almost at its height, and thinking about what might be going on in the house. Whatever it was, it was soon over. Before she had turned about the screen door slammed, and there was Lily—her white apron off, her Milan straw hat on, Mr. Duun with his hand on her elbow, and, at Mr. Duun's heels, Hodge.

"I'm going for a little ride with Mr. Duun, Mother," said Lily, and Mrs. Prosper watched Mr. Duun hand her up into the truck like an honored guest. When he had done that and closed the door he walked on around to the back of the truck and got out a smelt for Hodge. Then he climbed up into the cab with Lily, and slammed the door after him. He didn't at once start his engine, however, but sat leaning out of his window, looking at Mrs. Prosper. Mrs. Prosper thought he intended speech. Instead he reached across Lily, took down the little collar, and tossed it at Mrs. Prosper's feet.

"A gift from the groom," he said.

"Groom?" asked Mrs. Prosper.

"Groom-to-be," said Mr. Duun.

Mrs. Prosper stooped and picked up the collar. "A gift to the bride's mother in memory of her that wore it," said Mr. Duun; then he started his engine, and he and Lily drove on around the house and out the driveway on the other side.

Mrs. Prosper, who lived on irony, had her cupful then, pressed down and running over: the "bride's mother," and that collar, and known as she was; those three, all together and at one time. Mrs. Prosper stood for some time in the dry, burning sunlight without moving. Then she laughed. Not silently, but loud enough to cause Hodge, busy with his fish, to look up.

"Come, Hodge," said Mrs. Prosper, quickly stooping, "you'll wear the collar." But Hodge was faster than Mrs. Prosper. In one snake-like curve he was out of her arms and under the oleanders, carrying what was left of Mr. Duun's gift. So Mrs. Prosper had to enter the house without him, empty-handed except for the monkey collar.

*

Public-Address System

*

A NUMBER of people are blaming Bill Hare for
what happened to Leonard Hobart. They say
he's responsible. Bill Hare doesn't have to de-
pend upon hearsay for this information. He's president
of the Tenant Building and Loan Association and is in
his office on the main street of town eight hours a day.
That's a public place, every Tom, Dick, and Harry feels
free to go in—and does. They go in—Bill hasn't any way
of telling a client from a busybody since they look pretty
much the same and oftentimes are—and say, "Bill Hare,
don't your conscience hurt you the way this Leonard
Hobart business has turned out?"

It doesn't. But Bill is getting tired of saying so. He'll
say something else soon. Mrs. Hobart comes oftenest.
She'll say, "Mister Hare"—when Nadine Hobart says a
word she says *all* the letters—"Mister Hare," she'll say,
"I hold you personally responsible for what happened to
my husband." She came in yesterday. "Mister Hare," she
said, "I place the blame for what happened to Leonard
squarely upon your shoulders."

Bill Hare will take a good deal from Nadine Hobart
because of what she's been through. But not everything.

He watches her tear-shaped specs tremble on her fleshy nose and notes the way she builds her braids up into a kind of stockade on top of her head and remembers a few of the things Leonard told him about his wife. He thinks, Mrs. Hobart, you're a good-looking woman and you've been through a lot, but you keep *nagging* me and I'll tell you the truth. I'll tell you for one thing that you're responsible, far more responsible for what happened to your husband than I am.

From first to last, what Bill Hare did was done to help Leonard. He was more Quixotic than anything else—had far more to gain, personally, by letting the softball committee do what it wanted to do: that is, go into Los Angeles and buy a public-address system from a Los Angeles firm. But no. Not fair-minded Billy! "We must play ball with the local merchants," he told them. "We must give Leonard Hobart his chance." And since Bill Hare was chairman of the committee to buy the public-address system he was naturally listened to.

"You mean Hobart's Electric Shop?" asked Aldo Mattutzi. Bill said he did.

"Why waste time on Old Leonard?" asked Aldo. "I move we go right into L.A. where we can see the stuff at its source and in quantity."

"No sir," said Bill Hare. "The success of softball in Tenant depends upon the good will of the townspeople. We've got to play ball with them if we want them to play ball with us."

"Oh hell!" said Aldo. "In the first place Leonard probably don't carry the equipment. In the second place, even if he does and we bypass him he'll be the last person to raise a squawk."

"Mattutzi," Bill said reasonably, "you know that's not the way to handle this."

"Hobart's your next-door neighbor, isn't he?" Aldo asked, insinuating that Bill's reasons for going to Hobart's might be personal.

"He is," Bill said. "I've lived next door to Leonard Hobart for ten years but as far as I'm concerned he'd just as well not be there."

That was the truth. And it wasn't because Bill Hare was a big wheel in Tenant and Leonard Hobart a practically invisible cog. It was the truth because of time and silence and Nadine. Time: twenty-four hours in the day; eight or ten for business. Eight for sleep. Six left for his family (Bill has a wife and three children), for softball, for taking a drive, for tuberous begonias, for fishing, for the Royal Arch. Where was there any time for Leonard? Silence: Leonard was silent. Not even his shoes squeaked. In a room full of furniture he looked like furniture. When he was outdoors he appeared somewhat leafy. Leonard was a vacation for the eye and for the ear an intermission. Nadine: Bill heard *her*. In the morning he heard her tell Leonard which tie to put on. At lunch she told him what groceries to pick up on his way home. At night she reminded him to wash his hands before he ate.

"As far as I'm concerned," he told the committee, "Leonard doesn't exist. And if he hasn't got what we want I'll be the first to say let's go in to Los Angeles. But we ought to see him first and find out what he does have."

Bill naturally was given the job.

Leonard had a small shop, dark, and crowded with radios.

Amidst them he seemed somewhat varnish-colored himself. Bill looked this way and that trying to find him and saw him, finally, at the back of the shop taking the insides out of somebody's portable.

"Hi, Leonard," he said.

Bill saw Leonard look up, then quickly look downward, pretend in fact that he had not seen him nor heard his greeting. Bill walked down the narrow alleyway between radios to the back of the shop. Unconsciously he kept step to "Doing What Comes Naturally," sung by the Nightingales. That's a chorus of twenty girls and one of the radios was tuned in on their program.

"Hi, Leonard!" he called again. But still Leonard didn't reply.

Arrived at Leonard's workbench he said, "Hard at it, eh?"

Leonard then looked up. "Good morning, Mr. Hare," he said. "Radio's making such a racket I didn't hear you come in."

That was a lie. Bill knew it, then; and afterward Leonard told him so. Afterward Leonard told him almost everything.

"Remember the day you first came into the shop?" he asked Bill, afterward.

Bill didn't very well. "Yeh, I guess so," he said.

"I resented you that day, Bill."

"Resented me? I was just a poor customer."

Leonard disregarded this. "You were a big wheel in Tenant, Bill. And you had lived beside me for ten years and paid no more attention to me than if I were a stray dog."

Afterward, Leonard could say things like that to Bill

and laugh. They were friends then and Leonard could tell Bill things he had never told anyone else and in most of what he had to say Bill was interested.

"I thought to myself when you walked in that first morning," Leonard said, "here comes Bill Hare who'll expect me to drop everything the minute he says, Hi, Leonard."

Bill laughed. "Why hell, Leonard, didn't you want to make a sale?"

"Sure I did. But it was a pleasure to make you say hi twice, to get my attention."

Leonard didn't have any trouble making the sale. He could get the softball committee just as good a public-address system as any Los Angeles firm and he quoted them an even better price. Bill placed the order with him then and there, Leonard agreeing, of course, to install the system at the softball field.

Leonard was very pleased about the sale. Pleased to have made the acquaintance of Bill Hare and to have the prospect of working with and getting to know the committeemen. He went home happy that evening. He told Bill about it afterward.

It was raining as Leonard walked homeward from work that night, the first rain of the season, a sort of practice downfall, very slow and easy. On the empty lots the summer dust was cratered by the big drops. When the first autumn rain comes down the tiny shreds and particles of a long summer's grinding, the bits of leaves and cellophane and dried flower petals, the flakes of tobacco, hairs from bird feathers, horse's tails, lipstick brushes, the grape seeds, dried cherry stems, broken off thumbnails, all these things, pulverized, leap upward, an inch or so off the earth as the big drops hit them. Leonard watched this happen on his way home that evening. He had done so before, but he had never before had anyone to whom he could speak of it.

The whole town of Tenant seemed interesting to Leonard as he walked home that evening. First a building, then a vacant lot. Everything mixed. Loops, garlands, tendrils, lamp posts, swinging signs. Foothills at the end of streets. Frequency modulation beneath the lacy pepper boughs, empty bottles glittering in a clump of farewell summer. Beautiful uphill dream breasts behind the plate-glass windows. Busts, he corrected himself.

"Does your wife insist on busts?" he asked Bill.

"What?" asked Bill, who hadn't been listening very closely.

"As a part of your vocabulary," Leonard explained.

"Sally leaves my vocabulary pretty much alone," Bill said.

Leonard reached his own front porch that night and stood there, reluctant to go in: fall, the first rain, home town, big sale, acquaintances, friends! Next door was Bill Hare's house. Bill a neighbor of his, a business associate. A friend! Leonard closed his hand gently on a spattering of raindrops as if afraid he'd crush them. Why not go in, he thought, and lead the kind of life you've always dreamed about? What kind of a life is that? he asked himself. Why loving, he answered himself, lead a life of loving kindness. He went inside and it seemed possible.

Sometimes the furnishings of his living room disturbed him. There was a wicker settee in which the wickerwork strands seemed too numerous and to be traveling in too many directions. Sitting across the room from it he would find himself trying to follow one particular strand: discover where it began and where it was going. His eyes would hurt with the intensity of his concentration and still the pattern would elude him.

One evening, his eyes following, then failing to follow, the design of the wickerwork in the settee's arm, he had gone over and tried to trace the design with his fingers. Piece out the pattern by touch if sight were not enough. But Nadine had said, "Leonard for heaven's sake what are you doing? Creeping around the settee that way. And patting it."

"Patting it!" he had protested. "I'm not patting it. I'm just trying to feel out the pattern."

"Feel out the pattern? That's just as bad. What do you want to feel its pattern for?"

"I want to see if it *has* a pattern."

"Leonard Hobart," said Nadine, "are you crazy?"

"No," said Leonard. "No, I don't think so."

If he sat on the wicker settee the problem of its pattern escaped his eyes. But then he saw and worried about the picture on the wall opposite the settee: the picture of a vast, mid-ocean welter of green-gray swells. At the picture's lower edge there was one wave, poised, ready to break. Only it never broke. That was the trouble. There it hung, a white lip, threatening but stationary. Once he had run into the dining room to the wall behind the picture. But arrived there he had felt foolish. A painted wave cannot be made to break by getting behind it and pushing.

Tonight, however, neither the stationary wave nor the wickerwork settee troubled him. In fact, he didn't even see them. "Nadine, Nadine," he called. From the kitchen there came sounds of supper being prepared, but no answer.

"Nadine," he called again, "I'm home."

Nadine came to the kitchen door, her coronet of braids lustrous and her eyeglasses shining.

"Hello, Nadine," Leonard said. "Beautiful evening, warm, with a drizzle of rain."

"What are you saying?" Nadine asked.

"Raining," Leonard replied. "Beautiful evening, warm and raining."

"Is it?" said Nadine. "Well, I wish you'd speak up, Leonard, so I could hear you the first time. I wear myself out trying to find out what you're saying."

"And not worth the trouble half the time," Leonard agreed pleasantly.

To this Nadine did not reply, but observing his empty hands she asked, "Where are the rolls?"

"Rolls!" Leonard exclaimed clapping his hands to his pockets as if they might be there. "Rolls. I forgot them. Do you need them for supper?"

"Not if you don't mind stale bread."

"*I* don't," said Leonard turning back toward the living room and the evening paper, but Nadine told him, "Wash your hands. Supper is ready." So he had no time to read.

He was first at the table, even so. He and the stuffed pork chops and the creamed celery and the stale bread waited together. The children were not there and Nadine was calling them, calling up the dark stairs to young Nadine, aged sixteen, out into the rainy evening for Tom, aged twelve. Finally they were all at the table and the pork chops were passed, rich little pockets filled with food. Like a squirrel's cheeks, Leonard thought, then tried not to think as he cut into one.

"I had a piece of luck at the store today," Leonard told his family after the eating had started.

Young Nadine turned eagerly to her mother. "Timmy's coming. I told you he would. I'll have to have new sandals and a bag to match."

"Who's Timmy?" Tom asked.

"You wouldn't know, dear," his mother told him.

"Bill Hare stopped in. He wants—"

"If *she* gets new sandals *I* get a new football. Mine leaks so it's got to be pumped up every five minutes," Tom said.

"Good! Pump it up every five minutes. You can't be kicking it into people's faces if you're pumping it up."

"Do your face good to have a ball kicked—"

"Tom, dear," said Nadine. "You can have the ball. Now let your sister alone."

"They're installing a new public-address—" Leonard began again but Nadine had an idea. "I could dye that scarf for you," she told her daughter, "so that it would match your sandals and bag."

It wasn't until after the children had finished eating that Leonard had a chance to tell his wife about the sale.

"You seem pleased," said Nadine.

"I am. Bill could just as easy have gone into L.A."

"So it's Bill, now."

"Well, he calls me Leonard," Leonard defended himself. "We had a nice chat. I appreciate his swinging the sale to me."

"So he told you that, did he?"

"No, he didn't. But he's chairman of the committee. And whatever Bill Hare says in this town you can bet goes."

"You don't think Bill Hare's thinking about anyone but Bill Hare, do you?"

"What are you driving at, Nadine?"

"Bill Hare's buying the system of you so he'll have someone on hand to service it. You'll take care of it. Gratis, too, or I miss my guess. You'll spend your summer at the softball park. Any little flutter in the thing and they'll be calling on you."

"I like baseball," said Leonard. "That won't be much of a hardship."

"Baseball and servicing a public-address system are two different things. You'll be doing the latter. You mark my words."

Nadine and Leonard were both right. Leonard did spend a good deal of time at the park. And it wasn't, for him, a hardship. The system didn't go in until just before the opening of the softball season in late May. Leonard not only installed it but he went with Bill and Bill's committee for a number of nights after it was in to make sure that the loud-speakers were exactly where they should be, that the announcer's booth was properly and handily equipped, the connections dependable and so forth. Leonard was as anxious as Bill that both patrons and players be convinced that nothing out of Los Angeles could have been better.

Leonard enjoyed himself on those May evenings. The air was mild and soft. The grass (the softball diamond is located in Goodman Memorial Park) after its mowing and watering earlier in the day gave the place a fresh, country smell. Troops of kids followed the committee about; and in the midst of all the technical talk Leonard was the authority.

Leonard intended, of course, to be on hand for the opening night. He was an enthusiastic baseball fan in any circumstances and with a public-address system of his own installing receiving its first official tryout, he could not have been kept away. The game—the Tenant All Stars were playing the San Benito Champs—was not scheduled to begin until eight o'clock but Leonard planned to be at the field by seven-thirty.

At six-thirty, however, Bill Hare stopped in to ask Leonard to ride down to the park with him. "I thought it might be a smart idea to go down early and make a few tests," Bill said. "Just be certain everything's clicking."

The Hobarts were still at the dinner table and Nadine, at this request of Bill's, gave her husband a look which said plainly enough, What did I tell you? Bill caught the look and asked Nadine somewhat apologetically if she'd like to ride to the game a little later with his wife.

"Thank you, no, Mr. Hare," said Nadine. "Softball's a little outside my province."

When Bill and Leonard reached the diamond Bill said, "Maybe Burt's already here. If he is we'll get him to call out a few over the loud-speaker. Just to see if she's still got the power."

Burt Gayner was the announcer for the evening, a professional from Los Angeles hired to add éclat to the open ing game. But Burt hadn't showed up yet, so Bill told

Leonard, "I'll go out in the stands. You go up there and give her a tryout. Say the multiplication table if you want to. It don't matter *what* you say."

Bill still had the idea, at that time, that Leonard was a silent man for the lack of anything to say. Later, he realized, of course, that Leonard had been a silent man for the lack of anyone to listen to him. Bill walked up into the stands at the southwest corner of the field where tests had proved the acoustics to be bad and waited for Leonard's voice. What he expected to hear was, "One—two—three—testing."

Instead, what he heard was, "Tonight, ladies and gentlemen, the Tenant All Stars play the San Benito Champs in what promises to be a sizzling spine-tingling history-making softball classic. While we're waiting for the teams to put in their appearance on the field let me tell you something about the players.

"On the mound for the Tenant All Stars will be Al Tuck, big two-hundred-pound side-wheeler. Al's a spot pitcher, the boy who holds the league record for strike outs, a southpaw who's got control as well as steam. Give Al a low ball hitter and boom, upstairs the old apple comes. A high ball hitter and it's down in the basement."

Bill stopped, turned around, faced the announcer's booth. He stood stock-still, squinting across the twilit diamond, as the talk about Al Tuck continued. It wasn't what Leonard was saying so much—that was the spiel of a man who knew the Tenant team, all right, but who had read more baseball than he'd played it—it was Leonard's voice that impressed Bill. The voice of Leonard, the silent man. It had the authority of a natural phenomenon: of a cataract, or a thunderstorm, or a glacier, Bill climbed quickly down from the grandstand, then ran back across the field to the announcer's booth. He felt very excited, somehow.

After the game Bill took Leonard home. (The All Stars had won, Al Tuck, the spot pitcher, holding the Champs to six hits, one run.) They talked about Burt Gaynor, the announcer for the evening, who had not arrived until the fourth inning, and who had then been incompetent.

"Burt would've done a lot better," Leonard defended him, "if he hadn't been nervous."

"Nervous," said Bill. "Was he nervous, too?"

"A cop stopped him in Belvedere Gardens on suspicion of drunk driving. It upset him."

"Suspicion!" Bill exclaimed. "Well, I'm glad he was stopped. Five innings were more than enough for Burt."

"I thought he got better as he went along," Leonard said. "As it wore off."

"Look, Leonard," said Bill. "Burt Gaynor is no problem to softball in Tenant. Drunk or sober. You know that. Tenant got itself a new announcer tonight."

To this Leonard said nothing. It was eleven o'clock and in about half the houses they were passing the lights were still on, and in half of these the blinds were up so that they could see what was going on inside.

"Lots of card players," observed Leonard.

There were. Tables of four, two men and two women for the most part. High-school girls slamming cards at each other in a violent game of double Canfield. Solitary players, middle-aged men, moving cards from the top of a deck to the bottom. The wanted card never seeming to turn up.

"Lots of hair combers," said Leonard.

One hair washer. A man painting the ceiling of his kitchen. A woman ironing. A boy cleaning a rifle.

"You know who he is, don't you?" Bill persisted. "Our new announcer?"

They passed more card players, hair combers, workers, talkers, lovers.

"You'd want the job, wouldn't you, Leonard?"

Leonard replied reluctantly, as if talk might make the whole evening fade out like a dream.

"My voice was quite a surprise to me, Bill," he said.

"Me too," Bill replied.

"I'm not used to having people listen to me."

"How'd it seem, Leonard?" Bill asked.

Leonard tried to say. Out there, far out in the field *his* voice echoing against the stands. Bringing the heads of people about from their companions to face *him*. Drowning out lesser sounds: birds, wind in the park's trees, a kid's crying. *His* voice: the breath out of his own lungs, the vibrations given his breath by his own muscles. A part of him going where he could not go, doing what he could not do.

"Why, it's power," he told Bill.

"Sure, it is," Bill said, smiling. Then he had an idea. They had stopped at Leonard's place and Bill could see Nadine silhouetted against an upstairs window. "Maybe you'd like to talk this over with Nadine before you commit yourself to the job."

"No," Leonard said. "There's no need to do that. I'll accept it right now."

As the season went on Leonard's announcing got even

better. Not his voice. That couldn't be improved, but his manner and what he had to say. There was talk of his being invited to be the official announcer in other leagues. Bill was naturally proud of him and when softball fans dropped into the Building and Loan office to hash over the games, Bill would tell them the story of Leonard's debut as a broadcaster and of the part he had played in it.

"I lived next to him for ten years," he would tell his listeners, "and I never heard him speak. Didn't know if he *could* speak. Now listen to him."

Every one marveled at Bill's astuteness in discovering in such unlikely material a softball announcer, and Bill was willing to accept a fair share of the credit for Leonard's success. Then, when the criticism began to come in, he had to accept his share in that, too. It was natural that it should come to him, since he had been chairman of the committee that bought the public-address system. The criticism, at first was unorganized and sporadic and Bill paid little attention to it. Then Mrs. Florence Delia came to see him.

Mrs. Delia was president of the Goodman Park Neighborhood Association and as such came bearing an official protest. To her, Bill listened. He sat her down as formally as if she had been a stockholder, folded his hands on his desk and gave her his undivided attention.

"What's on your mind, Mrs. Delia?" he asked.

Mrs. Delia had several things on her mind. First of all she wanted Mr. Hare to know that the Neighborhood Association enjoyed the softball games. They enjoyed the broadcasts. They were proud of the Tenant All Stars. They were proud of Leonard's success as an announcer. Only, and here Mrs. Delia was both firm and warm as only an Italian matron can be, there was too much of it.

"At six o'clock, two hours before a game starts Mr. Hobart is out there at the field yelling balls and strikes," Mrs. Delia said. "Even when there is to be no game at all he does this. We are no longer able to hear ourselves think in the Goodman Park neighborhood. Mr. Hobart has a very fine, big beautiful voice, but we are getting too much of it."

Bill had heard all this before. He had even heard *it*, Leonard's practicing, Leonard's voice carrying as it did. He knew he would have to put a stop to it sometime and meanwhile he tried to placate Mrs. Delia and defend his protégé.

"Mrs. Delia," he said, "you can understand that a man needs to practice, can't you? Mr. Hobart is new at broadcasting. It's only natural that he should feel the need of practicing."

"He practices at the top of his voice," protested Mrs. Delia. "He makes the china rattle on our shelves. That is not natural, Mr. Hare."

Bill tried another tack. "Mrs. Delia, you are an Italian and you Italians understand artists. Your Caruso—for instance—rehearse, rehearse. Isn't that true?"

"Our Caruso," Mrs. Delia said, "sang. Mr. Hobart bellows. Bellowing is not a pleasant thing to listen to, Mr. Hare."

Bill Hare is an honest man. "I agree with you, Mrs. Delia," he said. "I'll speak to Mr. Hobart about it. I'll put a stop to it."

This was all Mrs. Delia asked. She left Bill with some compliments for Leonard's regular broadcasts. "Those we enjoy," she said. "It sounds like something very great going on when Mr. Hobart broadcasts. It makes my spine tingle like the late war and the sadness of good men dying."

This confused Bill but he said, "Thank you. Thank you, Mrs. Delia. I understand how you feel. I'll see Mr. Hobart at once."

By at once Bill had meant in a day or two. But he went to see Leonard that very afternoon, for hard on Mrs. Delia's heels came Nadine Hobart. She would neither sit, shake hands, nor speak of the weather. She was in a hurry, she told Bill, and what she had to say was painful to her.

"Mr. Hare," she said, "you are breaking up my marriage."

Bill was aghast. The last thing in the world he would willingly do was to interfere in any way with Nadine Hobart's marriage. "Mrs. Hobart," he faltered, "what do you mean?"

"Leonard," she said. "Before you got him started in this broadcasting business he was a good husband. Punctual, sympathetic, helpful. Now all that is changed. And above all Leonard is never at home any more. Broadcasting or practicing to broadcast! You must have heard him."

"Yes," said Bill, "I have."

"Well," said Mrs. Hobart, "put a stop to it. Besides my personal situation the neighbors are complaining."

"I know," said Bill. "To me, too."

"You're responsible for it Mr. Hare."

"I'll do what I can," Bill said.

"Do what you can? You started it. Now you stop it."

Bill closed his office about four that afternoon and went

around to Hobart's Electric Shop to have a talk with Leonard. Leonard, as on the first time he had called, was at the back of his shop doing some repair work. But this time he replied at once to Bill's "Hi, Leonard."

"Hi, Bill," he said, put down his work and came to meet his friend. "What's new, Billy-boy?" he asked.

"Well, Leonard," said Bill, without any beating about the bush, "we've been getting some complaints about the broadcasts."

"You mean about the practice broadcasts, don't you?"

"Yes," said Bill. "About the practices. The Goodman Park Neighborhood Association objects."

"Well, that's all fixed up, Billy," Leonard said. "I was going to tell you. The Association won't complain any more. I'm putting in a public-address system of my own."

Bill pushed his hat to the back of his head, then took it off. "At your house or the shop?" he asked.

"My house. It's already arrived. I'll connect it up this evening. It's a thing I've had in mind to do for some time. It'll be a great help to Nadine for one thing, calling the kids in to meals and so forth. And I'll find uses for it, too, no doubt. I've discovered that I enjoy using the darned thing, believe it or not. Over the public-address system, I don't mind admitting to you, Bill, I feel like a different person. Amplification—well, I don't know—it just seems to suit me, somehow."

"Are you planning to practice your broadcasts at home?" Bill asked doubtfully.

"I wasn't," Leonard said, "unless you think I ought to, Bill. I kind of had the idea that my softball technique was okay now."

"I think so, too," Bill said heartily. "Rehearse and

you're liable to go stale. The broadcasts are just about perfect as they now stand."

"Perfect! They're not perfect yet by a long shot," Leonard said, "but I have noticed one interesting development in them recently."

"What's that?" Bill asked.

"I don't know just what to call it—anticipation's maybe the word."

"Anticipation?" Bill repeated.

"Most announcers call out the plays a little after they're made, don't they?"

"Sure."

"I call them a little before."

"You what?"

Leonard repeated what he had said. "I call them a little before they're made, Billy. Haven't you noticed it?"

"No," said Bill. "I haven't."

"Not very much before, yet, less than a second, probably. I call ball and *after* I say it, the pitch turns out to be a ball. Inside curve, low, I say, and inside curve, low, it is. You've never noticed?"

"No," said Bill, "I never have."

"Watch tomorrow night's game, Billy. You'll see what I mean. They move when I give them the word. Not vice versa as with other announcers. It'll be an added attraction, when people catch on."

Bill felt uneasy and embarrassed. He knew Leonard was full of whimseys, he *liked* it in him, but, this seemed carrying a whimsey pretty far. He left Leonard and went immediately home. He had no appetite that evening and couldn't keep his mind on what his wife said. There was an old hollow feeling under his breastbone, not quite a pain, but unpleasant enough to send him to bed as soon as dinner was over. About midnight his wife awakened him. She had leaned over from the twin bed next to his and grasped his arm.

"Bill," she said, shaking his arm. "Bill. What in the world is that noise?"

"What's what?" Bill asked, only partially awake.

"That sound. What is it?"

It seemed to Bill more like a subterranean force than a sound. It was strong enough to be felt in vibrations along the headboard of his bed, against which he had pushed his shoulders in his hurried wakening. Then he realized what it was.

"It's Leonard," he said. "He was going to install a public-address system at his place this evening. He's testing it."

"Go on back to sleep, Nadine," Leonard said, the words issuing from the Hobart house like thunderclaps.

"Why is he shouting?" Sally Hare asked. "Why doesn't he turn it down?"

"I'm not shouting," said Leonard, as if answering *her*. "This is my normal voice."

At that Sally scurried over into Bill's bed. There was something frightening about that voice in the middle of the night, the more frightening because the voice was Leonard's. It suggested that there was no more dependence to be put on reason. It was not reasonable for such a sound to issue from Leonard Hobart's mouth. So quiet a man.

"I guess he doesn't realize how much he's being amplified," Bill said.

"Doesn't he realize it's the middle of the night, either?" Sally asked.

"I don't believe time means much to Leonard," Bill said.

Next evening Bill went early to the softball field. It was Saturday, the sixteenth of August, a warm, still night. Although it was a half-hour before game time the stands were already three-fourths filled and Leonard was in the midst of his regular pre-game talks. Listening to him Bill lost all the uneasiness which he had felt the night before. Leonard's introductory remarks were calm and factual, Leonard at his best. And his voice, or the voice which was the union of Leonard and the amplifying mechanism, it, too, had never been better.

"Tonight, friends," Leonard was saying, "we are to see the play-off for the Tenant softball championship, Elks versus Tavern Keepers. Battery for the Elks will be Kitto and Patrick. Battery for the Tavern Keepers Eby and Eldridge."

Bill, in his seat behind first, relaxed completely. I must've somehow misunderstood Leonard yesterday, he thought as he listened to him soberly relaying statistics to the crowd: batting averages, gate receipts, league standings. People were still pouring onto the field through the turnstiles and those already in the stands were discussing the coming game with animation. As one of the persons responsible for softball in Tenant, Bill looked about with pride. After the record-breaking crowds they had had all season they would be able to afford another piece of equipment for the field next year. Bill speculated a little as to what it should be. The lines past the turnstiles had dwindled, had ceased to be lines at all. The Elks team was in the field. Kitto their pitcher was warming up, and in the announcer's booth Leonard was telling the fans about Ben Woodford, Tavern right fielder and first man at bat.

"Ben's batting average for the season," he concluded, "has been .294, good but not sensational. On deck for the Tavern Keepers is Jim Lazarus. In the hole, Al Bailey."

Kitto finished his warm-up, the Elk fielders went out deep, for Woodford, when he connected, was known to take the ball for a ride. Kitto sent a final toss over to second, the umpire called, "Play ball," and the game started. Bill settled back to enjoy himself. Kitto was an amusing pitcher to watch, a tall lanky boy with an involved windup which took him, at its mid-point right down to the earth.

"Here comes the crank-up," said Leonard. "Kitto's starting off the game with his Sunday pitch. It's a fast one, it barely cuts the outside corner of the plate and Big Ben watches it go by. Strike one on Big Ben Woodford."

"He called that before the umpire, didn't he?" Bill's neighbor, a man in a yellow T shirt asked him.

"I couldn't say," Bill answered.

"Did *you* hear the ump call it?" the man persisted.

"We probably couldn't hear the umpire for the loudspeaker. He was probably drowned out," Bill said.

"The ump didn't even have his hand up yet, did he?"

"I don't know," Bill said uneasily. "I wasn't watching the ump."

Whatever had happened, the umpire evidently did not

object, for Leonard's magnificent commanding voice continued.

"Patrick, Elk catcher, is signaling Kitto for a repeat and he gets it, a knee-high sizzler right over the plate. Woodford swings but misses. Two strikes on Woodford."

"What'd I tell you?" Bill's neighbor asked.

Bill said nothing.

"Here comes another crank-up," boomed Leonard, "Big Benny is going to look this one over. He does. It's a fast peg, but it breaks wide. Ball one for Woodford. The count now stands one and two on Woodford, first man up in the first inning of the ball game, Elks versus Tavern Keepers, Elks at bat."

Down on the field umpire and catcher with masks up were having a talk. Kitto trotted off the mound to join them.

"Ump says *he* wants to call them," the man in the T shirt told Bill. Then as the three men resumed their positions he added, "Ump says he'll give the announcer one more chance."

"Kitto gets back on the firing line," Leonard announced to his listeners and Kitto, as if he had received an order, walked slowly back to pitcher's box. "Here comes the windup," Leonard continued, "it's another fast ball, a hummer dead over the plate but high. Woodford swings, he really leans on the old stick this time, but he misses. He misses by a mile. That's three strikes and out for Big Benny Woodford."

In the echo of Leonard's encompassing voice Woodford swung and connected, drove a liner deep into right field. Tate Pierce fumbled the pickup, finally made it, then in his hurry, overthrew. Woodford was safe on first with plenty of margin.

Leonard's amplified voice, mighty and reverberating, was undaunted by this fact. As if to compensate for the discrepancy between what had happened and what he had declared would happen, his voice became even louder, even more commanding. It vaulted over the grandstands, spiraled skyward, then hardening in an arc of solid sound settled just above the heads of the spectators, a weight beneath which they all sat, silent and unmoving as prisoners.

Bill had never suspected that the mechanism which he had selected and helped install was capable of so much power. It—or Leonard's voice amplified by it, not so much split the air with sound as filled it. The voice which had arched above their heads settled lower and lower. It became a yoke on their shoulders, a weight, a gravestone pushing them nearer and nearer the earth. The words Leonard had been saying, "Three strikes and you're out," he continued to say. But through repetition the words lost their meaning and finally, as words, they disappeared all together. The sound of Leonard's voice, amplified, became nothing but power, nothing but brute force. Bill could feel it belaboring him across his shoulders, thundering against his eardrums, and finally, pummeling him inside his head, in the innermost, private and vulnerable recesses of his mind.

Bill never knew, no one ever knew, how long it went on nor why they all sat there numb, unmoving for however long it did go on. Bill himself was the first to do something. Next was the man beside him in the yellow T shirt. To him Bill whispered—it was impossible to shout *above* the horrible din of that great, amplified voice, the only way to be heard was to get *under* it—"The poor fellow is out of his mind."

Together Bill and the man in the yellow T shirt scrambled down through the crowded stand, then reaching the ground ran at full tilt toward the broadcasting booth. Leonard wept when he was separated from the amplifier.

They took him to Norwalk that night.

At the time no one blamed Bill for what happened. Now they have begun to talk. They come into the Building and Loan office and say, "Except for you I guess Leonard Hobart would still be here selling radios."

Bill doesn't pay much attention to them. Nadine is different. She came in yesterday. She was in again this afternoon.

"I hold you responsible for what happened to my husband."

Up to now Bill has listened with patience to these tirades. Now he says, "Madam, *you* are responsible for what happened to your husband."

"I?" Nadine's usually firm glasses wobbled upon her fleshy nose.

"I, you, all of us," says Bill. "But especially you."

"What do you mean, Mr. Hare?" asks Nadine.

"Poor Leonard," Bill says, "we forced him—" He begins again. "No one listened to Leonard—" But suddenly he is tired of explaining. It is useless, he feels, to explain anything to anybody—particularly to Nadine.

"Good day, madam," he says and walks Nadine right through the doorway of the Building and Loan office and out onto the street. "What do you mean, Mr. Hare?" insists Nadine but Bill puts the plate-glass door between them and locks it.

"What *do* you mean, Mr. Hare?" Bill asks himself, ironically, imitating Nadine's demanding voice. He walks over to his desk, sits down, and begins to think about Leonard.

He puts his hat on his head, his feet on his desk. "What do you mean, Mr. Hare?" he asks himself, but flatly now and without irony.

Foot-Shaped Shoes

*

THE KNOCKING at her door continued and Kass reluctantly opened her eyes. There was such a dazzle of brilliant August light and bitter August heat in her room that she thought it was mid-morning, that Rusty had given up his crazy five o'clock trip. But no, the clock said five and it was her brother's red head that came cautiously around the slowly opening door.

"Kass," he whispered. "Kass, you awake?"

"Sure," she answered jauntily, then added, "I guess so."

"It's five."

"I know."

"But you don't have to get up for fifteen minutes. I said five to give you fifteen minutes extra before you had to get up. I remembered how you hated to get up the moment you opened your eyes."

"Well, thanks, chum," she answered drowsily.

Her brother came into the room. "Kass, you going back to sleep?"

She shut her eyes. "I am asleep."

"Kass, Kass."

She opened her eyes and smiled at him. He was shirt-

160

less, in skin-tight jeans. "Gosh, you've grown. What're your dimensions now?"

"Dimensions?"

"In space and time?"

"Oh. Six one, a hundred and eighty."

"Wowie! A heavyweight. The age?"

"Fourteen."

"Fourteen? How come fourteen? The last time I saw you I distinctly remember you were thirteen."

"That was six months ago. That was the night you got married. I'm older now."

"Well, me too, for that matter. *You* haven't gotten married since then have you? Or anything like that?"

Rusty laughed. "Father's the only one who's gotten married. I don't even have a girl."

"Why not?"

"I'm going to. I just haven't got around to it yet. I've been pretty busy."

Kass reached for her brother, pulled his cheek down to hers and hugged him. "You're my baby," she said.

The word "baby" seemed to make Rusty self-conscious. He backed away from her without returning her hug or snuggling, puppy-like, as he would've done six months ago.

"I know you didn't really want to get up early and go out to the ranch on your first morning home," he apologized. "I expect you're used to sleeping real late now."

He had backed half across the room and stood looking down at her, round-eyed, as if she were a patient critically ill or someone who'd just run the mile in four minutes. She supposed he had been suddenly hit by some speculations about her as a married woman, as opposed to the mother-sister he had always known. What was it like for a man and woman to sleep together? Was she perhaps going to have a baby? She had no idea how much a fourteen-year-old boy knew about marriage. And of course Rusty was no average fourteen-year-old. With his brain, there was no telling whether his silences meant he knew all there was to know about sex or whether he had been too busy, up to the minute, figuring out how to get to the moon on a rocket to know there *was* such a thing. It could be either way. *She* knew, though, and his stare made her self-conscious.

"Sleep late? A thing of the past. Bob goes to work at seven-thirty and I have to be up at dawn to put the toast on."

Rusty laughed. "O.K. See you in twenty minutes. Want to go out in your car?"

"Sure. Why not? It's brand-new, bright red, and will go one hundred and twenty miles an hour. You wouldn't mind that would you?"

"No," Rusty said, smiling, and tiptoed out.

She could dress in ten minutes, easy, so she lay back and looked at her old room, which was exactly the same, but as strange to her as if she'd never seen it before. As a matter of fact she never *had* seen it before. Had these shifting shadows cast by the jacaranda tree ever flowed in the same instantaneously flowering, instantaneously dissolving patterns across her blue rug before she was married? Had there been a maned horse in the knotty-pine ceiling? Rainbows in the mirror's beveled edge? A delicious crack in the footboard of her bed? Never, never! She had never seen anything before, in itself, but only as stage dressing for the imagined drama of being in love, of being courted and married.

Nothing in that unborn time had been an end in itself, all was means: Would it help? Would it hinder? Would a girl whose room had chintz curtains, a white enameled desk made by her father, and a Roman-stripe afghan which had once belonged to her mother be as appealing —to a man, that is—as a girl with her books on shelves supported by bricks, and a studio couch instead of a bed? If not, she had been prepared to change in a flash. She had been conscious throughout her girlhood of the eyes of all the potential lovers and husbands upon her, approving, disapproving. For those eyes, not knowing a thing about either lovers or husbands, she had brushed her hair dramatically, eaten daintily, written lush descriptive passages describing sunsets and bird song in her Five Year Diary. She had lived a hypothetical life. Nothing real, and the unreality she had conjured up was not really suitable, as it turned out, for the life she had been imagining.

But that was all past. She was alive, and through acting. No more dramatized hair strokes or faked nature loving. Bob had made her a real person and to a real person the world is real. She picked up one of her moccasins from the floor by the bed, seeing for the first time that it was made of separate pieces of leather skillfully sewed together so that the whole affair was not only soft but strong, and that—most remarkable of all—it was foot-shaped. She turned it round and about. I couldn't make one in a thousand years and this is the first time I ever gave it a glance—as a thing in itself. She threw it into the air, caught it, kissed it, said, "Bob, I adore you," then closed her eyes, shoe to cheek, to think of Bob for a minute.

A pebble on the window aroused her and, knowing who it was, she jumped out of bed, went to the window, and tossed the shoe to Rusty.

"A hostage," she said, "until I arrive."

Rusty went back to Kass's car, shoe in hand. She had left the car parked in the driveway—August nights in Hemet are bone dry—and he walked round it admiringly. If Kass had turned up with a ten-year-old broken-down Chevvy it would have been all right with him, but a big red convertible was more like Kass, and he smiled at the image of her, small and blond, behind the wheel, like the white-hot nub of a red-tailed comet. Besides looking right for Kass, it meant something else more important: it meant that lack of money wouldn't keep her from helping Alfred.

He had lifted the hood, when she came running out of the house, tough-footed enough not to mind the absence of one shoe. He put the hood down and said, "We go now."

"No," she said. "Not me. I've changed my mind. I'm not going."

Her face was wet; sweat, he guessed, not her shower, because her hair was dry. It didn't occur to him to say to her, "But you promised" or "But Alfred expects it" or anything like that, because what good was any act done just because it was promised?

He said, "Why not, Kass?"

"I don't want to see this Mexican kid."

"You would like him."

"That's just the trouble. I don't want to like him."

"You could decide before you went, so that liking him wouldn't . . ."

"I have decided."

"What I was going to say was that you could decide you weren't going to have anything to do with him—just go out and see him for the fun of it."

Kass went, "Hmmmph."

"You sound like Father."

"I feel like Father, like I'm getting a little sense. There is no place in my life for a nine-year-old Mexican kid. I'm sorry I let you think there was. But I got carried away, my first night home and everything. Father said no and he was right. I say no, too."

"Father's got his new wife. He's got to pay attention to what she wants."

"What she wants is very sensible. And if being newly married cuts any ice I'm practically a bride myself. I want to do what Bob wants. And I'm sure adopting a nine-year-old Mexican kid is the last thing that ever crossed his mind."

"You wouldn't have to adopt him. You could just take care of him."

"And even if Bob's one goal in life *was* to adopt a nine-year-old Mexican, there isn't room in a three-room apartment."

"I told you he was only the size of a six-year-old."

"No."

"He's used to sleeping on the ground."

"We don't have any ground for him to sleep on. We don't even have a hole in the ground."

"Did I tell you about the first time I ever saw Alfred?"

"You certainly did. He was up in that tree. What I'd like to know is, why is a Mexican kid called Alfred? Why isn't he José or Juan or Chico? If I were going to adopt a Mexican kid I'd at least want him to have a Mexican name. Not be Arnold or Albert or . . ."

"His real name's Alfredo. You could call him Alfredo if you wanted to. It was the umberella tree in the back yard. It was the Fourth of July and Father had some of the Mexicans in for a picnic. Alfred climbed to the top of the branches, then he crawled out across nothing but leaves really and sat there in the center of the tree on nothing but leaves really. . . ."

"Must've looked like a hen on a nest."

That wasn't the way he had looked. Rusty could see Alfred now, floating there in the crown of the tree, upheld only by faith and leaves, shiny and thin-boned as a cricket; but he didn't contradict Kass. What she thought Alfred had looked like didn't matter.

"What he sang up there was 'Columbia the Gem of the Ocean.' There were more verses than anyone had dreamed of and he knew them all."

"Oh Lord," Kass said.

Rusty defended Alfredo. "He's got a sweet voice. People like to hear him sing. What *they* worried about was his safety, sitting up there on practically nothing but leaves. Everybody yelled at him to come on down. And he yelled back, 'Caramba.' That's a Mexican swear word."

"I know, Rusty. I get around."

"He yelled, 'Caramba! Who wants to live forever?'"

Kass answered this vigorously, "Me! I do. I want to live forever. I want to live forever in my three-room

apartment with Bob, and with no little Mexicans climbing
up things, sitting on leaves, and yelling 'caramba' at me."

"I like it, though," Rusty told her.

"Like what? Singing, or what?"

"I like being willing to take a little chance. I like that.
It appeals to me."

"It takes all kinds, I understand," Kass told him.
"Some want to live dangerously and some want to live."

Rusty ignored this. "He's an awfully bright kid. He
does arithmetic with the seventh grade."

"This family's lousy with bright kids. One more genius
and we're sunk."

"He can play the guitar."

"That does it. Climbing chandeliers, yelling caramba,
and playing the guitar. Oh no, Rusty. Oh no."

"Nobody mentioned chandeliers, except you," Rusty
reminded her. "His mother doesn't take any care of him,
cook for him or anything. He just lives on scraps and
sleeps on rags."

"Where's his father?"

"He doesn't have any father. I mean around," Rusty
explained. "Also, I think his mother's a whore."

"Hore," Kass snapped.

"Like wrestle, and so on? The w's silent?"

"That's right. If you're really going to get in there and
mix with the underworld, you'd better learn how to pro-
nounce them."

"Alfred doesn't have anything to do with the underworld. You know that."

"O.K. I'm sorry. I know he doesn't."

"His mother might, though, for all I know. She goes
out every night with some different man. I mean stays

out. She'd be glad to get rid of Alfred. She'd probably even pay us. He could just disappear and she wouldn't say a word. Unless maybe hurrah. Tonight's the dance and tomorrow all the Mexicans are leaving and if Alfred just wasn't around she'd go without him. It isn't as if anybody wanted him."

"No," Kass said, "no. I won't do it. I can't do it. Don't ask me any more, Rusty. O.K. So he may really be the brightest, best little kid in the world. If you say so, I don't doubt it. I'm sorry his mother's a whore. I'm sorry he has to live on scraps and sleep on rags. I love you for loving him. I'll give you some money for him. I'll help you get him into an orphanage."

"No. He doesn't want to be in an orphanage—and his mother would take the money. He'd never see it."

"All right, then. That finishes it. You go on. Take my car and go out to see him. But don't talk to me about him any more. He's not my problem. I can't do anything about him and I don't want to hear about him any more. Or think about him."

She ran back to the house, her run a little lopsided because she'd forgotten her shoe, which was still on the seat of the car where Rusty had put it. Rusty drove the ten miles to the ranch slowly. He felt calm because he knew now what he could and couldn't do. He was on his own now and he had thought he might be and was prepared. He had only to find Mrs. Campos, if she was home, tell Alfred, and he would have given everybody a fair shake.

He turned into the ranch road, drove between the apricot trees, bare now of fruit, and parked beside the deserted cutting shed. The apricot season was over. A couple of the Mexican families were staying on for another week to help scrape and stack trays and to store the dried cots; but the others would pull out in the morning after the evening's farewell dance. Already, up in the last few tree rows at the base of the foothills where they had camped, the Mexican families were preparing to leave. What he saw and heard up there was somehow different from the sights and sounds of mornings when everybody had to be at work by seven.

Though Mexicans, contrary to all he had ever heard, were early risers, work or no work. And when they got up they took over exactly where they had left off the night before: singing, talking, fighting, playing the harmonica. They didn't seem, as Americans did, to go away from their daytime selves during the night. They didn't need a kind of decontamination period of orange juice, coffee, and radio news before they could start being their daytime selves. They seemed to stay the same, night or day, awake or dreaming. They awakened revved up, slid into high gear, and were off until the heat of mid-afternoon slowed them down. He liked that. It seemed to him a nice way to live.

He had been at the cutting shed some mornings at five, and knew that up there on the hill they would already be singing; their fires would be burning, and the sweet-sour smoke, which always smelled to him like stewing rhubarb, would be towering upward in clear blue columns. He had heard a coyote at five, yelping from the hilltop his farewell to night and the Mexicans' chickens; and he had heard Domingo answer him in the song the Mexicans called "Señor Coyote." And it had really seemed that the Señor, up there on the hilltop, gray and foxy, the early

sun at his back, had known he was being addressed, for
he had waited for the pauses between stanzas to reply. All
the Mexicans had stopped their work to laugh and ap-
plaud the duet sung by Domingo and the Señor; and not
until the singing was over had the coyote turned and
loped over the crest of the hill and out of sight.

It was too late now for coyotes. The smoke on the
heated air was transparent. The voices, singing or talking,
already tempered by the sun, were thin and sweet—like
sharpened knives. Human voices, animal voices; domestic
fires and the wild heat of the untamed sun; smoke, an
autumn thing, a thing of fallen leaves and coldness, drift-
ing upward now into the summer heat; everything at once
so balanced and so contradictory, and likes and opposites
so solemnly meshing, Rusty thought he might have to
run up some hilltop and there, like Señor Coyote, give a
great yelp of happiness. You surely weren't supposed to
just walk through stuff like that doing nothing, were
you But he didn't know what to do. Not yet, he didn't.
Except, he thought, to call it beautiful; which was true
but somehow not enough.

He headed for the tents on the hillside, walking down
the alleyway formed by the head-high stacks of drying
trays on one hand and the cutting shed on the other. He
took his Audubon birdcall, a spool-shaped cylinder of
wood with a metal pin in its center, from his pocket. By
rotating the pin properly, you could make squeaks bird-
like enough to cause birds to reply. Rusty rotated the
pin properly, and sure enough a bird did reply, a song
so exactly like a bird's imitation of an Audubon birdcall
that Rusty laughed aloud.

To reach Mrs. Campos's tent, which stood a little apart

from the others at the far end of the row that made up
the Mexican encampment, he passed his many friends: the
Pérez, Ramos, Rodríguez, Ortiz, Padilla and Flores families. They were packing, getting breakfast, eating breakfast, preparing for the dance, all at the same time and
mostly out of doors. Domingo Rodríguez, the coyote-
serenader, was tuning up his old truck. Manuel Ramos
was milking the family goat. Angel Flores was washing
her hair. Mrs. Estobar was washing her underwear. Chico
Pérez was painting a baby buggy red. They all yelled at
him, asked him to breakfast, asked him for advice, gave
advice.

"Hi-ya, Rusty" (they pronounced it Roosty), Chico
called. "What you think? Paint the wheels red too?"

Manuel Ramos said, "You asked Angela to the dance
yet tonight?"

Pablo Ortiz, sloshing stewed apricots over a tortilla
said, "You gonna be ready to pull out with us tomorrow,
Rusty?"

"I'm thinking about it."

"You're a good checker, Rusty."

"I like checking," Rusty said, modestly.

"We do peaches next."

"Yeah," Rusty said. "I know."

"In peaches you make a fortune, Rusty."

"What I want a fortune for?"

"Buy you a shirt, Rusty. Never seen you wear one yet.
You go with us, Rusty, and you be a big shirt and pants
man."

"It's an idea," Rusty said, and meant it.

"You could ride with us."

"You serious?"

"You be here tomorrow morning and see."

"I might, I really might. I'd like to."

"Okey doke," said Pablo. "You tell me 'no' first. I don't move tomorrow till I hear from you."

Rusty felt so happy and proud about Pablo's invitation that he thought for a minute that the tears which had come to his eyes might run down his cheeks. He started on toward Mrs. Campos's place, controlled his feeling, stopped and turned back to face Pablo.

"Thank you, Pablo. I sure do appreciate the invitation." Then he hurried on.

There wasn't much to knock on at Mrs. Campos's tent, but Rusty called her name and slapped his hand a few times against the canvas. When there was no reply he opened the flap and looked in. The tent, except for the usual confusion of bedcovers, clothes, dirty dishes, and empty beer cans, was empty. The air inside the tent was blazing hot and stank with a combination of smells, all stale and heavy: beer and chili and some nasty perfume. The smell alone made him feel uneasy. It was Mrs. Campos's smell exactly, and she made him feel that way, too. With most people he could tell where he was. With grownups he was a kid, ignored, or advised, or liked—he hadn't had much experience of being disliked. With other kids he was an equal. With Alfred, he didn't know exactly—he was a kind of father, maybe, or whatever Kass had been to him all of the years since Mother died.

Kass can't really blame me, he thought, about Alfred. I'm just treating him the way she always did me.

Kass used to say to him, when he would tell her not to take so much trouble with him, "I'm not doing it for you, kid. I'm doing it for me. When I play mama to you I don't miss Mama so much. Besides, I like you. I have fun with you." That was about the way he felt about Alfred.

So Mrs. Campos, of all the people in the world, was the only one about whom he wasn't sure what he felt. He certainly hated her, for the way she treated Alfred and for what she was; he wasn't sure he had a right to come between mother and son, and though he knew Mrs. Campos was a bad mother he felt apologetic to her because of it. And on top of all this, in spite of the hatred and disgust and apology, he felt a strange curiosity in Mrs. Campos's presence; as if, in spite of all of his real aversion, Mrs. Campos had some deep hold on him which she knew about and he didn't and which she could exercise if she wanted to. So far she hadn't wanted to, and maybe she never would; but the threat of that power made it more difficult for him to face her about Alfred.

While his nose was still inside the tent and while he was still breathing the scents which both repelled and attracted him, Mrs. Campos herself called to him. He turned around then to face her. She had come up the back way through the orchard and was still a couple of tree rows down the hill.

"Go on in," she called. "I'll be right with you."

"No thanks," said Rusty. "I just came to see about Alfred."

Mrs. Campos stood directly in front of him now, smelling like her tent, the perfume which, Rusty thought, was like some rotting flower. She was sweating and tired, but very revved up, drunk maybe—he couldn't tell.

"You want something, Rusty?"

Mrs. Campos was dressed like the waitress in Bill's Broiler: black satin skirt, white silk blouse so thin you kept looking at it to see if it was really there, big fake diamond earrings in her ears, fake diamonds in the high heels of her black platform pumps. Her shoes were gray with dust, there was dust on her skirt, and her white blouse was stained brown with streaks of sweat. She stood, hands on hips, with a big white bag—streaked and dusty too—hanging from one hand. This she kept in constant motion by a little outward thrust of her knee; that bag rising and falling. The curve of her long brown neck as Mrs. Campos looked at him over one shoulder out of her flat glittering brown eyes reminded Rusty of the time he had thought he was cornered by a rattlesnake. He moved back a step or two.

"Do you know where Alfred is?"

"Ain't he in the tent?"

"No."

"Don't ask me, then. I don't know and I don't care. He wasn't here last night. Run off, drowned in the reservoir. He's big enough to take care of himself. What you want, Rusty? Want me to push him around in a baby carriage? Feed him on a bottle? You're always asking, 'Where's Alfredo?' 'Has Alfredo had supper?' 'Do you let Alfredo drink beer?' 'Does Alfredo have some clean clothes?' What's the matter with you, Rusty? You're big enough to be interested in women, not little boys. You so interested in little boys, why don't you make a little boy, Rusty?"

Rusty backed still farther away from Mrs. Campos. "I don't think you'd care if you never saw Alfred again."

Mrs. Campos faced him directly then, and her knee and the white bag stopped moving.

"I wouldn't care if I never saw either of you again,

Rusty. Alfredo yelling, 'Where's Rusty?' Rusty yelling, 'Has Alfredo had supper?' Go on, beat it, Rusty. Get the hell out of here. Go find your little boy. Fall dead. I don't care. I'm going to get some sleep."

Rusty was trembling as he followed Mrs. Campos's route back to the cutting shed. He went to the rear of the shed, where the empty trays were stacked ten and twelve feet high. He looked around, saw no one, then detached from the center of one of the stacks he saw the loose side of a tray. Through this opening he was able to look down into a neat little cell formed by the removal of the bottoms from a dozen trays. On the final tray, in a room, not large, but homelike, furnished with two folded blankets, a carton of Cokes, a stack of sandwiches wrapped in waxed paper, Alfred sat cross-legged, playing double Canfield. He looked up at Rusty but played the card in his hand without saying anything.

Rusty looked at the layout and said, "You might win this."

Alfred nodded.

"You been O.K.?"

"Sure. I liked it."

"Well, I gave everybody a fair shake."

Alfred played a heart king and a jack of spades before answering. Then he said, "Nobody wants me?"

His voice was without feeling and he continued to look at his cards, but Rusty didn't answer his questions. He couldn't. Instead he said, "I got an even better idea. I'm going to work in peaches. Pablo asked me. I'm a good checker. I can earn enough money for both of us."

Alfred put down his cards at this, and looked up. "Your folks won't let you."

"They won't care," Rusty said. "They won't miss me. They're all messed up in love. They don't want to be bothered."

Alfred played another card. "You never lived in a tent, Rusty."

"I'd like to. I'd sure like it a lot better than feeling the way I do now at home."

"I can take care of myself," Alfred said.

"I know you can. I'd be going because I wanted to and because I liked it."

He didn't know exactly how to describe what he liked to Alfred. Alfred was probably too much of a kid to understand; besides, he didn't know if he could explain it to anyone, even to himself: about the quick waking in the morning, and Domingo and the coyote, and the rhubarb smell of the smoke—and much more he had no words for, for all of them working together, moving on together.

"*I'd* like it," he said again, "but it would've been better for you, all right, if you could've lived at home, or with Kass."

"I didn't think it would work out."

"O.K. Come on, now," Rusty told him. "Climb out while I'm here to help you. Your mother's not going to be looking for you. She's asleep."

"She wouldn't anyway."

"Come on, then. You'll break your neck if you try to get out alone. Come on. I got to go home and pack."

But Alfred wouldn't budge. "I can get out when I

get ready to. I'm going to finish my game first. I got a chance to win."

The minute Rusty was abreast of the back door and before he had stopped the car, Kass came running out of the house. She banged the screen door behind her so loud Rusty heard it over the Porsche's motor. He stopped the car, cut off the motor, and looked back at her. She had her other moccasin in her hand now and she ran tender-footedly down the graveled path to the driveway. She was slapping the shoe against her hand as she ran, and when she reached the car she slapped the door with it. She was crying and had been crying. Her eyes were red and her cheeks blotched and scalded.

"O.K.," she said, "you win."

"Win? Win what?"

"I'll take that damned kid, but I hate you for making me do it."

"I'm not making you."

"You are, too. You told me about him. What did you have to tell me about him for?"

"Well, I just told you. I didn't say you had to do anything. Besides, you don't, now. I've got other plans."

Kass looked at him scornfully. "Going to kidnap Albert, I presume, and live in a tree house with him or some such damn nonsense. Well, forget it. It won't work."

"His name's Alfred."

"O.K. Alfred. That treetop singer. Alfred's going to live with us and sing. 'Columbia the Gem of the Ocean,' and it'll be terrible. It makes me sick to my stomach to think about it."

She cried or hollered, Rusty wasn't sure which, in her misery.

"Don't do it then," he said.

"I've got to," she said, and then she really did cry. "Oh Bob," she said, "I hate you, I hate you! Why did you do this to me?"

This was too mysterious for Rusty. "I thought Bob was the one you loved."

"I hate him. What chance have I got when even shoes are real? All sewed together," she sobbed, "and foot-shaped."

Rusty stared at her.

"Did you ever look at a shoe?" she demanded. "Did you?"

"I don't know," Rusty said. "I never thought about it especially, if that's what you mean."

"That's what I mean. Look at it." She pushed it under his nose. "It's a miracle, isn't it? And I never knew shoes existed until Bob made them real. So what chance do I have with a poor little Mexican? I'll be opening homes for stray cats next. I hate him and I hate cats. And don't you sit there gloating either, Rusty."

"I'm not gloating," Rusty said. He saw the campfires and the singing, the early waking and easy fighting vanish forever. For a little while they had been near but he didn't suppose that, without Alfred for a reason, he would ever be near them again.

"I'm not gloating," he repeated, "but I'm glad for Alfred."

"Let's go tell him then," Kass said. "Let's not leave the poor little kid on tenterhooks. Where is he now?"

"Down in a bunch of trays playing double Canfield."

"Double Canfield!" Kass cried. "Oh, God, what have I let myself in for?"

But she had stopped crying. She put on the shoe she was holding, and began to hop along the hot cement of the driveway to the other side of the car.

"Here," Rusty called, and tossed her the shoe he had. She put it on and got in beside him. Two shoes seemed to restore her sanity.

"Have you had anything to eat this morning?" she asked, quite calmly.

"Couple of apricots."

"I haven't had anything and I'm starved. Let's pick up Alfred and go into town and have some strawberry waffles. If Alfred can leave his game, that is."

"He'll be finished," Rusty said, confidently. "He's a real fast player."

Horace Chooney, M.D.

*

ALTHOUGH Dr. Chooney had lived in the country for six months he was still unaccustomed to the sudden country alternations of sound and silence. He had never, as he remembered it, heard from his city apartment anything as startling as the abrupt scream and accompanying loud machinelike drilling which now filled the air just outside his bedroom window. Dr. Chooney, at once wide awake, he thought, sat up in his bed; still, before the sight of the big live-oak tree and its resplendent hardworking woodpecker had accounted for the sounds, two other possibilities had immediately come to his mind. The minute he had seen where he was, he had of course dismissed these and watched with pleasure as the industrious, systematic bird uncovered its bountiful and surprised breakfast.

At this hour of the morning Dr. Chooney missed his wife Harriet, who since their removal to the country had found it more convenient to occupy another sleeping room. Upon awakening, his mind often teemed with analogues and whimseys, and it was a real loss to have no one with whom he could share them. He always made an effort to recall them for her, but as is often the case

180

with such imaginative sparkles, they were not quite so good when rewarmed.

The height at which the sun came through the tangle of oak and madrone trees on the slope above the house told Dr. Chooney that he had overslept. Though there was no longer any need for early rising, the old habits still held, and he stepped at once from his bed and touched the push button which rang in the kitchen below and told Harriet that he was now up and would be ready in thirty minutes for his breakfast.

From his bedroom window Dr. Chooney regarded with pleasure the remoteness and solitude of his new home. There had been nothing in a large city practice to prepare him for it, and since he had left the city without premeditation he had had no opportunity before his arrival for even an imaginative sampling of country delights. Standing now looking out over his own wooded acreage, he was able to see its birds, trees, and occasional small animals in all their uniqueness; to focus upon them the same absorbed attention which he would have given in the past to some unusual lesion or malformation.

While the long-legged old-fashioned tub was slowly filling (the water pressure in the second story was bad), Dr. Chooney got out of his pajamas and walked about in his room enjoying the touch of the brisk morning air upon his unclothed body. As he passed and repassed the mirror in the combination washstand and dressing table he noted with satisfaction the unsagging firmness of his well-larded frame and its healthy mushroom color. Before he went into the bathroom, Dr. Chooney, in case Harriet when first he rang had been outside feeding her chickens or perhaps milking the goat, once more touched the bell; then, unflinching, he stepped into his cold tub.

Dr. Chooney used for his bath a bar of yellow soap and a coarse cloth, both intended for dishwashing. Dr. Chooney was in many ways a connoisseur of sensations, and he made a real effort to slight none, not even the smallest. For bathing, an experience cleanly, of course, but neutral, he had little regard: warm water, soft cloth, mild soap. These things did not interest him. Every experience, he believed, should be made positive through either pleasure or pain. If the pleasure itself had become an old story, all of its reality worn down into an undifferentiated smoothness, Dr. Chooney elected a flick or two of pain to teach his nerves a continued responsiveness. He relished now every stroke of the somewhat abrasive cloth; he delighted in the sensation as of a mild burn which the yellow soap left across his chest and forearms.

There had been whole weeks recently when Dr. Chooney had not seemed very real to himself: days when his personality, capable on occasion as he so well knew of the most amazing richness and intensification, became thin and diffused; long periods when he had felt almost completely bereft of that constellation of interests which makes a man so uniquely himself.

Red-striped now as any flagellant, Dr. Chooney stepped from his bath and gently dried himself. Psychically, he supposed he had been suffering somewhat as so precise an organization as a tiger might, had it found itself forced to exist for months on end as a mollusk of some variety—impotent, but never forgetful beneath the layers of jelly of its former subtlety and power.

Dr. Chooney finished his drying before the open window of his own room. There the zestful aromatic scents of laurel and madrone leaves, dampened earlier in the morning by fog and now heated by the sun, flowed up to him, and Dr. Chooney, inhaling, made them a part of himself. Dr. Chooney was a careful and methodical dresser. He had proceeded from the top drawer which held his underwear to the third from the bottom which held his white shirts when his wife entered.

He spoke to her a little shortly, which he certainly had not intended, but he had an aversion to unannounced entrances.

"I didn't ring, Harriet," he said without straightening.

"I know, Henning, but . . ."

Dr. Chooney closed the drawer, lifted himself, and looked down at his wife.

"Horace," she amended.

"Yes?" said Dr. Chooney. He put on and buttoned his shirt, very precise buttoning, calculated to prevent the appearance of any half-filled buttonholes later in the day.

Dr. Chooney would have preferred to have been more aware of his wife. She was a small, dark cloudy woman with a tender mouth. He berated himself for his faded responsiveness. In their former life in the city, where they had been somewhat gregarious, Dr. Chooney had heard it said occasionally that he stirred up Harriet as one might a placid, quiet animal simply to see it come to life. This was not so. He had never been interested in Harriet's impetuosity or lack of it. If he stirred her up sometimes, it was only as a means of becoming aware of himself. He smiled a little now at the naïveté of his friends' conclusions. Was frost interested in the boulder it split? Or wind in the height of the wave it piled up? No, no. His friends had not studied, as he had, natural forces and did not understand, as he did, that natural forces were interested in effects only as a means of knowing and testing themselves.

Still smiling as he thought of the incorrectness of his friends' suppositions, Dr. Chooney handed his wife a small white card. "Why wasn't this burned with the others?" he asked.

His wife read the card, then turned it over as if hoping to find something upon the underside to negate what she had just seen.

"Where did you find this, Horace?" she asked.

"Under the paper in my white-shirt drawer. How did you happen to miss it?"

"I don't know," Harriet Chooney answered. "I can't imagine. I've tried to be very careful. I was sure everything had been burned."

"Perhaps you left it on purpose," Dr. Chooney suggested.

His wife's small brown hand was trembling. "Horace, you know I never, never—"

Dr. Chooney cut his wife's protesting short. "Very well, then. Let's drop it. Let's speak of it no more. It was simply a mistake and doesn't call for so impassioned a defense. It would be better though if it did not happen again and if this were burned."

Dr. Chooney's wife first bent the card double, then folded it so that the bit of pasteboard was lost in the palm of her hand.

"You have a patient waiting," she said.

"At this time of the morning?"

"It's not really early, Horace. It's past ten."

"Who is it?" asked Dr. Chooney.

"No one we know," his wife said. "A Miss Chester from the place over the hill called Oakknoll. I think you ought to see her. You should build up a practice once again."

"You think so?" Dr. Chooney asked.

"Yes, Horace, I do."

"I'll have my breakfast now," he said.

"Horace, this girl is timid and nervous. She's waited thirty minutes already. If you don't see her now, she won't be back again," Mrs. Chooney urged.

"How old is she?"

"Perhaps twenty-five," Mrs. Chooney said.

"Show her into my office," said Dr. Chooney, "and bring us two cups of coffee."

Dr. Chooney felt very large in his small office, but efficient and commanding too. His thighs still burned pleasantly from the irritation of the harsh soap, and he could smell from the kitchen the fragrance of coffee beginning to boil. The office was filled with sunlight; his well-polished desk glittered, the madrone blossoms in the bowl on top of the case which held his medical books were translucent in the strong light. With an increasing sense of integration and well-being, Dr. Chooney seated himself and faced his patient.

"Yes?" he asked pleasantly.

Miss Chester, who herself sat stiff and unrelaxed before him, was not, he saw at once, twenty-five. Twenty-two or -three at the most. Miss Chester was one of those young women who have considerable breadth but no thickness. Her shoulders were wide, her waist narrow, and beneath her light summer dress her breasts, which did not seem organically related to her broad, flat chest, were very noticeable. She was his own color with some of the murk leached out. Her hair, by which women chiefly show their awareness of themselves and their times, was in a soft and dowdy pile.

Miss Chester's dress was of a kind Dr. Chooney could not remember having seen since childhood: soft, peach-colored, it did not expose the body but was a continuation of it. It appeared to have been made at home, someone saying, "A little more fullness here," or, "Does it bind now under the arms?" Miss Chester's dress gave Dr. Chooney as much pleasure as a disease. He could not have been more lingering in a diagnosis. At the neck the dress had small peach-colored frills which touched the skin and seemed almost as if they might be an extension of the flesh.

Unclothed, Dr. Chooney speculated, Miss Chester would look somewhat like a Botticelli Venus, formed not in a warm southern sea but in some cool northern pond.

"Yes," Dr. Chooney said again, agreeably.

"I am Flora Chester," the girl told him.

"Yes, Miss Chester," said Dr. Chooney.

"I haven't been well," the girl said, "or at least I've thought I wasn't well."

Dr. Chooney understood the doubt which comes over patients in doctors' offices. Unaccustomed to speaking of their ailments, they hear their own words, "I am not well," and begin to wonder if their disease is not a hallucination which has made it possible for them first to imagine, then to credit their symptoms.

"Just what did you think was the trouble?" Dr. Chooney asked.

"Perhaps I imagine it all," the girl told him, with a somewhat breathless, confessional rush. "Perhaps it is just something I dream up"—she looked up at Dr. Chooney as if she had used a daring piece of slang—"to fill my days."

"Are your days empty?" asked Dr. Chooney.

"Not empty . . . but not important."

"Just what," Dr. Clooney persisted, "are your symptoms?"

"Oh, they're really nothing." The girl paused as if asking Dr. Chooney permission to continue.

"Go on," Dr. Chooney said.

"Everything tastes like pasteboard," said Miss Chester. "I can't sleep, yet I seem to be always dreaming so that when I do sleep I wake up tired. Toward evening I feel less tired, but by then my head begins to ache."

Having told her symptoms, Miss Chester at once politely disclaimed them as a woman brushes aside a compliment. "It's probably just my imagination," she insisted.

"Why do you keep repeating that?" Dr. Chooney asked. "What kind of mechanism do you think the body is? Do you suppose it sends out false reports as to its lesions and aberrations Why should you imagine what is painful and distressing to you?"

"My father and mother imagine things," said Miss Chester.

"You live with your father and mother?"

The girl nodded.

"An only child?"

The girl smiled excitedly, as if Dr. Chooney had said something very personal to her. "Yes. Yes, I am."

"How old are your parents?"

"Sixty and seventy-two."

"What does your father do?"

"Nothing. Nothing, that is, except his hobby," said Miss Chester. "Father's a retired dentist. One day he just walked out of his office—with a man in the chair and his mouth propped open. He came home and said—this was before I was born, but I've heard my mother tell it—he came and said, 'I will never put my hand inside the mouth of another human being.'" She looked up at him as if she had just reported a revolutionary act.

"That doesn't strike me as being particularly imaginative."

"But now he really does imagine things," said Miss Chester. "For one thing, he's not really interested in anything but teeth. He listens to the radio just in order to be able to tell about the plates or bridges people are wearing. He thinks he can tell by the way they speak or sing. He writes them letters saying, 'You have never had your six-year molars removed,' and has them sign the letter if he is right and return it."

"Is he right sometimes?" Dr. Chooney asked.

"Oh yes, he is," said Miss Chester. "Almost always."

"Then he's really not imagining things, is he, Miss Chester?"

"My mother—"

"Look, Miss Chester. Let us first consider you. Your troubles, whatever you may think of your parents, are not mental nor imaginary. No little quirk is responsible for them. Turn this way, please."

"I've never been in a doctor's office before," Miss

Chester said, turning toward Dr. Chooney with stiff self-consciousness.

"You should have been," Dr. Chooney told her gravely.

Miss Chester smiled as if she had been praised.

Dr. Chooney leaned forward and with his cool, heavy-tipped fingers explored Miss Chester's slender throat: first at the jawline, then lower where the throat widened above the fragile collarbones.

"It is just as I thought," he told her.

Dr. Chooney was not surprised at the brilliant, quivering look his patient gave him—as if she were hearing a declaration of love.

"You mean there really is something wrong?" she asked.

"Decidedly wrong."

Dr. Chooney's fingers continued their skilled probing. This girl had probably never before been the object of so concentrated an interest, certainly never the object of so concentrated a male interest. Her parents old, lost in their own worlds, she without friends, this was doubtless the first time anyone had so leaned toward her or expressed concern for her well-being; the first time she had been so touched—with hands professional, of course, but conveying to her inexperienced nature feelings not wholly clinical.

"Feel just here," Dr. Chooney told her. He guided the long-fingered, soft hand to a spot beneath the jaw.

"The little lumps?" Miss Chester asked.

"Nodules," Dr. Chooney corrected her. "Indications of a serious glandular affection."

Dr. Chooney saw that his patient was both pleased and frightened.

"I don't really feel so very sick," she said.

"Pardon me, Miss Chester," Dr. Chooney said, "but you actually have no idea how you feel. You have had this disorder for so long that you no longer know what it is like to feel well. You have forgotten what health is."

Miss Chester put a hand to her face. "Don't I look well?" she asked.

"No," Dr. Chooney said, "to a doctor you do not look well. Lovely, charming," Dr. Chooney said, smiling charmingly himself, "but certainly not well."

The girl flushed. "Is this glandular . . . affection . . . serious?" she asked.

"Very," said Dr. Chooney gravely. He leaned back, fingertips delicately touching, and rocked gently in his swivel chair.

"Serious enough," Miss Chester asked in a low voice, "to be fatal?"

Dr. Chooney laughed, from deep in his chest. "My dear girl," he said.

Miss Chester smiled and once more leaned back against the dark chair, but Dr. Chooney was immediately grave again. "As a matter of fact," he said, "that depends entirely upon you. You can go on, as you have been doing, from bad to worse. Or, you can put yourself into the hands of a competent physician and become the girl nature intended you to be."

"It isn't too late then?" Miss Chester asked.

"Certainly not," Dr. Chooney assured her heartily. "Not if you care, not if you try. Look at this," Dr. Chooney said.

He opened a drawer of his desk and took out an envelope. "At one time I was something of an amateur photographer. I made it a practice to take pictures of my patients. They were not only helped by being shown graphic evidence of their improvement, but others with similar disorders were encouraged when they saw what had been done in the way of arresting their disease. Would you like to see some of the pictures?" he asked.

"Oh yes," said Miss Chester eagerly.

Dr. Chooney handed her a photograph. "This girl," he said, "had your affliction, though in a somewhat more advanced form."

Miss Chester gasped. "She looks dead," she whispered.

Dr. Chooney nodded in agreement. "Yes, doesn't she," he said. "Though that is largely a result of the bad lighting and her closed eyes. And as I've already told you, she was a considerably more advanced case than you.

"Now," said Dr. Chooney genially, "have a look at this." Before handing over the second picture, however, Dr. Chooney himself regarded it for some time: a really lovely study of Anne. Frail, eyes considerably sunken, but laughing. He remembered just her posture that afternoon on the lawn chair and the way she had flung up her arm as he snapped the shutter and what she had said afterward.

"Oh," said Miss Chester, "she's better, isn't she? Much better. She's lovely here."

"A very charming girl," Dr. Chooney agreed. "This," he said, "is the third. Plump, brown, playing tennis. You could scarcely ask for a healthier-looking girl than that, could you, Miss Chester?"

"Oh, no," Miss Chester said. "Here she looks"—Miss Chester paused, apparently searching for a word which would describe the change that had taken place—"quite normal. As if there were nothing in the world wrong with her."

"When that picture was taken," Dr. Chooney said, "there was nothing wrong with her. Well," he asked playfully, taking back the pictures, "is seeing believing?"

"Oh yes indeed," said Miss Chester. "I'm so glad you showed them to me. I can't thank you enough. I don't want to lose a minute getting started. What am I to do first?"

"First," said Dr. Chooney, "a prescription." He scrawled one swiftly. "Have this filled, Miss Chester, and follow the directions exactly."

"Shall I come back tomorrow?" Miss Chester asked.

Dr. Chooney looked through his engagement book. "No," he said, "not tomorrow. Could you come on Thursday at three?"

"Oh yes, Dr. Chooney, I'll be here. I won't let anything interfere." Miss Chester turned back from the door. "I feel better already," she said shyly. "I thank you so much."

Dr. Chooney, who had risen and was standing now beside his desk, said, "Hope is a great restorative, Miss Chester."

Dr. Chooney was still standing when Harriet came in with the tardy coffee.

"You're a little late," Dr. Chooney told her.

"I didn't bring it sooner on purpose," she said. "I didn't think it seemed professional—serving coffee to a patient you had never seen before—and I do so want," she explained, "everything to get started properly."

Dr. Chooney sat at his desk and his wife paused, waiting for him to clear a space upon which she could place

the tray she held. As she looked down, waiting, the tray
sagged, then slanted, as if all strength had left her wrists,
until coffee and cream together poured downward upon
the three pictures Dr. Chooney had just been showing his
patient. Dr. Chooney imperturbably shook the drops of
scalding coffee from his hands and himself regarded the
pictures, now so ranged upon his desk that the eye moved
from the girl—what had Miss Chester called her?—from
the normal girl to the frail one and from the frail one to
that girl who, lights or no lights, had the appearance of
death.

"Let me have that tray," said Dr. Chooney. He took it
from his wife and put it firmly down. "Now get a dish
mop of some kind and clear away this mess."

After his wife left, Dr. Chooney first took out his handkerchief and dried his hands, touching meditatively the
small yellow blisters which were already beginning to
form. Then he cleaned, but did not change the order of,
the three pictures. Looking at them, the well-being he
had begun to feel while bathing became more pronounced. He could feel quite clearly, along channels too
delicate for reason to follow, forewarnings of a delicious
reintegration. The tiger's outline had begun once more
to assume—from his well-stored mind Dr. Chooney chose
the poet's phrase—its fearful symmetry.

*

The Linden Trees

*

FRED NORBY stood at the kitchen door with his bathrobe wrapped so tightly about his thin body that
it provided him with a sort of auxiliary backbone.
He had been roused early from his bed by pain beyond
what he could bear, and, not wishing to awaken his wife
Emily with his groans, had crept downstairs.

Now he stood at the kitchen door looking out into the
bright morning. The alfalfa patch alone was not yel-
lowed by the sun. It was too blue a green to take any
gilding. But the round apricots, already beginning to
turn, were as fiery as tiger eyes.

All the world outside the house was awake. The gray
tomcat, who had been dozing on the steps, stirred
to catch and eat a bottle fly. He munched it slowly,
his eyes half shut, as if he were still occupied with
thoughts of the night. The sun shone rosily through the
big, ruby-veined ears of the jack rabbits who were
breakfasting on the alfalfa. The four linden trees at the
south side of the barn, garage it was now, were in full
bloom, and Fred Norby, now that his pain had let up a
little, was aware, above all else, of their scent.

It was a great relief to him to be so caught up by some-

194

thing outside himself that he forgot himself completely. This didn't happen often any more, and of course he wasn't aware of it while it was happening. Only afterward, after the moment had passed, and he was once more the man to whom certain things had happened—and for whom this other certainty waited—did he rejoice and think, "For a second there, maybe even longer, I escaped. I lived in that linden smell. I remembered Father's planting those trees a long time ago, and saying how they'd been thick in Iowa when he was a boy, and how there was no honey to beat that from linden blossoms. I always planned to get me a hive of bees some day—when the press of work let up—and find out the taste of linden honey for myself. Now I suppose I'll never know what it's like but I recall Father's saying it was heavier than most."

He opened the screen door and stepped outside. Though it was still very early, heat waves were already dancing over the tin roof of Harm's garage. Old Cassius, the cat, laid his warm, supple weight across Fred's instep. The old man's moment of self-forgetfulness was gone; he was identified with the linden smell no longer. Slowly, he hoisted his foot until Cassius hung across it like a furry snake, making no move to escape. He eased him carefully to the ground, and walked painfully down the steps. In the rhubarb bed he had seen some withered stalks that needed snapping off. He thought that perhaps in a little job like this he could lose himself again, be a man like his neighbors, out to do a little weeding or hoeing before breakfast; but it was no use. Such escapes did not come by seeking. He was what he was, kneeling here by the rhubarb bed, a sick man; too sick to do any job that really needed doing. "Difficult or unnecessary jobs are the only ones I have stomach for now," he thought, as he tugged at the slack, rubbery stalks. But they were too much for him. He could neither break them, nor pull them up.

Dizzy and swaying, he got to his feet and walked back to the steps across ground that seemed so yielding his feet became imbedded in it. He pushed Cassius aside and sat with closed eyes. "It's a funny thing," he thought, after the wave of weakness had passed, "that we aren't better prepared for this— It's a wonder we can't accept it quietly, not knowing anyone who's escaped it—seeing as it's touched all we know."

He buried his hand in Cassius' dry hot fur, and felt beneath his fingers the cat's heartbeat even more hurried than his own. "I believe, in spite of everything, we all half expected to escape. More than half expected, believed completely. Thought it would come to everyone else, but pass us by. Without us, without me, how's anything else to exist?"

He stretched his hand clear of the shadow of the eaves, into the sun's morning brightness. "Heat. The only heat's the heat I feel. And the only cold I've ever had is that that's made me shake. Hard to believe there's any other. Hard to believe it won't stop with me. Hard to believe I don't have to keep on existing just to keep them going."

He sank his head against his hand. "No, that ain't the trouble," he said aloud. "The trouble is they're going on —and me not here—me leaving before I've had half my fill."

He rubbed his fingers strongly together as if to imbed in the very bone some grains of sunlight—something that would last him, after the flesh was gone.

"The trouble is," he thought, "I've got no child. I've got no way of continuing. I stop here. Them with children keep on living—they survive. Eyes just like theirs go on seeing—and hands they've given shape to go on feeling. But not for me—" and he rubbed his hands together, dryly and sadly. "Eyes just like theirs," he said.

And then he thought of Norby. Little Norb. Only last week he had come up and said, "Can I take your glasses off, Uncle Fred?"

"Sure," he said. "Sure you can, Norb. Do you want to try them on? Your eyes giving you trouble?"

Norb had laughed at this—a quick little snort. "No," he said. "I wanted to look at your eyes. Grandma said I had your eyes. She said, 'Norby's got Fred's eyes.' So if I've got yours you've got mine and I want to see what they look like."

Norby had held the spectacles carefully in one hand and with the other balanced himself on the side of the bed, while he looked long and intently into his uncle's eyes.

"Well, Norb," Fred had said at last, "are they yours?"

"They're in your head," Norb said, "so they must be yours. But," he said, wagging his head seriously, "they are i-den-tical."

"I laughed then," he thought. "That was another of the times I was able to forget. I was nothing but a laugh then. It swallowed up everything else—pain, everything. Think of a little sprout like that using a word half as long as himself. Identical.

"Identical," he mused. "Identical. Well, I suppose they are. Same kind of piebald mixture of blue and brown."

He felt a little easier and leaned back against the door, cautiously, afraid to relax completely, leave himself open and vulnerable to a pain thrust.

"Those eyes of Norby's are going to go on seeing things a long time after mine're shut. He's ten now. Why, he ought to be here for another sixty years. He ought to see the year 2000. He'll see the new century—not much doubt of it. Except for me all the Norbys are long-lived. Just to think—I've looked into eyes that are going to see the year 2000."

And then the idea came to him. He struck his palms together with almost a gesture of health. "Why haven't I thought of this before?" he said. "Why haven't I?"

As he sat there, completely filled with his discovery, taken far away from his present condition, Emily came downstairs. She had awakened and missed him and hurried, fearful and foreboding, about the house looking for him.

Now she was calling his name, trying to keep the anxiety out of her voice and failing. "Fred," she called, "Fred, where are you?"

He didn't hear her until she got to the back door and pushed the screen against his shoulder trying to open it.

"Here, Emily," he said, "what are you up to? Trying to push me on my face? Taking advantage of me because I'm sick?"

Emily hadn't heard him use this bantering tone for months. It was as if the past months had been a bad dream from which she was just awakening. Oftentimes she had thought, "This will suddenly pass away and everything will be as it was before," and for a second she felt that had happened. Here was Fred, up early, sitting out in the sunshine and joking with her just as in the old days.

She wanted to believe, to carry on the conversation in the tone in which he'd started it, but she couldn't. "Fred, Fred, what are you doing out here? I woke up and you were gone and I was terribly worried."

"What do you think I'm doing, Emily? I'm enjoying the sun. Now you get me some breakfast and I'll come in and talk to you. I've got a wonderful idea. It just came to me. I can't see why I never thought of it before. It changes everything. Now you just give me a hand up and I'll come in and watch you cook."

Emily was surprised to hear him ask for help, and glad. It made things easier and happier when he'd take the help he needed without bitterness. He slid over on the steps until she could open the door and putting his thin, dry hand in hers, let her take most of his weight in hoisting him to his feet.

"You always were a husky girl, weren't you Emily? If you hadn't married me you'da been a lady athlete. An Olympic champion in something or other."

Emily smiled a little as she helped him into the kitchen. "I used to beat all my brothers running and jumping."

"Sure you did. You could yet." Fred smiled, too. Funny about Emily. Most women liked to be praised for their looks, or their cooking, or their mending, but Emily liked to be praised for her muscles, told what an athlete she'd of made.

He eased himself down into the breakfast nook. "Now, Emily, I tell you what I want for breakfast. Fried hominy and bacon. Hominy fried until it's good and brown."

Emily looked at him pleadingly. "Fred, you remember

what the doctor said? You'll just have to pay for it afterward."

He shook his head at her. "Emily, you know as well as I do, it don't matter a hoot what I eat. Nothing I eat's going to make any difference—and I got to pay for it all afterward anyway—no matter what it is. So it had about as well be something that tastes good while I'm eating it. Now you go and start it cooking. And I want coffee, too. Bacon and grits and coffee."

Emily got some cushions from the living room and put them at the end of the bench next the wall, and lifted his feet up so he was half lying down.

"This feels pretty good," he said. "Now you hustle the breakfast along."

Emily had tears in her eyes while she measured out the coffee and water and cut and chopped the bacon. It seemed at once so much like old times, and like the end.

But Fred wasn't paying any attention to her. He was talking about his idea.

"Emily, you know how everyone's always said Norby was just like me? Same laugh, same cowlick, same way of pointing one foot further out than the other? And he's got my eyes. No doubt about it.

"Of course these outside things don't matter much—but they's what made me think of it—so I naturally speak of them."

The smell of frying bacon filled the kitchen. He shut his eyes and drew in a deep breath. "That's the first time food's smelt good in a coon's age. Fry aplenty."

"But, Fred," said Emily, "what is this idea?"

"It's about me and Norby. I ain't got much longer here. No, no, Emily. We've both knowed it a long time. No use shutting our eyes to it. But look, Norby's going to be here—say sixty years more, might even be seventy. Going to see the year 2000 and maybe more. Well, I'm going to talk to him. I'm going to have a talk with him as soon as he can get over here."

Emily stirred the hominy into the browning bacon and spoke above the hissing spatter. "Fred, what can you say to Norb?" All her happiness in finding her husband up, and talkative and hungry, dropped from her. She was afraid his mind had been touched by his long sickness. "Norb's a child, Fred. What can you say to him about—" but she couldn't go on.

"About dying, Emily? No use being scared of that word. I was. I have been. No use denying that to you. You've seen it plain enough. But this idea, this thing I want to talk to Norb about changes it."

Emily slid the skillet back and forth across the gas flame. "What idea, Fred?" she asked gently.

"It's hard to put in words, Em. I'm afraid it won't sound like much in words. But it's real all right. However it sounds, you remember its real, real as fried hominy. I'm going to talk to Norb. I'm going to tell him to look at things for me—smell things, touch things. I'm going to tell him to think about me when he's doing it. Maybe he won't be able to do that—much—but when he can . . .

"The things I've missed, Em—the things there ain't time for now. I know now what's important, and I'll tell him. He can do them for me. See 'em with my eyes. And what's the odds, Emily, whether I do it myself or not. He'll do it for me.

"Then I want to tell him about the year 2000. Then, that night, January first, I want him to go out some place

—away from town, some place out in the open where he can see the stars—I want him to stand in some open field where there's trees and woods about and look at the stars and say some words I got in mind. I'll write 'em out, maybe, for him. Why, Emily, it'll be as good as being there. You know right now if I had to choose between my seeing something and Norb's seeing it—I'd choose Norb. Well, I choose Norb for the year 2000.

"Then afterward I want him to come into town. Needn't be this town. Any town'll do. I want him to go some place where there are people—people all together, and shouting and happy. You know how they are on New Year's Eve? Kind of silly. But most of them full of good thoughts about the coming year. And I'm going to leave him a little sum—say fifty dollars—to buy champagne with—that's another thing I've never tasted—and he and his friends can drink it. And in a way—this is kinda hard to explain, Emily, it'll be as if I was. Why, I can almost taste it now, that champagne Norb will be drinking in 2000."

Emily put the food before him; the hominy delicately browned, the coffee black and steaming. She couldn't help being practical, even about the year 2000. "Bertha will never let Norb taste that champagne, Fred. She's strong against liquor."

"Bertha won't be here then, Emily. She'll be with me— and Norb will be a seventy-year-old. Out from under Bertha's thumb."

Emily poured herself a cup of coffee and sat down opposite her husband. The apricot tree outside the window broke the sunshine that fell across the white tablecloth into gold nuggets.

"I can't tell you, Emily, all about it. I don't want to try too much for fear if I spill it all now there won't be any left to tell Norb. But you call Bertha right away, won't you? See if Norb can't come in this morning. It may be some time before . . . I may never feel this good again."

It was late afternoon before Norb trudged into town, hot and dusty. He'd been picking berries all morning for Bertha. Emily gave him a couple of glasses of lemonade before she sent him upstairs to Fred.

"Norby," she said, before he went up, "your Uncle Fred wants to talk to you. You know Uncle Fred's not well, and maybe what he says'll sound funny to you. But you be a good child—you listen. Maybe you can't understand everything he'll say to you. But you try. You try as hard as you can."

Norb licked the last drops of lemonade from his upper lip.

"Uncle Fred and me's got the same eyes," he said.

"All right, Norb, you remember that, and go upstairs to Uncle Fred now."

Emily walked about outside while the two were talking. She was too restless to sit still. She picked three or four apricots, hard as donnickers yet, but beautifully colored, to put on the window sill over the sink to look at.

"I don't understand it myself," she thought. "I don't understand it at all, and I don't see how a child Norb's age is going to make head or tail of it."

She stayed outside as long as she could and when she went in she found that Norby had left. He had gone out the front way, closing the door so quietly behind him she hadn't heard it.

She ran up the stairs full of misdoubts, fearful that Fred

would be sad, bitter again, full of pain; afraid that he hadn't been able to say what he had in mind, or that Norby had been too little to understand.

She heard Fred's heavy breathing before she'd got to the head of the stairs, and hurried to his room.

But he smiled at her. "Get the hypo, Em," he said. "It's pretty bad." She gave him the injection skillfully and, inch by inch, he eased back against his pillows.

"It's all right, Em," he said finally, seeing she was afraid to ask him how the talk had gone. "It's all right. Everything's fine."

"Did you tell him all you had in mind, Fred? Were you able to make him understand?"

"No, Em, I didn't tell him as much as I'd planned. About all I told him was about the linden trees."

"The linden trees," Emily echoed.

"Yes, about getting a hive of bees and having linden honey. My father did, and I always planned to, but I never got around to doing it. Norb's going to do it. He's going to taste linden honey."

"Did you tell him about the year 2000?"

"Nope. No, I didn't mention about the year 2000."

"Oh, Fred," Emily said, so sad for him.

"I didn't mention it on purpose, Emily. As soon as I started talking, as soon as I laid eyes on Norb, I seen how silly all that was. All that champagne at midnight. I don't have to tell him—nor nobody like him. They got my eyes, regardless of color, and they'll use 'em in my way without a word from me. See the things I missed—year 2000 and beyond, and I'll have my share without saying a word. All I needed to speak of was the honey. And the lindens."

*

Breach of Promise

*

EVERY afternoon between two and four, depending upon the amount of business or conversation he had encountered on his route, the mail carrier came by in his ramshackle, mud-spattered car. He didn't drive up the lane to the house, a lane a quarter of a mile long and crossing at one point a brook, which after heavy rains was something more than a brook, but put the mail in the wobbly tin box, set the flag, honked three times, and drove on.

Ordinarily I waited for these three honks before I walked down to the box. But now and then, because I was at that time so eagerly hoping for a certain letter, I would convince myself, in spite of the fact that I had been listening intently, that the mail carrier had passed without my hearing him. Invariably, after I had walked to the box on these occasions to find I had been mistaken, the mail carrier would be unusually late. Then, because my work had already been interrupted and because my eagerness for the letter I awaited always made me hopeful that the mail carrier would be along in another minute or two, I didn't return to the house. Instead, I paced up and down the lane, stopping usually at the brook to examine the veining in some curious pebble or to watch an island of foam, seemingly as imperishable as the pebble, float by.

At the time, I would be scarcely aware, however, of the objects I scanned. All of my consciousness would be focused in a fury of attention on the wished-for letter: imagining its size, shape, color to the eye, weight to the hand, the heavy downstrokes of the writing, even the postmark, Yorba Linda, California.

The letter, not the one which I wanted but the one of which I am writing, came on a day when I was in this manner examining pebbles at the brookside. The mail carrier saw me and honked three times but, nervous and irritated after what had seemed my long wait, I continued obstinately to bend over my pebble. He honked again. I picked up the pebble I had been admiring and with it in my hand walked down to the mailbox.

"You got another letter here addressed to that other name," he told me.

He held this letter close to his chest, as if it were a winning card in a crucial game. The mail carrier had never been reconciled to the fact that I received letters addressed in two ways: to my "own" name, and to what he called "that other name," the name I used in my writing. The letter I had hoped for would not be addressed to "that other name," so I didn't care how long he held this square white envelope to his chest.

"It's addressed care of the Seulkes," he said (the Seulkes were the people with whom I was boarding, the house at the end of the lane), "so I reckon it's for you."

He ended on a rising note and looked at me, through spectacles as blurred and spattered as some old windowpane. "It's from Persis Hughes," he said. "You know her?"

"No," I told him, though I knew that a Mr. Hughes owned a large farm, down the road a mile or so and that he had a grown daughter.

"Funny thing," he said. "Persis writing you when she don't know you."

There was no use telling him that writers get letters from people they don't know, so I agreed with him. "Yes," I said, "it's a funny thing."

"You'd think she'd just walk up the pike if she had anything to say to you and save her three cents."

"Yes," I said again.

He finally handed me the letter from Persis Hughes, but he hadn't finished with talking yet.

"I notice it takes four days for a letter from California to reach you," he said.

"If they don't airmail it," I agreed.

"You get homesick, back here by yourself?" he asked.

"I'm pretty busy working," I told him and he didn't notice that I hadn't answered his question.

"Working?" he asked, and I could see that he thought I had found myself a job of some kind in town.

"Writing," I said, and from the way he repeated, "Oh, writing," it was plain writing wasn't his idea of work. But he drove on without any more questions, leaving me standing by the mailbox, Persis Hughes's letter in one hand, my prettily veined pebble in the other. On a sudden impulse I opened the box, placed the smooth little stone in its tin emptiness and tightly closed the lid. I did this without thinking, but I suppose that bitterly, subconsciously, I was thinking, I asked for bread and you gave me a stone, and that I felt some relief in thus being able to objectify my emotions, to symbolize my self-pity.

I didn't open my letters from Persis Hughes until I reached my room. Though if the letter I wanted had come I would have read it six times over before I reached the house. My room at the Seulkes' was a perfect place for reading unwanted mail. It was sad, sad: strange, unpleasant colors, peculiar furniture, odd smells, and a most distressing, a really horrifying picture.

This picture was of the Seulkes' only son Albert, aged twelve, taken three days before he died of lockjaw. After Albert's death Mrs. Seulke had had his picture enlarged, covered with convex glass, and framed. And now Albert, looking, it seemed, already swollen, feverish, and in pain, watched me the whole time I was in the room.

A marble-topped "center table," a wicker rocker with crocheted back and arm tidies, a wooden chair, one of the dinette set which the Seulkes used in their kitchen, these, together with a large brass bed, made up the furnishings of my room.

I lived on that bed like a castaway on a desert island, like a lone survivor on a raft. It was my desk, chair, filing cabinet, table, sofa, home, world. Neither of the chairs was fit to sit on and the marble-topped table was too encumbered with decorative feet, claws, and legs to permit anyone with feet and legs of his own to get near it. It was on this bed, under Albert's picture, that I read Persis Hughes's letter.

Dear Miss or Madam [the letter began]:

I have heard that you are married but since I do not know for sure about this and do not want to call you Madam if you are really Miss, I address you thus.

I know you are a writer. I have read several of your stories in magazines. Some of them were interesting to me, and I suppose all must have been interesting to somebody because I do not think editors pay money for stories unless they are pretty sure about this.

This is not a "fan" letter though, to say I like your stories, for frankly some of them I do not because they do not seem to me to be about real life, but about some idea you have which you think is "real life." Or maybe you know it isn't, but write about it because you think it is better than real life. Or maybe more interesting.

What I want to ask you is this, wouldn't you like to *do* some *good* by your writing? That is, not just *write about* goodness. You usually do write about good people, etc., but I don't think this does any real good in the world and it may do harm. People may read about all these good characters of yours and say to themselves, "Well, if the world is such a good place a little badness from me won't do any particular harm."

And wouldn't you like to find out more about real life, too? Not just your own ideas about life which you think will make a good story, but *real* life, the way a woman suffers it?

I know a writer writes for money. So what I have to ask you is, not only wouldn't you like to do some good with your writing and find out more about how things really are than you seem to know (judging by your stories) but also make some money?

I could have invited you for a social call, to have supper with me, then have asked you these things. But I think that would have been sailing under false colors, which I do not care to do. Now that you know that my purpose is mainly not social would you care to have supper with me on Tuesday of next week at six o'clock? I will be honored by your presence. Please reply.

Sincerely,

Persis Hughes

When I finished Persis Hughes's letter it was dark. I had read it a line or two at a time, not caring about it, thinking only of my own letter, the one which had not arrived. I remembered all those letters in stories and novels which never arrive or rather which are, ironically, delayed or lost until their arrival means nothing. I had almost convinced myself that my own letter had been held up in a like way, that all I needed to do was to send a telegram saying, "Your letter delayed, wire contents," to have by bedtime an answering wire and the words I had awaited the past weeks.

Almost, but not quite. By the time Persis Hughes's letter was read I had given up this silly dream. Would I like to know life, "the way a woman suffers it"? This made me smile. Persis Hughes was not much over twenty, if what I had heard was true. Still, I knew I would go to see her. For the mail carrier had been right. I was lonely here, heartsick.

Mr. Seulke drove me down the pike toward the Hughes's on Tuesday evening. I didn't tell him where I was going. Persis Hughes's father was a widower and I did not care to be twitted about him, as I would have been had Mr. Seulke known my destination, for nothing so interested him as what he called "he-ing and she-ing."

Mr. Seulke was very imaginative about such things. The first time I had hired him to drive me I asked him to take me to a small stream for the afternoon and pick me up later. With a sudden downward look Mr. Seulke had asked me, "Who you meeting, sis?"

At first I didn't understand his meaning and answered quite literally that I was going only to walk along the stream because it was beautiful and to note the kinds of trees and bushes which grew by it.

"That's your story, sis," he had said. "You stick to it."

I asked Mr. Seulke to let me out a short distance from the Hughes's farm. "You needn't come after me," I told him. "I have a way home." Persis Hughes, when I accepted her invitation, had told me she and her father would drive me back to the Seulkes'.

I can't write what Mr. Seulke said then, though to him it was no more than a half-humorous gallantry and nothing that any woman in that neighborhood would have taken amiss.

The Hughes's house was a nice place to be walking toward in the dusk. Chrysanthemums, bronze and gold, though grayish in the dark, were staked up along the path which led to the front door, and light, soft, and yellow from kerosene lamps, shone out through the windows. Persis Hughes herself answered my knock and asked me in. She seemed neither nervous nor emotional, the two things I had feared. A gusty fall wind was blowing and she shut the door quickly behind me.

"Father's old-fashioned," she said. "He likes supper early, and he eats it early, so there'll be only the two of us to eat now."

She put away my coat and purse and led me into the dining room. It was a real dining room, a room planned only for eating, and there was nothing in it which did not

have to do with eating or one's comfort while eating or
afterward: a big, fumed-oak sideboard, six fumed-oak
chairs, a china closet through whose curving glass sides
cut glass sparkled. Under each of the two windows was
a Boston fern in a wicker fern stand and between these
was a narrow couch upholstered in red rep on which one
might rest or nap after eating. The table itself was round,
covered with a white cloth whose corners touched the
floor and lighted by a hanging kerosene lamp. In one
corner of the room the isinglass eye of a small wood stove
glowed rosily and its fire made an occasional dry tick,
tick.

Persis Hughes seated me opposite her at the table. Between us was a very fine meal: an old hen, baked with
dressing, glazed parsnips, baked squash, gravy, a casserole
of tomatoes, slaw, a sponge cake covered with boiled custard, and besides these a number of jams and relishes.

"Did you cook all this?" I asked Persis.

"Oh, yes," she said. "Who else? There'd be only my
father to cook if I didn't."

"Do you like cooking?" I asked.

"Not particularly," she said, "but it has to be done and
I like good things to eat. So I cook as quickly and well as
I can."

She carved the hen deftly, filling my plate with dark
meat, white meat, dressing, gravy. I watched her as she
did this. Afterward, but not then, I tried to see Persis
Hughes through a man's eyes, which is a mistake, a thing
a woman can never do. A woman, summoning all the
latent masculinity she possesses, focusing it like a spyglass
to peer through, remembering every item of female ap-

pearance ever lovingly described by man, will still see awry, unlike a man.

No, this particular spyglass is useless, and at that time it did not occur to me to look through it at Persis Hughes, anyway. I thought only, as I watched her carve, that she was very pretty. Persis Hughes was plumper, perhaps, than she should have been. She was hazel-eyed and had wavy sorrel-colored hair which she piled high on her head in a loose knot.

It was I, who for a time, in spite of what she had said in her letter, tried to keep the evening "social." "How long have you lived here?" "All of my life." "Where did you go to school?" "Local high school and the Cincinnati Conservatory." "Oh, you play?" "Yes." "What instrument?" "Piano, that is I did." "Why did you give it up?" "I can't write music and I don't want to go through life going do-do-do to another man's tune." I suppose I showed my surprise at this.

"Would you want to spend the rest of your life reading aloud what other people wrote?" she asked.

"I don't know," I replied. "Perhaps if I were good at it. One likes to really succeed at something."

She refilled our plates and as she did so she asked, "Did you ever see yourself unexpectedly in a mirror and not know yourself?"

I had, of course, and I said, "Yes. It's an awful experience, isn't it?"

"Did anyone," she asked, "ever see herself in a mirror, not recognize herself, but think, what a beautiful, stylish woman that is coming down the street?"

This was something I had never thought of. "I suppose

not. We're only surprised at our ugliness not at our good looks."

"Then," said Persis, "we all actually look far worse than we have any idea we do."

"I'm afraid so."

"Writing is a kind of mirror isn't it?" she asked.

"A mirror?" I repeated, seeing how this was at once true and not true.

"I mean," she said, "a man might see himself truly for the first time in his life in a story, mightn't he? See how he really was, wicked and ugly perhaps, instead of handsome and good."

"He might, but he'd probably not recognize himself. Just as we'd never recognize ourselves in the mirror on the street except that the awful woman approaching us is wearing our hat, walking in our shoes, carrying our purse."

"That's just it," said Persis eagerly. "*He'd* recognize himself in the same way. He'd read the story and think to himself, why that's what I said, that's what I wore that day, that's where we went and what we ate. He'd have to recognize himself by these things. Then, seeing himself as someone else saw him he'd see how bad, how foolish he'd been. And he would be filled with remorse."

I began to understand Persis Hughes's letter—a little. "If he *did* recognize himself," I asked, "and he *was* filled with remorse, what would he do then?"

"Change," she said promptly. "Mend his ways. Do what he promised."

She left the table to get more custard for our cake and poured us both coffee. She took no more than two bites of her own dessert, then carried her coffee over to the sofa and sat there bolt upright, sipping it. "Please go ahead and eat," she said. "I'm not hungry."

I did eat. The cake and custard were very good.

"I thought perhaps you would write this story," she said.

"What story?" I asked.

"Dallas's," she said. "Dallas's and mine."

"Who is Dallas?" I asked.

"A man," she said. "The man who promised to marry me."

"I don't know him. I don't know your story."

"You could meet him," she said. "He doesn't live far from here. And I'd tell you everything about us. I've thought over everything so much these past weeks I could talk to you all night and not a word would be untrue. I see and hear it all of the time. But you wouldn't know how that is, probably."

Not know that long, never-dissolving panorama of memory? That sound track which runs on and on repeating the very words which are most painful to hear? That film which replays, even against the closed eyes, particularly against the closed eyes, the very scenes one longs to forget?

"What good would it do if I were to write this story? How would it help you or anyone else?"

"Dallas would read it. He reads a great deal. And if he didn't happen to have the magazine it was in, I'd see he got it. Then it would be like the mirror. He would say to himself, 'If that is how I really am, God help me, I will change.'"

"Why do you want him to change?" I asked.

"I want him to do what he promised. I want him to

marry me." She saw that my coffee cup was empty and refilled it from the pot she had left to keep warm on the stove.

There were so many objections to her scheme that I didn't know which to point out first. "Even if I wrote it," I said, "this story, you couldn't be sure a magazine would print it."

She wouldn't believe this. "It would be so real, so true," she said, "they would have to. They could see it was nothing anyone had imagined. That it was what a real person had suffered."

"Do you like to read about suffering?" I asked her.

"Yes," she said, "I do. I don't feel so alone then."

"Editors don't think that," I told her. "They think people want to read about happiness."

"Editors!" she said scornfully. "What do they know about people? Happiness, happiness, happiness! It breaks my heart to read about happiness."

"It breaks my heart to write about it sometimes, too," I said.

"Then why do it? I didn't intend to say this, but all those happy stories of yours! They sound silly to me. Besides," she said changing her tack very swiftly, "this might have a happy ending."

"Even so," I told her, "written in the best way I know, no one might want to print it."

She had a new idea. "It might be even better to have it printed in the *Republican*. That way Dallas would be sure to see it."

The *Republican* was Lane County's weekly paper. "I didn't know the *Republican* ever printed stories," I said.

"It doesn't. But it would if I paid them. Oh, I have the

money to do it all right," she said, as if I had questioned her. "My mother left me," she stopped, as if her native hill-country suspicion and shrewdness had just reminded her that she was talking, after all, to a stranger with whom reticence about money matters was advisable, "a considerable sum," she finished. "I will also pay *you*," she said, "in that case, whatever a magazine would. And this way you'd have a sure thing. Not have to take a chance on an editor's liking it."

She put her coffee cup down on the floor with a gesture of finality, as if everything had been settled.

I said there had to be more in a piece of writing than promise of pay, otherwise writers wouldn't be writing at all but doing something that paid regularly the first of every month.

"You could do good, too," she reminded me, "by writing this story. Doesn't that interest you?"

"How?" I asked.

"You will help a man keep his word. And you will help save him from being ruined. For if he doesn't marry me, I will sue him for breach of promise. And if I do I will take from him everything he has. I can do it," she assured me. "I have his letters."

She picked up her cup again trying to find a few more drops in it. I refilled both our cups. Coffee keeps me awake, but I didn't expect to sleep anyway that night.

"I know exactly what the story should be called," she said.

"What?" I asked.

" 'Breach of promise.' "

"That isn't a very interesting title," I said, "not very pleasant or inviting."

"What do I care about that? Interesting! Pleasant! That title will catch Dallas Hindshaw's eye, because he knows very well what I will do if he doesn't marry me. 'Breach of Promise,'" she repeated. "Yes, that's it."

I said nothing. What is there to say to the naïveté which outlines and names a piece of writing for you as specifically as if the work involved were of the same order as that needed for spading a garden plot or scrubbing a piece of linoleum? Perhaps Persis Hughes saw some of this in my mind. Anyway she said rather sadly, "Doesn't our story interest you?"

I couldn't help smiling. "I don't know your story," I told her, "the story of Persis Hughes and Dallas Hindshaw."

"What do you want me to tell you about Dallas and me?" she asked.

"Whatever you like." I put my empty coffee cup on the table, pushed the table nearer the wall, turned down the wick in the lamp, pulled up a second chair for a footrest, and prepared to listen. "Tell me whatever you like."

Persis lay back against the red sofa's bulging, built-in hump. The wind had died down, but not enough to stop the rustling of some vine against the wall of the house or to end the slight movement of the overhead lamp.

"I remember it all so well . . . the train we met on . . . his first words, everything. The only trouble is that our story is so strange, so unusual, it's hard to tell you. It isn't as if it were everyone's story."

But that was exactly what it was, everyone's story . . . my story. "Dallas was already on the Seymour train when I got on." . . . Does it make any difference whether the train runs between Cincinnati and Seymour or San Fran-

cisco and Salinas, if *he* is on it? . . . "It was snowing—that
made it seem so much more close, private, shut away from
everyone else." . . . What difference does the weather
make? In rain, in a wind storm, in a time of quiet, not a
leaf stirring, if *he* is there everyone else is shut away. . . .
"Dallas had such a nice way of eating. I've never enjoyed
seeing other people eat, but Dallas's hands went flying
around the table, helping me, helping himself, and when
he chewed there was no sign of it except a kind of shadow
on his cheek. It was a pleasure to watch Dallas eat." . . .
Whatever *he* does is a pleasure to watch: things unbear-
able in anyone else, how pretty they are in him; flip, flip,
two aspirin on the back of the tongue, a gulp of water
washing them down, and the smooth Adam's apple momentarily jutting out under the skin, the only grace in
that is *his* grace . . . Ted's grace. "Dallas loved my faults,
freckles, stubby eyelashes, anger, he didn't exclude
them." *He* loves the whole person, always, unites what is
severed and makes what was fractional complete. . . .
"Dallas says there is no one else, so why doesn't he marry
me? When he wanted to so much? All I need do is wake
him up, show him himself in the mirror. Wake him up
from this crazy dream he's in."

This crazy dream . . . this crazy dream . . . I put more
wood in the stove. They were burning apple wood. The
wind came up again and the lamp's arc widened. Back in
the house a clock kept striking, quarters, halves, and
wholes. After the hour struck there was always a little
quaver, a kind of audible tremor as if the effort of that
transition had almost overwhelmed the clock's mechanism.

Persis Hughes took down her hair, wound it up again

in a tighter knot, took it down and braided it. Her father came to the door, with so big a yawn I could scarcely make out his face.

"Good night, girls," he said. "I'll lay down with my clothes on for a little snooze, call me when you want me." I stopped listening to Persis Hughes and thought my own thoughts and listened again and couldn't tell where my thoughts left off and her words began, so moved back and forth between the two and mixed them up thoroughly.

"That is Dallas's and my story," she concluded, unbraided her hair, sat up, leaned forward so that her face parted her long wavy hair the way a rock parts a waterfall. "Now you know it well enough to write it."

"Too well," I told her, "to write it."

"How can you know it too well?" she asked.

I couldn't say I had lived it.

"It's like the multiplication table. I know it by heart. I wouldn't write that."

"Do it for me," she urged.

"I can't. You can only write about what you don't know, and find out about it in the writing."

"You won't do it then?"

"I can't."

"You won't!"

"Very well, I won't. Besides, it wouldn't help you any."

"All right, then, I will sue him. You like to write about good people but you won't be troubled to do good. I will sue Dallas Hindshaw, and everything he has I will take away from him."

If she could not understand writing, I could not understand suing. We were at a standstill. "Do you love Dallas Hindshaw?"

"Were you asleep?" she asked.

"Then why do you want to ruin him, make public everything that is private and sacred?"

"I am honor bound to do so," she said. "It is a terrible thing to do but I am honor bound to try everything to bring him back."

"Bring him back!" I said. "You will make him hate you."

"If he won't marry me, I hope he will hate me enough to want to kill me. I hope every morning he will wake up thinking how he could kill me, put his hands around my throat and strangle me, or open up my dress and plunge a knife in my heart."

"You are crazy," I said. But I knew she wasn't crazy. She was speaking the truth.

"All right, I am crazy. If Dallas Hindshaw doesn't love me he must hate me. He must *do* something about me."

"You will be suing him for money. It will look to him and everyone else that you care for his money. That you can be paid with money for not having his love."

"Dallas's money is part of him. He worked for it, he invented this machine, peddled it about from house to house. If I have his money I have part of him. But I do not want a part of him. I want Dallas. Write our story."

"No," I said.

"Will you go to see him then? You might change your mind."

"I won't change my mind. And how could I go see him? What excuse have I for calling on a man I've never seen?"

"Women go to see him all the time to buy this machine. It shreds up vegetables, makes them come out finer than shavings. You could go to his house to buy one."

She was suddenly exhausted and sleepy. She fell down onto the sofa as if she were boneless, her head resting on the deepest swelling of the hump so that her hair flowed backward over it, touching the floor.

"Shall I tell him you sent me?" I asked angrily. Had I moved away from the painful emotions of my own life to be caught up in a pain that wasn't even my own? Was I to become that absurd creature, a woman without a husband who knows how husbands should be handled? The childless woman, full of advice to mothers?

"Whatever you want," she said, closed her eyes, and slept. It was three. I put another stick in the fire, blew out the lamp, and settled onto my two hard chairs. In California it was one, the October air warm; those who slept were quiet in their beds and those who were wakeful had company to solace their wakefulness. Had *he* company?

Toward morning Persis Hughes turned on her side and I saw that she was no longer sleeping. I asked her the question which had been in my mind.

"What happened?"

"What happened?" she repeated drowsily.

"Between you and Dallas? Why does he no longer love you?"

Then she was wide awake and furious. "I tell you he does love me."

"But he won't marry you? What happened?"

"Nothing happened," she said, "nothing, nothing, nothing. Don't ask me that again."

I didn't, but I knew better. Something has always happened when we deny it so strenuously. Something we cannot bear to face.

At daybreak I walked home to the Seulkes', undressed, slept till noon under Albert's accusing picture, awakened, ate a package of dried figs, spent the afternoon writing a long letter, put the California address on it, and at dusk destroyed it. Then I washed, dressed, and went downstairs to supper.

When supper was over I said, "Will you drive me over to Dallas Hindshaw's, Mr. Seulke?"

"You planning to spend the night out again, sis?"

"No," I said, "tonight I plan to spend in my own comfortable bed."

Usually I tried to keep Mr. Seulke's conversation in channels of seemliness. But as we drove along that evening I thought, you're sixty years old, Mr. Seulke, and these are matters you've had on your mind since the age of ten or younger. If you've learned anything, Mr. Seulke, if you've got any knowledge in fifty years of thinking, speak up. If experience is a lamp, turn up the wick, Mr. Seulke, light the way for stumbling feet. Shine your light on Persis and Dallas and Ted and me. Shine it on hate and love and deceit. Shine it on hope deferred, Mr. Seulke, that maketh the heart to sicken. Shine it on a wife away from home, Mr. Seulke, lost and waiting and full of pride.

But Mr. Seulke, the minute he saw nonresistance in me, was interested in nothing but the weather, spoke of nothing but the weather. It was a mild evening, the sky curded with clouds. Occasional long drops of rain like warm fingers (there was no glass on the right-hand side of Mr. Seulke's Tudor) touched our faces.

Mr. Seulke wiped the drops from his brown face. "But it won't rain," he said. "My mother could foretell the weather and I've heired enough of her gift to prophesy wet from dry." Sniffing the air and prophesying, mild as the evening itself, Mr. Seulke drove the Tudor skillfully along the narrow graveled roads toward Dallas Hindshaw's. He pointed out Hindshaw's house from a distance. As we came nearer I saw it was small, a cabin really, with an open porch extending across its front.

"Hindshaw," said Mr. Seulke, "is an interesting fellow and of an inventive turn of mind. He's made considerable, I understand, with this vegetable reamer of his. A pity he's humpbacked."

Rousing from the lull of the weather talk, I said, "Humpbacked? That must be another Hindshaw. The Hindshaw I know isn't hunchback."

"Know?" asked Mr. Seulke. "My understanding was you'd never seen him."

"I haven't," I said, thinking of the six hours talk in which he had seemed to be present, "but I've heard him spoken of considerably."

"Persis Hughes?"

"Yes," I said.

"Hindshaw jilted her," said Mr. Seulke, "and you can take for sour grapes anything she has to say about him."

But this fox had said the grapes he couldn't get were sweet, not sour; that had been the whole burden of Persis' story!

"See for yourself," said Mr. Seulke, pointing, "he's

humpbacked," and I saw on the porch steps a figure, even in the growing darkness, plainly misformed.

"I'll wait for you, sis," said Mr. Seulke, and there was nothing for it but to walk up that long, shell-lined path toward the man who sat motionless, watching me approach.

"Mr. Hindshaw?" I asked.

The man on the porch step was smoking a pipe. One hand was buried in the long black and white hair of a small dog which lay beside him, the other was lifted above his head clasping the post he leaned against. He was gazing out across the countryside which his cabin, situated on a little rise, overlooked. He shifted his eyes from the landscape to me but didn't get up.

"I've come to ask," I said diffidently, "if I could buy one of your vegetable reamers."

Mr. Hindshaw then got to his feet. Except for his deformity he would have been a very tall man. As it was, he was taller than I, dark, withdrawn, much thickened and broken about the neck and shoulders.

"I'm sorry," he said. "I don't sell them here any more —only in stores."

That seemed to end the visit. Mr. Hindshaw stood, obviously willing for me to leave; the dog got up, ready to walk to the gate with me; a lean, big-faced gray cat at the other end of the porch folded her feet beneath her in anticipation of the return of solitude. Still I stood there thinking, why won't you marry her? She'd rescue you from all of this, she'd have lights in the house at this hour, a white cloth on the table, the table set, and two bowls on the back porch, one for the cat, one for the dog. She'd be willing to play a note or two for you on the piano, after you'd eaten, and lie, without talking, her hair hanging over the edge of the sofa while you smoked your pipe. She's ten years younger than you; if she's naïve you could teach her whatever it is you think she'd be better for knowing. It isn't everyone in the world who'll love you, Mr. Hindshaw, and Persis loves you, desperately. So much, to judge by her talk, she doesn't even know your back isn't straight. You loved her once, promised to marry her, and she hasn't changed. What's come over you, Mr. Hindshaw, why have *you* changed?

With all the craft and skill of a person whose own plans miscarry, I stood there making plans for Mr. Hindshaw, even thinking that he might say, "It was all a mistake," and that I might carry this word to Persis. But Mr. Hindshaw said nothing. His live pipe dying unsmoked in his hand. Mr. Hindshaw waited for me to leave.

"Persis Hughes told me about the reamer."

Mr. Hindshaw turned, knocked out his pipe on the post behind him. "That was kind of her," he said, and once more waited.

"She's very beautiful," I said.

"Yes, she is," agreed Dallas Hindshaw.

"She will sue you," I said, "for breach of promise if you don't marry her." I felt bewitched saying these things, as if I had not the power to choose what I would say, as if I were Persis Hughes herself.

"So Persis tells me," said Mr. Hindshaw.

I hoped he would sick his dog on me, throw his pipe at my head, get rid of me. I could not mention his back, say, Persis loves you, hunchback and all, where will you find another like that? I did say, "Persis loves you just as you are."

Then I ran down the steps and down the path toward Mr. Seulke's car but I heard Dallas Hindshaw say, "I'm afraid you're mistaken."

Mr. Seulke said, "You left in kind of a hurry, sis."

"Yes," I said, "I did."

"Get your reamer?"

"He doesn't sell them at his house any more."

"I could have told you that," said Mr. Seulke, "but I figured you wanted an excuse to talk to the fellow." He turned into the home driveway. "Well," he asked, "what do you make of our jilter?"

I didn't know what to make of the jilter or of Persis, or of Albert with his unanswered question, or of the empty mailbox, or of Mr. Seulke, purely a weather man nowadays. I lived on my hard bed, did the writing and notetaking I had come to do, and was glad, as winter drew on and the trial of Hughes *versus* Hindshaw for breach of promise was announced, that I was called away. The books I had asked for were available at the state library; they didn't circulate, I would have to come up to the capital to use them. I'll go tomorrow, I thought, and not come back until the trial is over. The thought of the trial had been a horror to me, like the wreck along the highway, which the eye, knowing it will be sickened, still seeks out. I'll go tomorrow, not come back until the trial is over. And not have my mail forwarded, I thought. Since reason had not worked, I would try magic. If I made the gestures of not caring about my letter, went off without leaving a forwarding address, no longer listened impatiently for the mailman, perhaps it would come.

I lived in a hotel room near the state library, a room

very high and lodged between two jutting wings of the hotel like a matchbox in a crevice of the Apennines. It was a great pleasure to be free of hoping for the letter I had no right to hope for, free of the temptation to attend the trial, and able to work on the old books. I went to the library early and stayed late, writing down much that I needed to know and much that was useless but which I could not resist. My notebooks were filled with long lists, I was happy, almost drugged, as a child becomes repeating a series of words until finally they are without meaning, nothing but a loop of sound binding him to mystery.

The wonderful names in the old newspapers; the names a writer can never achieve, names which only a loving mother can imagine: Alert Miller, Talkington Trueblood, Cashie Wade, Leadona Leahigh, Else Grin, Omer Bland.

The names of fish: bass, salmon, pike, buffalo, red horse.

Of apples: Imperial, Winesap, Baldwin, Romanite, Russet, Northern Spy, all these ripening in October.

The useless facts: A good deer skin fetched 50 cents, raccoon 37½ cents, muskrat 25 cents.

Then, coming in after lunch one day, another list, in a folded newspaper left on my table caught my eye: "Dearest, dear heart, sweet sorrel, Puss-Precious, my burning bush, long-loved, long-loving. These," the article continued, "are but a few of the terms of endearment culled from the love letters of Dallas Hindshaw and addressed by him to Persis Hughes. These letters have formed the high light of the breach of promise suit in which Miss Hughes, daughter of Clayton M. Hughes, prominent Lane County farmer, is attempting to obtain $10,000.00 of Mr. Hindshaw in lieu of marriage, which she says he promised her." My eyes went from one list to the other, from my list, got out of the books in the state library, to this other list, the words written first in the letters of Dallas Hindshaw, and copied now in a city newspaper. They went from "muskrats, Northern Spies" to "dear heart, dear Tawny, long-loved, long-loving." Was Persis right? Walled up in a crack in the Apennines, did I avoid what she called "life, the way a woman suffers it"? Should I stop reading about the past, go back to the Seulkes', go to the trial, go down to the mailbox? Was there a letter waiting for me there? And if there wasn't, write myself? Say, "Dear husband, having no word from you these past weeks I hasten to assure you that I regret my hasty leave-taking, my long silence. It is enough that you love me. You need not also . . ."

But perhaps there *was* a letter waiting. Was it this, instead of the trial which took me back to the Seulkes'? I don't know. There was no letter, anyway, and the trial had ended the day before I got back. Persis, who had asked for ten thousand dollars, had been given five.

"That poor fool, Hindshaw," said Mr. Seulke, on the evening I returned, "he asked to have his money taken away from him." But I was too tired, after my trip and after searching through my mail for the letter which had not arrived, to listen to him, and I went upstairs to my hard bed and wrote nothing myself—letter *or* list—but relived old scenes.

Next afternoon the mailman honked three times and I flew downstairs, but Mr. Seulke was waiting to tell me about the trial.

"That poor fool, Hindshaw!" he began again. "Wouldn't have a lawyer, and set on representing himself! And for all the good he done himself he'd better've given the girl the money in the first place and spared making himself the laughingstock of the county with all those letters of his read out loud."

"Did he say he hadn't promised to marry her?"

"In a way he did," said Mr. Seulke, "but small good it done him, letter after letter saying, 'My sweet pigeon, I can hardly wait till we are married.' Sweet pigeon!" said Mr. Seulke laughing. "Sweet vulture is what he thinks now, I reckon."

"What defense *did* he have?" I asked.

"None," said Mr. Seulke flatly. "He had no defense, only a quirk in his mind. He wouldn't marry Persis Hughes he said because she was changed. She wasn't the girl he had asked to marry him in the first place, because that girl accepted he was humpbacked, and this girl, the one he was refusing to marry, did not accept it. He called up two dozen witnesses to testify that she never would mention his hump, talked about him as if it didn't exist, and tried to make out, in her own mind, and to others, he was straight-backed. 'I've got a hump,' he said, 'and the person who don't accept my hump don't accept me.' "

"Why didn't she?" I asked. Why didn't I? *He* was made that way when I married *him*.

"Why didn't she what?" said Mr. Seulke.

"Accept his hump? Accept the fact his back was crooked?"

"I don't know *why* she didn't," said Mr. Seulke, "but I know when it started. And I know it was the cause of Dallas Hindshaw's refusing to marry her. I was there and I saw it happen."

I remembered my question that night at Persis Hughes's and her "Nothing happened, nothing, nothing, nothing."

"What was it?" I asked.

"It was a dance at Zenith and I was as close to them as I am to you. Dallas was a good dancer and a young fellow passing by clapped Dallas on the back and said, 'This frog sure can hop.' He meant it as a compliment or at most a joke and Dallas took it so. But Persis slapped the boy not once but a half-dozen times and screamed, 'It's not, it's straight.' Hindshaw grabbed her, 'My back's crooked but my mind's straight,' he said, and that was the beginning. That's what broke them up."

"Did Hindshaw tell this at the trial?"

"Not in so many words, but he said, 'I do not intend to be half-wed to somebody who sorts me out and marries what suits her, only. I could sue Persis Hughes,' he says, 'with as much justice as she sues me, for she has not kept her promise to my hump. And as I was made shorter than most men,' he says, 'by reason of a horse stepping on me when I was a boy now I will not be still further whittled down by a woman marrying part of me only and maiming me beyond the first damage.'

"So it went," said Mr. Seulke. "But Hindshaw had no real defense and nobody thought the girl didn't have a legal right to the money. But nobody would've wanted to stand in her shoes to get it."

Mr. Seulke followed me out onto the porch, sniffed a few times, and said, "It's going to snow."

It was already snowing, a first, soft, downward feathering.

"What do you make of it?" asked Mr. Seulke. "You seen and talked to them both."

"I don't know, Mr. Seulke, I don't know what to make of it." I didn't want to make anything of it, meaning was striking too close.

I stood there on the porch, the big flakes blowing against my face like cold cobwebs. Mr. Seulke stood there, too, not speaking, so presently I went down the lane toward the mailbox. I remembered saying to Persis Hughes, "I understand it all too well, it's like the multiplication table," and remembered Dallas's words, "She didn't keep her promise to my hump." Do you understand that? I asked myself.

I jumped across the brook, cold now, as it ran across its pretty stones, and specked with falling snow. I hesitated, as I always did, to open the box, then did so quickly. The only letter in the box was one from Persis. In my disappointment I couldn't pick it up for a while, but stood looking at it, and the orange-veined pebble beside it. Finally, I took it out and opened it.

Dear Miss Marsden [it began]:

Though I know now that this is only your writing name, not your real name, it seems more natural to me because I used it first, so I keep on doing so. I understand that you have left the Seulkes' but trust that this will be forwarded to you.

I am sorry you did not come to the trial and still sorrier you would not write the story. But it is too late to worry about this now. I did as I said I would and as I think I was duty bound to do, that is, show Dallas Hindshaw that I was willing to do anything to get him to marry me, even sue him.

I don't regret having done this but I find I don't want his money now and I want you to know it. So will you seal up and mail this envelope which I have enclosed and addressed, after you have read what is in it? You will see I am not keeping the money.

Since you live quite a ways off I don't expect we'll see

each other again and I want to wish you the best of luck in everything, and hope you understand I did what I was honor bound to do.

Sincerely and with good wishes,
Persis Hughes

I read the letter Persis Hughes had enclosed as I had been told to do, replaced it, and sealed the envelope. It was addressed to Dallas Hindshaw. All this trouble, all this sorrow, and who had moved a step forward? I, I told myself, I have moved a step forward. It was the truth. When I put the letter back in the mailbox I took the stone out, and at the brook I stooped down and laid it once more beside its brothers at the water's edge, then I walked on up to the house. "Sort him out," and make him pay for refusing the sorting—and give the money back. It made no sense.

Mr. Seulke still stood on the porch, arms folded, watching the weaving patterns of the falling snow. "Well, did you get your letter, sis?" he asked.

I had never spoken to Mr. Seulke of my letter, nor of any letter for that matter, but I felt neither evasive nor glib now.

"No," I said, "it didn't come."

"What do you figure on doing now?" he asked.

"I'm going home," I said.

"Home? I didn't know you had a home, sis."

"I have."

"Home and husband?"

"Home and husband."

"That's more like it, sis."

"It is," I said.

I went upstairs to write and stop my waiting.

*

The Singing Lesson

*

L IBERTY SCHOOL is built on a piece of low, unusable, alkaline land. There are no other buildings in sight. In spring it rises like a lighthouse above great fields of ripening barley; in fall its shadow is long morning and evening across far-reaching stretches of stubble. In winter it stands solitary in the center of a pool of shallow, wind-scalloped water.

The wind always blows about the schoolhouse. It lingers there as if the school were the last building it would be able to touch before plunging over the world's edge, as if it were reluctant to trade domestic for universal architecture.

Scalloping the water, the wind spoke to the teacher in the schoolroom at the Liberty School. It said far. It said distant, strange, remote. It said someday.

"Miss McManaman," suggested Peter, "we'd ought to be practicing our singing lesson."

"I know we ought," said Miss McManaman, but she didn't move. Rain had been falling all day—slowly and dispiritedly, with none of the clatter and excitement of a storm. Elongated drops hit the gray pool of water which surrounded the schoolhouse with a melancholy plop-plop.

"Mr. Harmon," urged Peter, "will be here tomorrow."

"I know he will," said Miss McManaman, continuing to stare at the rain.

On Thursdays Mr. Harmon, the music supervisor, drove out from town to give the Liberty School its weekly singing lesson. He was a severe, talented young man with perpendicular red hair rising above a somewhat greenish face. He had a voice so high, pure, and thin that when he sang the sound of it crept between the joints like electricity—or a razor blade. But Mr. Harmon did not sing often. "I come to hear you sing, Miss McManaman," he said. By which he meant Miss McManaman's pupils, for Miss McManaman herself could not sing. She had a disappearing voice. After four or five good notes, it vanished, fell like a waterfall over a precipice and was heard no more.

"Why is this?" Mr. Harmon would ask savagely, for he was married to his music and felt his awareness of Miss McManaman's black eyes and cream-colored arms to be a kind of infidelity. "Why is it that a healthy young woman like you should have a disappearing voice? How do you account for it?"

Miss McManaman couldn't account for it—but it was a fact which she recognized. Playing the piano with one finger she taught Peter Mr. Harmon's assignments, and Peter, singing, taught the school. On Thursdays, shorn of his musical significance, Peter would sit once more at his desk, and Miss McManaman, resolutely opening and shutting her mouth, would lead the singing. But it made her unhappy: it was underhanded, and it wasn't, she felt sure, what music should be.

"Miss McManaman?"

"Yes, Cletus."

"Can I be excused?"

"May," Miss McManaman said, and nodded. With the schoolyard under water the boys' and girls' outhouses could be reached only by wading—and everyone had to be excused often. Miss McManaman had said no at first to all this taking off of shoes, wading out, replacing shoes —but there had been an accident and now once an hour, if necessary, was the rule. And as soon as his hour was up necessity smote each pupil again and off he waded.

"Take your shoes and stockings off and leave them off," Miss McManaman ordered suddenly. "You'll be less likely to take cold with bare feet than with damp shoes and stockings. Put your shoes and stockings by the fire to dry."

The children circled the stove with their shoes and hung their stockings over the edge of the woodbox. The woodbox, in addition to wood, held three semi-drowned squirrels, a family of motherless field mice, an animal no one had ever laid eyes on before, and a ground owl which was assuredly dead.

Coyla, however, pleaded to keep it. "A live ground owl," she told them, "don't look very much alive. A dead one, I think, would have to look deader than this to be dead forever." So they kept the ground owl, giving it the benefit of the doubt and warming it as thoroughly as the known living.

"Teacher," called Peter, who had no shoes and stockings to dry but had made a trip to the woodbox to inspect the refugees, "come quick."

Looking out of the high windows onto the rain-pricked, gently lapping water, Miss McManaman felt dreamy, too easeful to move.

"You come to me, Peter."

Peter ran. "What d'ya think?" he asked. "The one we don't know the name of is having babies. Two already," he said with pride. "We saved it just in time."

"That's fine," said Miss McManaman dreamily. "Put something over that corner of the box. A coat or something."

"Why?" asked Peter.

"Animals don't like the light when they're having babies."

"Why?"

"Make it snappy," said Miss McManaman.

"Will we sing then?"

"Yes," said Miss McManaman, sighing, and went to the piano.

"We gotta sing that?" Peter asked, reading the words of the song over Miss McManaman's shoulder.

"Yes, we do."

" 'Cherries are ripe, cherries are ripe, the boys and girls all say.' "

Peter read the words so that even to Miss McManaman's ear they sounded fantastic.

"Listen, Peter," she said, "this is the tune." And she picked it out with one finger as spryly as she could. "Pretty, isn't it?"

"Sour," said a resonant voice behind her. "Sour as cat piss."

Miss McManaman swung about on the piano stool. That wasn't a word to be used in the schoolroom, though it was not, she knew, a word which would startle her pupils.

"Not your playing, Miss," said the little man in the doorway. "That was refreshing. Full of feeling. Ping, ping," he said. "Tum, tum. Like a gander pecking on a lard pail. Not plushed over. Simple and melodic. I was speaking of the tone of the piano. "Sour," he reaffirmed. "Sour as . . ."

"Please," began Miss McManaman.

"Swill," said the little man. "Pig swill. You understand that, Miss? Or Mrs.?"

"Miss," she said, "McManaman."

"Irish. She was Irish," he told her.

"Please," began Miss McManaman again. "To whom . . . ?"

"Wilbur Smiley. Smiley by name but damned melancholy by nature."

"You mustn't . . ."

" 'You mustn't swear, Mr. Smiley, before the dear little children.' "

"Well, you mustn't," she said.

"Paugh," said Mr. Smiley. "Where'd you learn the bad words you know, Miss? Right here," he said, pointing.

"In the boys. *And* the girls . . . What's the worst you know, children?"

A dozen hands went up.

"Ta ta, children," he reproved them.

"You see?" he asked Miss McManaman. "It's in 'em. Working like yeast in a barrel and frothing at the bunghole. Treat 'em like human beings," he advised. "Or cure 'em if you're a mind to. Make 'em spend a day writing bad words on the blackboard. That'll take the brimstone out of them."

"Really, Mr. Smiley," began Miss McManaman, "what *is* your . . . ?"

Mr. Smiley handed her a card.

"Wilbur Smiley," she read, "Piano Tuning. Vocal Music. 276 Railroad Avenue. Evenings by Appointment."

"Fooled you, didn't I?" asked Mr. Smiley. "Sent out by your superintendent, Professor Barr. Musical outfit you got around here. Except for the piano."

Mr. Smiley, leaning, it seemed, from the ankles, reached over Miss McManaman's shoulder and with a slight flick of his hand sent a spatter of sound out into the room.

"Be a waste of money. You do all the playing here?" he said.

Miss McManaman nodded.

"Be a pure waste," said Mr. Smiley.

He walked across to the stove. "Don't get your dander up," he advised Miss McManaman.

He was a small, red-brown man with a peaked head, dusty hair, and deep-set eyes which went about the schoolroom, lapping it up: jut and cornice, chalk dust and children, Mr. Smiley took them all in.

"Mind if I stir up the fire?" he asked. "I ain't hot-blooded like the rest of you here," he said eying a row of bare feet.

"We ain't hot-blooded," began Cletus, believing a slight to have been put upon them, but Miss McManaman interrupted him. "They have to wade," she explained.

"Often, too, I bet," said Mr. Smiley, taking it in.

With one hand he was poking up the fire, while with the other he felt about in the woodbox for fuel.

"What's this?" he cried. He let the poker stand in the open stove and bent over the woodbox.

"Fur-bearing wood," he announced.

He lifted the coat from the corner it roofed over. "Three already," he told them, "and more expected."

He took the ground owl in his small hand and soberly regarded it. "Ashes to ashes. Dust to dust. The life cycle complete," he informed Miss McManaman. "Birth, death, and the intermediate whistle stops. Don't know, though, as life's going to hold much surprise for these kids. They'll already've seen it all in the woodbox."

Mr. Smiley filled the stove with eucalyptus chunks, unwound his green scarf, laid aside his long black overcoat, and walked to the front of the room.

Here an experienced teacher, Miss McManaman felt, would have asserted herself, said, "Would you care to hear the fifth grade spell, Mr. Smiley?" or "What can you tell us, Mr. Smiley, of the art of piano tuning?"

But Miss McManaman was not experienced. She leaned against the piano, said nothing, traversed the slight distance which separated her from pupilhood herself, listened to the wind and the rain, lifted her eyes to Mr. Smiley's face as if waiting to be asked by him to recite.

"What was I interrupting when I came in?"

" 'Cherries Are Ripe,' " said Peter. "The singing lesson."

"Ah, well," said Mr. Smiley, "this ain't cherry weather."

With no hemming or hawing, no clasping of hands or arching of his chest, Mr. Smiley began to sing. He stood before them, his face a little sad, his eyes still looking about the schoolroom as if all he saw interested him, and sang words they could not understand in a voice so beautiful Miss McManaman pressed her hands to her heart. She could not say whether what she felt was bliss or pain. Both, she thought. As if all the things of which she had dreamed and for which she had waited, without having a name for them, were now spread before her, named, shining, and palpable. And that was bliss. But at this very minute of knowing and naming, she saw also that they would vanish: melt, run away, be lost forever. And that was pain.

"Singing," she said to herself. "Singing." This, then, was what was meant by the word they used each Thursday—the meaning she had missed and struggled toward.

Mr. Smiley, his song finished, stood for a minute regarding the Liberty School pupils. Then, turning about, he stepped to the blackboard and with three or four large swoops erased Miss McManaman's silent reading lesson and drew—in the space he had cleared—two hearts.

He then stood aside so all could see. "This," he said, pointing to the first, "is your heart . . . Thomas . . . George . . . Jane . . . Henry. A fine muscle . . . empty, easy, beating free."

Then upon the second heart Mr. Smiley made with his piece of chalk the slanting dashes Miss McManaman's pupils used to show that upon a landscape they had pictured, rain was falling.

"This is my heart," Mr. Smiley said. "These are my tears. Tears," Mr. Smiley repeated quite impersonally. "My heart is full of tears."

He began to sing again. His second song was simpler than his first; it was gentle and flowing, like rain in the early morning, or a river under trees. It sounded to Miss McManaman like the beginning of things, like first days: the new key in the rusty lock, the fresh flag hoisted, the September bell tolled. It sounded like her first day at Liberty School.

Waiting for her the morning she had begun teaching was a hay wagon. It stood on the school grounds like a frigate come to rest. Three people looked down at her from its high seat: a stout old man with a flaring semicircle of white whiskers, a ruddy woman of middle age, and between them a small boy with bright eyes and a red mouth. Mother and son dismounted by means of a ladder, slowly and with dignity.

"Miss McManaman," said the ruddy woman, "this is George Washington Berryman, the fruit of our old age. We are raising him to be a great man. We want your help."

"I will help you," Miss McManaman had said, with the feeling of taking a vow.

"If he can learn," said his mother, "well and good. If he can't, train him to be holy. Or it could be both. But that's not likely," she added. "One or the other's as much as can be hoped for. Remember your name," Mrs. Berryman told her son. "Don't do anything he'd be ashamed of."

Mrs. Berryman didn't kiss her son in parting, but laid her hand for a minute on his shining, egg-shaped head. Then Mr. Berryman helped his wife to remount and drew up the ladder after her like a skipper preparing to cast off. On the plank bridge at the edge of the schoolyard he reined in his horses for a minute and Mrs. Berryman, pivoting about on the high seat, called back a farewell message to her son.

"Stay pure, George Washington Berryman," she said in a clear, sad voice. "Stay pure."

The five Rosses came unaccompanied across the fields: downy-eared, round-eyed, their brown cheeks frosted with crumbs.

"The first day of school," Miss McManaman chided them.

"Us Rosses," Jennie, the oldest, explained, "always eat whatever's in our lunch pails for dessert on the way to school. Then it's done with and we don't have to worry about it any more."

"Why do you worry," asked Miss McManaman, "about dessert?"

"It's not the dessert," said Jennie. "It's when to eat it. Should you eat it first recess? If you do, you kick yourself. If you don't, you think about it till second recess. Should you eat it then? Second recess is awfully near to noon. At noon you got all the rest of your lunch. Maybe you should save it to eat going home. If you do, you can't enjoy it, the rest of 'em beg so. Us Rosses always eat it the minute we're out of sight of the house. That way it's done with. Don't have to worry any more about dessert all day long." Jennie brushed the crumbs from her face.

Mrs. Renzo brought Ada to school the first day. "Ada's backward," said Mrs. Renzo, "she's a little slow. But she's deep. Ada's got ideas'll surprise you. She's got strange, deep ideas," said Mrs. Renzo.

Miss McManaman had gazed at Ada's face. It had every appurtenance faces have, yet it seemed primitive: an early, trial face to which, century after century, endearing and humanizing details would be added. It was a small granite face, made by a hurried man with a sharp chisel.

"What I figure," said Ada to her teacher, "is this. God is a bird. A peacock probably and the stars is his tail."

"See," said Mrs. Renzo. "See? Deep and strange like I said."

Peter, in his green fedora, led the Mendezes across the early morning fields. Behind him, and stepping in time to the harmonica which he played, were Felicita, Pablo, Josephina, and little Fructoso.

"Good morning," said Miss McManaman to the Mendezes. "Here bright and early. Would you like to look at your new readers?"

"To hell with reading," said Peter, tapping the spit from his harmonica. "Numbers is what counts. Numbers is the way you read real things."

"Oh, I must teach him to read," thought Miss McManaman now, watching Peter's listening face—seeing it shining as though the music to which he listened were summer sunlight. "I must teach him to read. There are things numbers can never say."

Mr. Smiley finished his second song and went again to the blackboard. There he drew a human foot, narrow-heeled, long-toed, and with an arch like a culvert. It was a beautiful foot made to spring away, to fly, and never linger.

Mr. Smiley, from the heart, his heart, the one which

was filled with tears, drew a stream full and lapping over which ran beneath the culvert of the high-arched foot and was lost in the far reaches of the south blackboard.

"From my heart," he said, "the tears she has no use for. They flow under her foot," he said, tracing the stream, "but never touch her. She walks dry shod."

"Is your name Agnes?" he asked Miss McManaman.

"Not Agnes," she said. "Mary."

"Her name was Agnes," said Mr. Smiley, and sang again.

Was it the tears under the arch like a culvert he sang, was it the arch which unbending carried the weight? Or was Agnes herself his song?

Whatever it was there was no sadness in it. Or, if sorrow was there, it was sorrow swallowed, digested, ruminated, until it had become bone and blood—for singing and seeing. Agnes . . . where was Agnes? Lost, gone, turned to another perhaps . . . but here was Agnes, unknown, a name only, a pallid name, alive in the rainy schoolroom, lifting it out of chalk dust, shivering the blackboards, setting all the Rosses, Mendezes, Tritonas, Hanrahans on the edges of their seats: showing Ada a non-peacock God, showing George Washington Berryman his mama's pure dream. Sounding to Peter numbers he had never dreamed of.

Once in October when the wind off the stubble fields had been hot and dusty and the children had fought and squirmed all day, Miss McManaman had gone to the girls' outhouse and closing the door behind her had stood with her face pressed against the smooth pine boards, looking out at as much of the world as was to be seen through the crescent-shaped aperture in the door. And as she stood thus it had suddenly seemed to her that she was in one of those prisons of which she had read: a prison so small one could never lie down; so remote a human voice was never heard; a prison where for twenty years her only sight of the world would be this finger's breadth of sky and field; her only assurance that all had not vanished from the earth, the hand which slid to her each night a bowl of food.

Just at the moment when the sky had seemed on the point of closing in about her, she had flung open the door and rushed back to her pupils.

"We are free, boys and girls," she had cried. "We are free."

They were startled by her words. "Of course," they said. "What did you think?"

"Sometimes I forget it. Oh, boys and girls, let us go outside and run up and down in the wind and never forget it."

Listening to Mr. Smiley sing, Miss McManaman wanted to say to them once again, "We are free, boys and girls, we are free." Listening to Mr. Smiley's song . . . and not to his alone, she knew, but to that other one's, the song noted down a hundred, or two hundred, years before by a hand seeking to record—what? Not Agnes, who was Mr. Smiley's song, nor the light, unfaithful, springing foot, nor the tears beneath the culvert, nor Wilbur Smiley's rain-pocked heart—or was that it? Was that all there ever was to sing, whatever hand set the notes down, whatever throat swelled with the beautiful, glancing sounds? Was that all—Agnes, the beauty, the tears, the rain? . . . Miss McManaman, listening, could not be sure.

But she wanted to say to her children, "Remember, boys and girls, remember. Remember today. Remember the schoolhouse half afloat and the wind and the animals who were born whose names we did not know and remember me who loved you and Mr. Smiley, a grown man, with a heart still alive and beating."

Mr. Smiley, while Miss McManaman was wondering and dreaming, had come to the end of his song and had rewound his scarf about his neck and picked up his coat.

"Say 'peach pit,' " he told the Liberty scholars, "when you get a strong longing for a dirty word. It's got an ornery ring to it, somehow. Then sing. That'll do the trick. You'll feel like you've just said your prayers."

Miss McManaman walked to the door with him. "The bill will come for piano tuning," he told her candidly.

She scarcely heard him. "Oh, Mr. Smiley," she said, "I can never tell you . . . you do not know . . ." Then she started over again. " It was so beautiful . . . and I have to teach singing. And I can't," she said. "I have a disappearing voice."

"Let it, let it," said Mr. Smiley, undisturbed. "Too many voices in the world already."

"It makes me so ashamed. Mr. Harmon expects . . ."

"Ed Harmon," said Mr. Smiley. "That musical saw."

"He knows so much, though. He can look at a song and sing it. He looks at a note, then opens his mouth and says it, the way I would a word."

"Vacant veins, however," said Mr. Smiley. "Sound's his whole stock in trade."

"I can't sing," Miss McManaman persisted. "Mr. Harmon says . . ."

"Why, Mary," said Mr. Smiley, "don't you know you got more music in one of them little white arms of yours than Ed Harmon's got in his whole body and shock of hair? You got grace notes in your eyes, Mary, and whole ballads in your hands. You sing with them."

Mr. Smiley turned and faced his car, which, to avoid wading, he had driven astraddle the walk right up to the porch.

"Clearing a little in the west," he said.

Miss McManaman looked and in the far west saw a thin streak of clear green.

"Say her name sometimes, will you?" asked Mr. Smiley. "Say 'Agnes, Agnes.'"

"Oh, I will, Mr. Smiley," said Miss McManaman. "I promise I will say her name and I will remember singing."

"So long, Mary," said Mr. Smiley.

Miss McManaman did not leave the porch until Mr. Smiley's car was far up the road. When she went inside again Peter was standing at the head of the room.

"I'm going to teach the kids one of Mr. Smiley's songs," he told her.

"Can you, Peter?" she asked. "Do you think you can do it?"

"Sure," he said. "Different words, maybe, but the same tune."

"It's the tune that counts," said Miss McManaman.

She walked to the stove and held out her hands to its warmth. There in the woodbox, his eyes yellow and unblinking, the ground owl gazed up at her. She opened her mouth to say, "Children, the owl's come to life," but Peter had started singing. I'll tell them later, she thought, happily.